"Why can't you stay away from me?

"Ross, you told me yourself that you're like all the men in your family. It was your intention to stay away from *me.*"

"I *can't* stay away from you!" He seemed tormented. "You put on that damn perfume and look at me with those haunting eyes, and I'm ... I'm Peter coming under Willow's spell all over again. He couldn't resist her sorcery, and I'm no better. I don't care what happens— I want you!"

Arianne's hands grew icy. "You compare us to our ancestors? You think Willow seduced Peter through sorcery, and that *I'm* putting a spell on *you?*" She swallowed convulsively. "Then, once you're finished with me, are you going to drown me?"

His eyes became cold and hard, pinning hers.

Oh, Lord. What had she done? She shouldn't have challenged him. Not if she valued her life. Ross was Peter Briarcliff's descendant. Perhaps he *was* capable of ...

Dear Reader,

Welcome back to Shadows. It's hard to believe it's been a year since we first took you on a walk to the dark side of love, but it has been. And in honor of our first anniversary we have two very special books to entertain—and scare—you.

Lindsay McKenna is a name that needs no introduction, and we're thrilled to have her contributing to the line. *Hangar 13* is almost indescribable, mixing the truly terrifying threat of a restless spirit with the transcendent power of love. You'll hang on every word.

Lori Herter makes her full-length-novel debut with *The Willow File*. Is the past destined to repeat itself, even when repetition means tragedy? Or can the power of love overcome all obstacles and free two lovers from the curse of their ancestors' folly? Read this extraordinary book and the answers will be yours.

And in months to come, keep returning to Shadows to enjoy our unique mix of ingredients, the mix that chills you and thrills you, as our authors create memorable tales set in that mysterious region we call the dark side of love.

Enjoy!

Yours,

Leslie Wainger
Senior Editor and Editorial Coordinator

Please address questions and book requests to:
Reader Service
U.S.: P.O. Box 1325, Buffalo, NY 14269
Canadian: P.O. Box 1050, Niagara Falls, Ont. L2E 7G7

Lori Herter

THE WILLOW FILE

Published by Silhouette Books
America's Publisher of Contemporary Romance

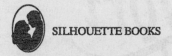 SILHOUETTE BOOKS

ISBN 0-373-27028-3

THE WILLOW FILE

Books by Lori Herter

Silhouette Shadows
The Willow File #28

Silhouette Romance
Loving Deception #344

Silhouette Books
Silhouette Shadows '93
"The Phantom of Chicago"

LORI HERTER

was an only child and learned to entertain herself by daydreaming. Now happily married, she has found a good use for her well-developed imagination by writing romance novels. Formerly from Chicago, Lori and her husband, Jerry, a certified public accountant, live in California with their three cats.

To Suzanne, Rita, Lou, Jill Marie and Chelley
for their enthusiasm and support

PROLOGUE

1901

A late evening breeze swept onto the beach over sand still cooling from the hot July sun. The mild wind ruffled through the tall palm trees that graced the grounds of the Aragon Hotel. The San Diego seaside resort, painted white with red tiled roofing, was built in 1893 in Victorian gingerbread style with cone-shaped towers, turrets and long balconies.

Over one of the pointed towers a half-moon hung silently against a starlit sky, while far below on the hotel's deserted beach, a man and woman argued. They had been slowly walking together, but now they stopped at a point near the edge of the sea's lapping waves.

"You're making a terrible mistake, Peter."

Willow Monroe's earnest brown eyes shone with emotion as she said these heartfelt words to her lover, Peter Briarcliff. The breeze played with tendrils of hair that had loosened from her upswept hairstyle. The dark brown wisps wafted along her fragile neck and around her delicate features. She was remarkably beautiful, but so frail that even the sea breeze seemed to buffet her diminutive, small-boned frame. Her long, white cotton dress accentuated the paleness of her face in the light of the half-moon.

"I wish I could believe I was making a mistake," Peter replied. Tall, black-haired, with a robust physique and manly bearing, he seemed incongruently ill at ease. "I wish to God I could have found some way out of this dilemma. I didn't want to write you that letter. The knowledge that I'm hurting you gives me much anguish. But there *is* no other choice. There is no way we can be together."

"Just because of what my doctor told you?" she asked.

"Willow, he told me you would die in childbirth," Peter said in a tone that showed his reluctance to be so blunt. "Your heart—"

"Oh, I know what he says about my heart! I don't believe him. Why didn't you talk to *me* about your fears instead of going to him? Without telling me, too. He had no right to give you his opinions about my health without my permission."

"I told him we were engaged to be married," Peter explained, impatience in his tone. "He agreed that I, as your future husband, had a right to know the parameters of your physical condition. But what he told me was far worse than I had feared. I knew that you tire easily, that you suffer from heart palpitations—though you always make light of these things. We had talked of having a family, but I secretly feared that giving birth would be difficult for you. So, I decided to ask your doctor." Peter's face sobered. "He said a childbirth would be your death sentence. Your little heart is just not strong enough."

Willow's fiery eyes filled with tears. "Ridiculous! I'll go to another doctor."

Peter took hold of her slim shoulders. "No, Willow." He spoke now as if to a young girl. "A new doctor would only say the same thing. Anyone can see how weak you are. I knew it a year ago when we met, when I got my shoes wet pulling you back onto this very beach, because a wave had knocked you down while you were wading. It was clear to me then that you had the strength of a kitten. But that was part of your charm. Your eager spirit and your fragile beauty captured my heart, and I put your obvious ill health out of my thoughts. I assured myself you would improve because you seemed determined to do so."

"I *will* improve," she insisted.

Peter shook his head. "I would like to believe everything could turn out as our romantic dreams wish them to. But they can't. If we were to marry and you died giving birth to my child, I would never forgive myself. I would blame myself, because I had caused the baby to be conceived. To think we've already risked—"

Her eyes brightened. "Yes, Peter, think of that. When you visited me in Los Angeles. Those secret hours we shared...."

"I'll never forget," Peter whispered, a self-conscious shadow haunting his eyes.

"Your caresses made my heart thud against my ribs," Willow said, her voice energized with remembered passion. "My parents were out and could have returned at any moment. I trembled with fear and desire in your arms. When you carried me to my bed, I couldn't catch my breath. I felt faint. I didn't even know how to be intimate with a man, and I was frightened. But I wanted so much to make you happy."

Willow grasped Peter's jacket lapels and her voice filled with awe. "You caused me to feel such ecstasy, I grew afraid that my body couldn't endure it. I writhed in pleasure and agony. I thought my pounding heart would burst. But instead my body exploded with joy." She pressed her thin frame to his and looked up at him with feverish eyes. "I survived your love. My heart endured our passion. How weak can my heart be? Childbearing can be no worse a risk for me than your lovemaking."

Taking her shoulders, he held her away from him. "This is foolishness, Willow!" he said, shaking her a bit. "Of course giving birth is a far greater risk. I should never have . . . thank God you aren't with child now."

"You cut me to the core saying that! I want to have your baby." She grasped his lapels again, pleading. "I want to marry you. I love you so much."

"No, Willow," he said, pushing her away once more in a resolute manner. "I told you in my letter—I'm going to marry someone else."

"I don't believe you could love anyone else."

"Love . . . love has nothing to do with my decision. She comes from a prominent family here in San Diego. My parents approve of her, and—"

"And they never approved of me, did they? I'm from Los Angeles, and not even the best part of town. My mother is of Mexican descent, and that makes me not quite the right sort of wife to marry into your elite Anglo-Saxon family."

"My family accepted you," he argued in a defensive tone. "They consented to let me give you the Briarcliff brooch."

"With great reluctance, I'm sure. And now they want it back. You want it back, too, so you can give it to your *new* fiancée."

"I'm truly sorry to ask you for it," Peter said in a softer tone, yet his manner was still firm. "Don't you think this embarrasses me, to ask you to give back a gift that was meant to signify our future union in marriage? But that marriage can no longer be. The brooch *belongs* in my family. It's part of our tradition. My grandfather—"

"Gave it to your grandmother when they became engaged," Willow finished his sentence for him with impatience. "I know the brooch is to go to the bride-to-be of the eldest Briarcliff son. But *I* am your bride-to-be, Peter. I am the woman you love." She pointed to the large opal brooch pinned to her dress between her breasts. "I've worn it over my heart every day since you gave it to me. I wore it for my engagement photograph for all to see, because I was so proud to be the bride of Peter Briarcliff. I love you. I've given myself to you. Our wedding plans have been announced. I can't believe that you could throw away the future we've planned together, the happiness we've shared, to marry some...some heiress!"

"It's not what I want," Peter retorted. "But it is what I must do for your sake. I couldn't marry you and not lie with you as a husband." He lifted his shoulders in a helpless gesture. "You stir my desire so, I couldn't keep away from you any better than I did that day in Los Angeles. But every time, you would risk getting in a family way. And then you would risk death."

Willow dodged a wave that almost reached her foot before it faded into the sand and the sea. "I'll take the risk, Peter," she said, regaining her footing. "How can I live without you? How could I tolerate the thought of you married and living with someone else? It's *me* you should be with." She lifted his hand to touch the brooch fastened snugly between her breasts, which were surprisingly full and round for a woman so frail. The large opal gave off bright, translucent flames, even in the moonlight. "You gave this to me," she said in a soft, husky voice, then moved his hand to cup her breast, "because you wanted me. Remember when you caressed me, Peter? You unbuttoned my dress. You touched me so sweetly and told me how lovely I was. My breasts were exquisite, you whispered, and then you kissed them. You made me delirious with your words and your kisses. And then you took me to bed."

She leaned against him and whispered in his ear. "Take me to bed now, Peter. My room is empty. My parents are playing bridge with my sister and her husband in the card room. They won't be back for at least another hour. Take me to bed and love me again."

"No!" Peter exclaimed, shoving her away from him, throwing her off balance.

When she had regained her equilibrium, she said with defiance, "Your rough manner only betrays how much you want me. You're fighting yourself, not me."

"We must speak no more of this, Willow. The time has come. I've met with you here, as you asked. I felt I owed you that much, to affirm in person, with my own lips, what I wrote in my letter. As you see, nothing has changed. I'm bound for your sake to break my engagement to you. I intend to marry another, if only to make certain my relationship with you comes to a close. And now—" he held out his hand "—I must ask you to give me the brooch."

Willow's eyes grew hollow and she took a step backward, away from him. "You...you're only misguided because of the silly things my doctor told you. Or perhaps your family has talked you into marrying that heiress instead of *un*wealthy me." Her eyes took on new courage and she stepped toward him again. "I see I must wait until you come to your senses, and you realize that *I* am the only woman for you! No, I will not give you the brooch, Peter. I must keep it because I'm meant to wear it, because you chose me to be your bride."

A couple of late-evening strollers passed by them on the beach. Peter ignored the strangers and retorted in a raised voice, "I will marry someone else. You must accept that, Willow!"

Willow stood in silence for a long moment, her expression slowly changing until it grew stricken. "Did you ever love me?" Her voice suddenly lacked confidence. "You first told me you loved me that day in Los Angeles when we... You insisted you wanted to marry me. Did you only say those things to ease my fears? Has it been only physical desire on your part all this time? We wrote each other such caring letters. I thought they were love letters. I thought... Perhaps I've been mistaken in the character of your feelings for me."

"There's no use discussing the past anymore," Peter said in a terse manner. "The point is, we have no future."

"I know what it is," Willow said with renewed assurance. "You did love me and you still love me, but you can't admit that now. You've buried all your feelings for me, because that's the only way you can let me go and then turn the knife by asking me for the brooch. My answer is still *no*. I will not give it to you. I'll wait until you remember you love me, and then you'll realize you can't marry another woman, heiress or not."

Peter's face had grown impassive, hard and angular in the silver glow of the moon. "Willow, you are no longer my fiancée." His cold, unemotional voice put a chill on the mild summer night. "The brooch belongs in my family." He stepped toward her, hand outstretched. "Give it to me. And then we will say goodbye."

"Never!" Tears streamed from her raging eyes. Her breathing grew labored, unsteady. She raised her hand to her heart, near the brooch, and hesitated, as if catching her breath, as if waiting for her heart to steady itself. Then she looked up, letting her hand drop to her side. Her chest rose with pride as she took in a breath. The opal caught a ray from the half-moon and glistened.

"I will never give it back!" she insisted with cool defiance. "You gave it to me after I accepted your promise of marriage. *You* have dishonored that promise. But this brooch proves to me that you did love me. The brooch is all I have of you."

"Willow," Peter said in consternation, his broad shoulders looming over her as he took hold of her wrist, "give it to me!"

She stepped backward, breathing hard as she fought to get away from him. He gripped her other arm and jerked her toward him.

"Violence?" she spat in his face with vehemence. "Is this what our love has come to? Very well! If you want this brooch, you'll have to take it from me!" She gasped, chest heaving, and her heels dug into the wet sand. The bottom of her dress became soiled as she bent her knees trying to twist out of his grasp. Her voice began to falter as she exclaimed, "Go on, Peter, prove you've stopped loving me! Rip my brooch from my heart! I dare you!"

CHAPTER ONE

Ross Briarcliff squatted, bending his tall frame and dropping one knee to the dusty floor for balance, getting his light gray summer suit dirty in the process. Just his luck—it was the *bottom* drawer of the antique office cabinet that the old man was telling him to look at, the drawer marked The Willow File. Smirking, he touched the yellowed label on which the words were typewritten and wondered what long-ago file clerk had given himself, or herself, a chuckle when they affixed it to the drawer. Or perhaps they took it all very seriously. Ross pulled the drawer open, breaking a small, thick cobweb that some tiny spider had built between the corner front edge of the oak drawer and the oak cabinet that held it.

"Sorry about the cobwebs," Alex Howatch apologized as he leaned on his gold-handled walking stick. "With the economy being what it is lately, we don't have the staff anymore to keep our storage rooms dusted. Have to give first priority to the guest rooms and the lobby and so on."

"No problem," Ross muttered. He'd met Alex, the manager of the Aragon Hotel, yesterday and found him to be surprisingly chatty in a folksy, past-generation sort of way. Alex fit the part, too, with his distinguished-looking head of white hair and gray mustache. He represented well the Victorian courtly charm that kept the century-old hotel so popular with tourists. Even local San Diego residents came here for a weekend of picturesque relaxation.

And then, of course, there happened to be a mysterious ghost story that gave the place that intriguing ooh-ah factor. That was why Ross had come here, to get some idea of why the revolting spook tale wouldn't die. He suspected Alex, who had been the hotel's manager for decades, did all he could to keep ghost gossip alive. Every time an article appeared in the newspapers or the ghost story was covered on some TV show, often around Halloween, Alex was always featured, indicating he gave reporters his full cooperation. The elaborate historical exhibit off the ground floor lobby also provided a major clue as to the ghost story's importance to the hotel.

As he scanned the open drawer, Ross was surprised at how few contents it held. Indeed, it looked half-empty. But then, they'd put so much on display in the hotel museum, there was probably nothing left for storage. The drawer contained some stained dining room menus from 1901, some browned and disintegrating old newspaper clippings and a weathered cardboard shoe box identified by a typewritten label as "Willow Monroe, artifacts." Leafing through the clippings, Ross recognized some of them as the ones that had been duplicated and enlarged for display in the hotel museum. Ross glanced up at Alex, who was standing a few feet away looking dapper in his seersucker suit, patiently observing Ross. The old gentleman had apologized a few minutes ago for making Ross bend down to open the drawer, mentioning a touch of arthritis in his knees.

"Who arranged to have these newspaper articles enlarged for the historical exhibit?" Ross asked him.

"I did," Alex readily replied. "One of my duties as manager is to preserve the Aragon's rich history. Reporters often asked to see the newspaper write-ups of the...the events of July 6, 1901, so I thought perhaps the general public would find them of interest."

"Isn't it sort of a morbid topic? A hotel guest who drowned off the hotel's own beach? Wouldn't it make people afraid to swim here?" Ross already anticipated what Alex's reply would be, but wanted to bait him with these questions anyway, just to be sure he'd sized Alex up accurately.

Alex shifted his weight from one leg to the other. He was a slim, rather delicate man, with a quiet elegance. "Well, I suppose you may be right. I hadn't thought of that, frankly. It's just that people are so interested in the Willow Monroe story, the . . . the mysterious circumstances of her death."

"By that you mean, some people think she was murdered," Ross concluded in a sardonic manner.

"The matter was never resolved, was it?" Alex said with an affable smile. "No one was ever charged with her murder."

"Exactly." Ross's voice took on a dour, authoritative tone. His great-grandfather, Peter, had been suspected of drowning Willow, because a couple of people had passed them by on the beach and heard him arguing with her about the brooch she was wearing. But no one actually saw Willow drown. Her body had been found early the next morning, washed up on shore. She was stone cold, and the Briarcliff brooch was no longer pinned to her dress. "She probably drowned herself," Ross conjectured, stating the Briarcliff point of view. "Or got swept away by a large wave and couldn't swim back. She had a weak heart."

"Yes, yes, those theories have been postulated as well as the . . . the murder theory. I sympathize with how your family must feel about your ancestor being connected in an unpleasant way to the tragedy. Please let me assure you that we make every effort to present all sides in an even-handed and unbiased way."

"Thanks," Ross said tersely. "But why milk this tragedy at all? Why not just let it be forgotten? If you did, the ghost story would surely die with it."

One side of Alex's mustache rose as he made a slight half smile. "No, Mr. Briarcliff, I don't think so. I get reports of phenomena coming from Room 302 on the average of twice a month. Just the day before yesterday a woman—quite upset, too—told our receptionist she was passing by that room and felt a cold spot, which she said chilled her to the bone."

Ross rose to his feet to look at Alex eye to eye, though the old man was quite a bit shorter than he. "That's just what I mean. You keep this ghost story alive, even broadcast which exact room Willow stayed in, and people go by it out of curiosity and imagine they feel something odd. It's all the power of suggestion."

Alex promptly nodded. "You're quite right, I'm sure. Even the unexplained scents, the sound of weeping or the lights going on and off that guests have reported can all probably be chalked up to imagination. Or even attributed to natural phenomena. I believe the reported cold spots may come from the ocean wind whooshing through the hall windows, which we leave open in pleasant weather. The south wing of the hotel, in which Room 302 is located, has an unusual configuration. I've long thought that its structure causes the wind to whip by it in an accelerated way. So, you see, I quite agree with you. In fact, I find these complaints a genuine nuisance. One has to calm the guest down and so on. And the persistent reporters! Some of them want to stay overnight in Room 302. They bring in all their TV equipment, which, when they turn on their high-powered lights, wreaks havoc on the hotel's old electrical system. Oh, you have no idea what we go through here."

"Then why do you encourage such a ghost story if it causes so many problems for you?" Ross asked, raising his eyebrows.

Alex smiled and shook his head in an affable way. "The Willow story has long been part of the hotel's history. One can't dismiss history," he said in a benign tone. "Willow Monroe did die here, one way or another. Neither of us can change that fact."

Alex inclined his white head momentarily in a pose of thoughtful humility. Ross couldn't help but be impressed with the old man's natural grace.

When Alex looked up, he said, "You've been very open with me about your purpose for investigating the Willow story. I appreciate your frankness. As I said, I completely sympathize with your family's point of view, and I'll do whatever I can to help you debunk the whole story. Our files and artifacts are entirely at your disposal."

"I'd gladly dispose of them!" Ross couldn't help but say with malevolent humor.

"Ah, yes," Alex said, chuckling at the joke. "I didn't mean permanent disposal. But any time you want to see anything concerning Willow, by all means, please just ask."

"I'm a little surprised at your cooperation," Ross said with suspicion. "Haven't you found that the ghost story is actually good for business?"

Alex said nothing, but made a charming, noncommittal shrug of his shoulders.

Exhaling, Ross looked down at the drawer and realized he'd forgotten to open the cardboard shoe box. "Anything in here?" he asked, bending again to open it.

"Not much, if memory serves. We did put most every-thing in our little museum."

Ross lifted the partly torn lid and found an ornate, small bottle with a fading, flower-entwined label that read *Eau de Toilette, Violette*. The cap was missing. Ross sniffed the bottle, for he thought he could smell a faint floral scent in the air now. But the smell did not seem stronger when he brought his nose to the edge of the old cologne bottle.

"It's believed that was Willow's," Alex told him, obvi-ously relishing the opportunity to display his knowledge of historical details. "A maid found it in Room 302 after the Monroe family left to take Willow's body home to Los Angeles. In one of the old L.A. newspaper clippings in the pile there in the drawer, you'll see that a friend eulogized her at her funeral, saying...let me see if I remem-ber...'She was sensitive, frail and beautiful, an ephem-eral nymph who always smelled of violets.' "

"Touching," Ross said with a deadpan tone as he dropped the bottle into the box. "So how come it's not on display in the museum?"

Alex scratched his nose in an amused manner. "Well, it was, actually. It was an odd thing. We had the bottle fas-tened with a small wire to a display board behind glass, along with her white gloves, the replica of the brooch and the hotel's registration book turned to the page with her signature. But the *eau de toilette* bottle always fell off the display. We tacked it up again at least three times, and the next morning it always had fallen off." He chuckled. "We began to wonder, you know, if Willow didn't want it on display. So we finally gave up and put it back in the box."

Everyone's loony around here, Ross thought to himself as he picked up the only other article in the box. This Ross had seen many times since childhood. It was the engage-ment photo of Willow with the Briarcliff brooch pinned to her dress. Even the Briarcliff family kept a copy of this picture, because it was the only photo in existence of the opal brooch.

He glanced at Alex again. "By the way, who had the replica of the brooch made for the museum display?" He was referring to the life-size copy, using an artificial opal, which Alex had mentioned.

"I had it made about eight years ago," Alex replied. His tone grew solicitous. "Perhaps I should have asked for permission from your family?"

"Perhaps," Ross agreed ominously. "I have another bone to pick. Why is a drawing of the Briarcliff brooch now being used as a logo on the perfume boxes in the hotel's perfume shop?"

Alex shook his head gravely. "I'm afraid I had nothing to do with that. You see, the perfume shop is a separate business under private ownership. The owner merely rents space at the Aragon. The hotel takes no responsibility for the products the shop sells."

"Mmm," Ross grumbled, pressing his lips together. Another party to deal with. "Who owns the perfumery?"

"Arianne Lacey."

"Is this Arianne working in her shop today?"

"Yes," Alex replied, "I saw her on my way in this morning." He hesitated, stroking the stiff hairs of his mustache. When he looked at Ross, his keen hazel eyes revealed concern. "Something you should know. Arianne is one of the nicest young women I've met, and..." He paused again, as if reluctant to continue.

"What about her?"

"Well...you see, she's related to the Monroe family."

Ross had never heard the last name Lacey. "How closely related? Is Lacey her married name?"

"No, she's not married. She's quite young, about twenty-four, I believe."

Ross exhaled with impatience. "So how is she related?"

"She told me she's descended, on her mother's side, from Willow's sister, Katy. Katy was Arianne's great-grandmother."

"Terrific," Ross muttered, anger rising inside him. Now he had a Monroe to personally deal with on top of everything else.

He ought to keep an open mind, he supposed, but members of the Monroe family had so often spoken to the media about Peter Briarcliff over the years. Katy Monroe Thornton had had five children, all of whom seemed to have reproduced, so there were any number of cousins available to tell the bitter story their family had passed on to them about poor Aunt Willow. They were often interviewed in the same news pieces that Alex had been interviewed for. Invariably, they described how Willow was cruelly jilted and then—they believed—murdered over the Briarcliff brooch, and how ruthless Peter Briarcliff never paid for his crime.

Most of the family seemed to be residents of the Los Angeles area, where Willow and her parents had lived. Ross had had no idea one of the Monroe descendents was here in San Diego, much less working at the Aragon Hotel, of all places. *Probably wants to be near her dear old auntie's ghost,* Ross thought with dark amusement. She must have some reverent attachment to Willow—and some gall!—to use the Briarcliff brooch as the logo on her perfumes. Well, he'd see to her, all right.

Ross coolly thanked Alex and left the musty file room. It was almost noon, and he decided to see this Arianne person immediately. If he stewed over the matter during lunch, he'd only work up his anger further and give himself indigestion.

He walked through the hotel's stately old lobby, whose wall panels, staircases, balcony balustrade and ceiling were all made of original, hand-worked oak. A wide hall led from the lobby to the south wing of the hotel, the wing that bordered the beach, the ground floor of which made a gallery for the hotel's shops. He passed by the ice-cream parlor, a gift shop, card shop, a florist's and finally the Aragon Perfumery, as the business was called.

Opening the glass door, he stepped into the shop. He suddenly found himself in a new, unexpectedly sensual atomsphere laden with the scents of perfumes. It took him off guard and made him wary, somehow. Perhaps he connected perfume to feminine wiles.

The woman he'd almost married several years ago always wore some exotic, spicy scent that put him in a romantic mood far too fast. Weakness for women, especially seductive women, had been a trait of nearly all the Briarcliff men, beginning with Great-grandfather Peter and his disastrous attraction to Willow Monroe. Ross, experience had proved, was no exception. Fortunately, he had come to his senses in time to find out his fiancée was only angling to marry him for his Briarcliff name and money. And Ross eventually realized, once he was well out of range of her perfume, her dazzling red hair and her voluptuously upturned breasts, that his feelings for her didn't rise any farther than his zipper.

Choosing the wrong woman to marry was practically a Briarcliff tradition. Ross felt certain that he'd inherited this tragic lack of discernment from his ancestors. After his close call, he'd vowed to avoid making any further matrimonial mistakes by never choosing a wife.

Remembering his purpose, he glanced around the shop for a moment. No one was behind the counter, though there appeared to be a closet-sized storage room in back of the counter. He'd never been inside the perfumery before. His family made it a point to avoid the hotel altogether. Yesterday he'd happened to walk by the small shop and noticed the hall window display, where he'd been incensed to see the Briarcliff brooch being used as the perfumery's logo. As he slowly turned to look around him now, he felt surrounded by mirrored displays of glistening perfume bottles and pastel-tinted crystal atomizers. A crystal chandelier hung above him. Piped in piano music played a romantic Chopin sonata. The heady mixture of scents, the piano playing, the glitter of lights reflected from colored glass, the floral wallpapered walls, all made him think for a "Twilight Zone" moment that he'd entered an expensive, old-fashioned brothel.

Ross remembered his great-uncle Louis, a cigar in his mouth and a glass of brandy in his fat palsied hand, describing with relish his favorite bawdy house. He'd told his ribald tales nearly twenty years ago, when Ross was a wide-eyed twelve-year-old. After a sumptuous Thanksgiving dinner, all the Briarcliff men had gathered in the library to have a traditional smoke. Louis loved to reminisce about the many "ladies" he'd encountered at his favorite "club." With a dose of raunchiness, he confided just how they'd spun his head and made him eager to spend his money on them. Gorgeous women, blond or brunet, big eyes or big breasts, paid for or seduced—all contributed to the life-long pleasure of unrepentant Uncle Louis.

His first wife left him because of his womanizing. His second wife tried to shoot him. His last, scandalously young and beautiful wife gleefully outlived him, however, and spent the rest of her days squandering his wealth.

Great-uncle Louis was the quintessential Briarcliff.

"May I help you?"

Ross, involved in his thoughts, was startled by the sound of the pleasant, inviting, feminine voice. He stiffened, bracing himself. He felt oddly vulnerable meeting a female from the Monroe family in such an atmosphere as this. But when he turned, instead of a young woman behind the counter, he found a plump middle-aged lady with short blond hair.

"I was in the back room. I didn't realize anyone was here," she apologized.

"I want to speak to Arianne Monroe," he said.

"Arianne Monroe?" the saleswoman repeated, looking perplexed. "Do you mean Arianne Lacey?"

"Lacey," Ross corrected himself with annoyance.

"She just left for lunch. I'm Doris. I work part time for Arianne and often fill in for her at noon. May I leave a message for her?"

"No," Ross said, irritated at the delay. Anxious to get out of the shop, he did not leave his name and told the woman, "I'll stop back later."

He had lunch alone at the hotel's beachside restaurant, then went to the historical exhibit. He'd looked it over briefly yesterday and decided to spend more time examining all the displays and the accompanying write-ups more thoroughly. If he was to undermine the old story that wouldn't die, he needed to find out exactly what he was up against.

After spending a couple of hours reading about the hotel at the turn of the twentieth century and looking at a series of old photographs, he came to the display, which covered one wall, devoted to Willow Monroe. He paused in front of an enlargement of the photo, blown up to a height of about five feet, of Willow wearing the Briarcliff opal. Her dark eyes peered down at him from the sepia-hued photo, knowing and a little mysterious.

She was, indeed, quite beautiful even by modern standards. Frail, with large eyes that seemed to speak without words, she reminded him a bit of Audrey Hepburn in one of her first movies. Ross could understand Peter's initial attraction; she probably brought out his protective instincts. The day they met, he'd helped lift her up from the sand when a wave had knocked her down on the beach. Somehow in that small event, she caught his fancy and fixed her hold on him. *She felt so feminine and fragile as I assisted her to stand, her eyes both amused at herself and appreciative of my help, that I found myself eager to look after her. She made me feel as if I had grown in stature and strength in a moment's time,* Peter had written of that first encounter.

But Peter's diary, which Ross had taken from the Briarcliff library and was currently reading, indicated that Peter soon learned that Willow's health was poor. A sexual union and children, he ought to have guessed even then, were out of the question. Why did he let the romance evolve? Why did he go so far as to offer to marry her and give her the family brooch? In other words, what happened to his common sense?

Peter was the first Briarcliff to lose his sense of direction, at least when it came to women. Probably still reeling from his ill-fated encounter with Willow, he went on to marry an heiress who, within a few years, he grew to despise. To escape his sometimes violent relationship with his arrogant and shrewish wife, he became obsessed with increasing his wealth. He tripled his real estate holdings using any and all means and made himself a multimillionaire. Thus he furthered his reputation for ruthlessness, already established by the Monroe family who insisted, but could not prove, that he had caused Willow to drown.

Eventually Peter rid himself of his wife by arranging to have her committed to an asylum for the mentally ill. Peter's two handsome sons led equally mercenary lives and were particularly noted for their heartless treatment of the various wives and mistresses they attracted because of their wealth and notorious charm. His only daughter also made a devastating marriage and eventually went mad. Peter died fabulously wealthy, but bitter, angry and alienated from his children.

Yet Peter's parents and his grandparents, according to Briarcliff family history, had chosen their spouses wisely and made sound, lasting marriages untarnished by scandals or violence. And Peter, in his youth, had seemed to be a steady young man who had done well scholastically and showed every promise of being a solid, admirable citizen. Somehow, Peter's judgment had been knocked off balance and then took on the warped pattern that continued into the present generation of Briarcliffs.

And the turning point was the day he met Willow.

What could she have done to him, to set him so gravely off course for the rest of his life? Ross asked himself as he studied her photo. What charms did this woman with her damaged heart possess? What hidden power lurked within her frail frame? What sorcery?

Ross would probably never know, and studying her picture was beginning to give him the willies. He left the museum and went upstairs to the old file room, with Alex Howatch's permission, to get the newspaper clippings he'd found in the Willow File. He spent the rest of his afternoon in Alex's outer office, photocopying the clippings. The dated machine was touchy and kept getting jammed, requiring Alex's elderly secretary to come and fix it for him repeatedly. By the time he was finished, it was dinner-time.

As he relaxed and sipped a glass of wine in the hotel café, which featured large windows that overlooked the beach, he realized he'd never gotten back to the Aragon Perfumery. Mentally shrugging, he decided tomorrow was time enough to deal with Arianne Monroe—or Lacey, or whatever. She was only one small part of the major project he'd taken on to try to put a better light on the Briarcliff family name.

Ross's older brother, William, had recently declared his candidacy for the United States Senate. The only white sheep in a family of black sheep, William was a reputable businessman who had married a fine young woman, and he'd managed to stay happily married to her for over a decade. More than that, they had two beautiful, well-adjusted children. Ross was proud of him and secretly envied him.

William, even as a boy, had had a selfless streak, always giving Ross the biggest chunk of a divided candy bar or putting off his own homework to help his younger brother with his. In his college days, William became an activist for environmental issues. Later, as he took over managing family business matters for their ailing father, Norman, William also became concerned about the poor and homeless. He developed what Ross believed were some innovative ideas for furthering both these causes. When William decided to run for the Senate to advance his ideas through politics, Ross eagerly gave his brother his full support, having no doubt that William would make an excellent, responsible politician who would well serve his home state and his country. Ross hadn't even recognized his own, unexpected sense of patriotism until William became involved in politics. He'd thought of himself as jaded and cynical, and his growing depth of commitment to his brother's idealism surprised him.

Ross had studied law and served as the family's legal counsel and troubleshooter, for there was always someone suing one of the Briarcliff clan. Peter's sons had had children, who in turn had children and so on; now the extended family, most of whom had expanded their inherited wealth, was quite large. Ross was never at a loss for work. He also knew he would inherit an immodest fortune when his father died. His financial future and career were set. He had no worries—other than finding personal happiness.

But Ross was too realistic to expect to achieve that. He wasn't altruistic like William, whom he very much admired but could never emulate. Ross saw in himself all the telltale Briarcliff flaws. He could be overbearing and highhanded—often was in court; he was generally a cold person, not given to emotion other than impatience or anger; and he had an eye for women, which he feared would be his downfall.

But if Ross couldn't rise above his family's faults, he knew William could—in fact, had. He wanted to do all he could to help his brother become a senator, hoping that the scandal-ridden Briarcliff name could stand for something positive for a change.

Unfortunately, the political party opposing William in the Senate race began slinging mud immediately. They made a phony tape of a supposed telephone conversation between someone who sounded like William and a woman claiming to be his mistress. The press and his political opponent eagerly compared it to past Briarcliff sex scandals, which were thoroughly rehashed, and it was implied that William was no different. William had never been unfaithful, and his wife proudly vouched for him. But the public, used to tawdry Briarcliff stories through the decades, was conditioned to believe the tape and feel sorry for his wife.

Ross managed to disprove the tape's authenticity with the help of a private detective who uncovered the woman's identity. Ross easily demolished her credibility once he discovered she'd never even met William. But William's candidacy had been tainted nevertheless, mainly because the public had been reminded of his family's notorious history.

Ross decided to help by making an effort to polish up the tarnished family image. Many of the historic scandals were based on partial truth, but had been greatly exaggerated. A prominent San Diego newspaper had agreed to let him write a series of articles giving the Briarcliff side of each story and correcting untruths. While he couldn't deny his ancestors had flaws, he could at least make sure those flaws were portrayed fairly and without embellishment.

He'd decided to begin with the most infamous scandal and the one that had started it all—the supposed murder of Willow Monroe by Peter Briarcliff.

Ross finished the glass of wine and leaned back in his chair, tired after his long day at the Aragon. He'd become painfully aware that he had his work cut out for him. Despite Alex's claim to the contrary, everything Ross had read and studied today seemed to favor Willow. Peter was portrayed as a villain.

The waiter brought his dinner, and Ross dove into it, deciding to shove Willow out of his thoughts for the rest of the evening. Reliving history put him in a bad humor.

As he chewed his medium-rare steak, he gazed out the window at the summer sun, hanging like a large orange ball over the flat blue horizon of the Pacific. It was almost sunset. The sea looked tranquil and the palm trees along the shore waved softly in the gentle wind. A few bathers were still on the beach, most of them gathering their belongings.

The serenity of the view soon had a calming effect on Ross, as did the second glass of wine he sipped with the last of his dinner. Perhaps he'd have a walk along the beach in the setting sun before he went home tonight.

All at once the figure of a young woman caught his attention; that is, he realized he'd been staring at her for the last few minutes. She appeared lithe and slim, wearing a long, colorful skirt that billowed in the breeze as she faced the sea. Elbows in the air, she was unfastening her long, dark brown hair, which had been tied up in the back. When she'd loosened it, she ruffled her fingers through it until it fell down past her shoulders and blew in the wind like her skirt.

She looked so graceful, like a vision of the essence of feminine beauty, that he found himself slowly lowering his glass to the tabletop and smiling as he watched her. The wind shifted, blowing her hair into her face, and she turned, so that he could view her profile. She was too far away for him to see every detail, but her face appeared to be quite lovely. Ross's eyes sharpened as she began unbuttoning the white blouse she wore. She pulled the blouse apart and drew the lower edges out of her skirt, wearing it now like a light, open jacket. Beneath he saw the sudden splash of color from her revealed bright pink tank top. When he glimpsed the profile of her softly jutting breasts as the breeze blew back the blouse, Ross's pulse quickened.

God, this woman looked beautiful—how could he meet her? Yes, a walk on the beach was a great idea.

He realized in a fleeting, self-conscious moment that he was behaving like a true Briarcliff male—instantly devising a plan to meet a female who had caught his eye instead of first questioning whether she might be married or otherwise unsuitable for him. Well, so what? This was a woman who stirred his blood, and there was no use fighting heredity. Ross intended to meet her. And if she was as beguiling as she appeared to be, and if she was willing, he intended to have her.

Though he'd made a pact with himself never to marry, it didn't mean he'd sworn off women. No way. Great-uncle Louis had always seemed to be the happiest of the Briarcliff men, and Ross believed he knew why.

He motioned to his waiter, paid the check and left the café. As he walked out of the hotel to the beach, he took off his necktie and stuffed it into his pocket. By now the young woman in the long skirt was a small figure walking up the shore. Carrying her shoes in one hand, she strolled barefoot along the edge of the gently lapping waves, sometimes drawing up her ankle-length skirt to keep it from getting wet. He started walking in her direction.

As Ross followed her, he began to debate with himself. Old Uncle Louis, he had to admit, *wasn't* the happiest Briarcliff male. Ross's brother, William, was. William always seemed to have an inner peace about him, even in the midst of the false scandal that rocked his budding political career and might have rocked his marriage, as well. But it hadn't. His wife, Marlene, had stood by him without question, and William looked upon her as the foundation on which his life was built. How had he managed to find such a warm, trusting, admirable woman to marry? William had met her at college and they'd dated for a long while. He hadn't chased her down the beach on a hot-blooded whim, as Ross was doing at this moment.

Ross's pace slowed, then he stopped walking and turned his face to the sea. He reminded himself that he wasn't like

William, who must have been brought into the family by some foreign stork. Ross would always be attracted to the wrong women for the wrong reasons, like the rest of his male relatives. Even his father, Norman, had had a wretched first marriage that had ended in an ugly divorce, well-covered by the newspapers. His second marriage, out of which William and Ross were born, had been stable and lasted until their mother died over five years ago. But it wasn't what one would call a loving marriage. Norman was too cold a man to be affectionate or to let anyone ever think he gave a damn about them. He didn't even have his Uncle Louis's humor and zest for life.

Ross often felt he took most after Norman. The best he could aim for, he'd concluded, was to learn to enjoy life through wine, women and song—as Great-uncle Louis had, despite his failed marriages.

Still, these thoughts had put a damper on Ross's quest to meet the beauty on the beach. He felt depressed now. He was too soured, like his cynical father, and too admiring of his saintly brother, to ever take up the sort of life Louis led. Who was *he?* What sort of Briarcliff was he destined to be? Ross wondered. At age thirty-one, he ought to know. He understood all the pitfalls to try to avoid, but what was the right path for some modicum of content-ment?

Ross stayed for a long while in the same spot, brooding at the setting sun and darkening sky instead of walking up the shore as he'd intended. All at once the woman he'd admired passed in front of him on her way back. The flash of pink and white and the swing of her long dark hair caught his eye as she walked into his dreary reverie. The exotic floral scent of her perfume invaded his senses and lingered in the breeze after she'd gone. He had the strange sense that a slice of paradise was passing him by. He closed his eyes for a half second, then turned and began to follow her.

Taking long strides, he caught up to her, walking just behind her left shoulder. The sea was on their right. He wondered what to say, how to begin. Ross wasn't usually shy about introducing himself to a woman, but he'd never been in a sort of dream situation like this before. Her alluring perfume kept wafting over him in her wake, and he began to feel as if his shoes had somehow lost contact with the sand.

As if she'd sensed someone was following her, she began to walk at a faster pace, though she kept facing ahead. Ross felt at a loss. They'd be running soon, if he didn't think of some approach.

Then all at once she lost her balance. With a small cry, she fell against him, dropping the sandals she was carrying. Ross quickly took hold of her, not believing his luck. Hands on her slim upper arms, he helped steady her until she stood firmly on both bare feet again. She was so slender, her frame seemed to be made of bird bones. Perhaps the breeze had knocked her off balance.

"Are you all right?" he asked, feeling the softness of her arms beneath his fingers.

She turned out of his grasp and looked up at him, her silky brunet hair swishing, her large brown eyes full of alarm and confusion. "D-did you push me?" she asked in an accusing tone.

Ross was dumbfounded. "No. You fell toward me. How could I have pushed you?"

She seemed at a loss for an answer and looked quite frightened. Her delicate face, her flawless skin and cheeks made rosy from the breeze, her slightly trembling mouth and shocked, vibrant eyes invaded Ross's senses like a heavenly army storming a pagan citadel. No woman had ever affected him so instantaneously. The words *ephemeral nymph* came to him from somewhere, as if he'd heard them recently, though he couldn't remember where. But they fit. She looked so lovely, all he could do was stare at her.

"You were following me!" she said, stepping back into a small wave sliding up the sand toward her feet. The sand gave way beneath her and she was thrown a bit off balance again.

When he reached to steady her once more, she avoided his touch and walked around him onto drier sand. As she stepped into the sandals she'd dropped, she asked, "What do you want?"

"Nothing," Ross assured her. "I just...I wanted to meet you."

"Why?"

He knew he'd better make this sound good. "I saw you walking by yourself and..." She eyed him warily for a telling moment. He floundered, and no more words came to him. Suddenly he blurted out, "You're so beautiful."

As if thrown by his compliment, she looked down at the sand and gathered the white blouse about her, folding her arms above her narrow waist. "Thank you. I have to go now." She turned to walk away.

"Wait," he said, taking hold of her elbow. "Can't we at least introduce ourselves?"

"No," she said, looking at him with suspicion again. "I don't give my name to strangers who follow me on the beach."

"Has this happened to you before?"

Her wondrous eyes grew confused. "What?"

Ross smiled. "You've had men follow you before as you walked alone on the beach?"

Her eyes darkened in consternation. "No, I meant I make it a rule not to talk to men I don't know. Like you."

Ross felt himself regaining his usual composure and confidence, seeing that she seemed discombobulated by their encounter, too. Beneath her stern words he could tell from her wavering eyes that she didn't quite know how to handle the situation. Maybe she found him just as attractive as he found her.

"We can remedy that," he told her, stepping sideways to stand directly in front of her. "We can *get* to know each other."

She shook her head, stiffened her posture and began walking away. Ross followed. "Wait. Let's give this a chance. I'm a single guy. I don't have anyone in particular that I'm seeing right now," he told her as he walked alongside her. This was true. Ross dated several women, but no one in particular. "I'd like to meet someone new."

"I wouldn't," she said in a devout manner.

"Are you married?"

"No."

"Engaged?"

"No," she said, sighing with annoyance. "I just don't like being picked up by some stranger on the beach."

"This isn't a pickup," he countered. "I'm only trying to introduce myself."

"I don't *want* to know who you are."

"All right. We'll keep it a mystery. A sunset rendezvous between a man and a woman. No names. Just mutual fascination."

"In your dreams!" She said the words tartly, but Ross noticed that her pace wasn't so fast as it had been earlier.

He took hold of her arms and made her stop. They were beneath the pointed tower near the south end of the hotel's beach. The sun had grown very slim on the horizon in a last reddish glow. "I'd love to dream about you," he told her softly. "I'd love to make the dream come true."

Her eyes flashed at him, exasperated and amused. "You really are the limit!"

He grinned. "You think so? You're a little inexperienced. I'll show you what the limit is." He gathered her against him, feeling her soft breasts jut into his chest. Before she could object, he caught her mouth with a kiss. As he pressed her head back, he felt her resist. Turning, she broke the kiss, but he kept her in his arms.

"Let this happen," he whispered in her ear. "It's only a kiss. Just a kiss. We're on the beach, and there are still some people around, so you're in no danger. Kiss me and see what happens."

She turned her head to face him again, but kept her beautiful eyes lowered, perhaps from shyness or not wanting to look too forward. Ross did not stop to analyze and aggressively claimed her mouth again with his. Once more, she tried to back away. But soon her resistance grew weaker, and she gradually wilted against him. His head reeled with the softness of her mouth, the female suppleness of her yielding body, the perfume that made him feel he was at the gates of paradise.

Time stopped. He thought the earth certainly must have paused in its orbit. For a few heady moments Ross knew true bliss. Unable to hold himself in check, he began to take advantage of her unexpected cooperation, for indeed, she was kissing him back. He could feel the heat and return pressure of her lips. In response he slipped his hands beneath her open white blouse to run his fingers along the clinging knit material of her tank top. He slid his hands over her back and the sides of her birdlike rib cage, feeling the heat and tremulous expansion of her chest from her uneven breathing. He drew his hand upward and gently moved his thumb over the side of her breast, its generous swell flattened against his chest.

God, she felt delicious, he thought, deepening the kiss, wanting her so much he felt raw stirrings in his groin. When she breathed out in a sigh through her nose, her chest contracted. He took advantage and slid his hand over her breast, gently caressing its softness. The hardened peak of her nipple pressed through the knit material of her tank top. He found it with his thumb and teased it.

Her breathing grew quite ragged and her heart was pounding so, he could feel her chest reverberate with each beat. This was getting out of hand, he realized in his haze of accelerating desire. He'd have her down on the sand in a few minutes if they kept this up, and he didn't even know her name. Still, he wouldn't stop, not just yet. He slid his mouth hotly down her chin and along her smooth neck. Pushing down the low scooped neckline of the pliant pink top, he exposed the upper part of her breast, pressing up on the precious mound of flesh to make it plump. His mouth burned as he kissed her skin. She whimpered and made a halfhearted effort to push him away, which he ignored. But when he slid the pink material even farther down with his thumb until he touched her nipple, she gave a cry of alarm and squirmed away from him.

"Stop!" she told him sharply, covering herself with the blouse, as if with a sudden sense of shame. "H-how dare you!"

Ross looked at her, still breathing hard, recovering his senses. "I'm sorry. But... you were responding..."

"I may have been stupid enough to let you kiss me, but I never intended—"

"All right, I went too far," Ross admitted. "But I wouldn't have if you..." No, he didn't want to blame her, even if she had been cooperating those last heated seconds. "Why *did* you let me kiss you?" There, let her think about that.

"I don't know," she said, a bit petulant as she wrapped her white blouse even more protectively around her. "The romantic setting, I suppose. The way you whispered in my ear—you're obviously experienced at this sort of thing! You took me off guard. It won't happen again, believe me."

He reached to touch her hand. "Don't say *that.* I want to see you again."

Her slightly bruised mouth dropped open. "The *nerve!*"

Ross shrugged. "It's a family trait. You'll get used to it."

"I certainly will not," she said as she began to walk toward the hotel.

Ross quickly stepped to her side as she hastened her pace. "You have to admit there's something undeniably hot between us. You can't let that pass unexplored."

"Oh, yes, I can!"

"Will you be here tomorrow? Are you staying at the hotel?"

She didn't answer and kept walking. He assumed she must be a hotel guest. "I'll be working here tomorrow again," he told her. "Meet me at this spot on the beach at sunset tomorrow night."

"No!"

They were nearing the hotel entrance and he took her arm to make her pause. "If you don't, you'll always wonder what might have been. Meet me here tomorrow," he urged. "Don't tell me who you are, if you still don't wish to. But I want to see you again. I promise I won't take advantage of you. I'll do my best to be a gentleman."

He paused to exhale, his breath surprisingly unsteady. His desperate desire to see her again astonished him. No woman had ever affected him like this. It was almost scary, but he knew he wanted to get on this roller coaster ride, wherever it took him.

She kept her eyes averted and shook her head.

"Don't say no," he whispered in the manner he had used before. Maybe it would work again. "Don't deny the spark that ignited between us. Are you afraid of desire?"

She slid her eyes up to his, looking at him askance. "You promise to be a gentleman and then talk about igniting desire!"

"I mean I'll take things at your pace."

"We won't take things at any pace," she told him with finality and began walking again.

He prevented her and took her into his arms once more. She tried to back away, but he wouldn't let her. He had one last arrow to aim at her. "What if we're meant for each other? Do you want to let what might be one of the most memorable relationships in your life pass you by, because you're afraid?"

Her expression changed. Her eyebrow quivered. He'd gotten to her, he could tell.

"Don't be afraid of life. Don't be afraid of me. I won't hurt you, I promise." As he said these words he found himself meaning them more than he ought to. As long as he didn't wind up promising to marry her, he was okay, he silently affirmed. "Meet me on the beach tomorrow at sunset," he whispered and softly kissed her forehead.

She raised her eyes to his warily, studying him. She looked like she wanted to believe him. *Believe me,* he said to her with his gaze. Her mouth quirked with a hint of repressed humor. Her eyes took on a knowing look then that gave him a sudden sense of déjà vu. She seemed to be saying, "I'd be crazy to believe you, but—" and he couldn't guess the rest.

Pushing herself out of his arms, she walked to the entrance of the hotel. Ross decided he'd be taking things too far to follow her any farther. He called after her, "Give me a chance. Just one more chance. Tomorrow at sunset. I'll be here."

As she opened the door, she gave him a last furtive glance and disappeared inside.

Still slightly dazed, Ross turned and headed to the beach. He paused in the darkness at the place where they'd kissed with such unexpected abandon. Looking up, he noticed the hotel tower looming above. And then he realized—this was the spot on the beach where, legend had it, Willow was last seen arguing with Peter. Like an invisible wall falling on him, Ross suddenly knew what had given him that sense of déjà vu a few moments ago. The knowing look in her dark eyes was exactly the same look Willow had in her engagement photo, the photo he'd spent so long staring at. And now that he thought of it, she resembled Willow. Her nose might be more upturned, her mouth more full—but her eyes, her hair, the perfume...

Good God. Had he just kissed Arianne Monroe?

Arianne Lacey hurried through the door and down the hall to her perfume shop. She wanted to look in the mirror and make sure her clothes weren't disheveled before going home. The gall of that man to kiss her that way, to fondle her! Her pulses began to race again at the memory of it. Why had she let him go so far? she asked herself in the mirror as she checked to see that her pink top was properly in place. She buttoned up the white blouse and tucked it into her gauzy cotton skirt's waistband.

She didn't know what was the matter with her, to have tolerated a stranger's advances that way. But what a stranger! Tall, dark and handsome, just like all the fairy tales. But despite his expensive-looking three-piece suit, he wasn't any candy-box prince. He seemed to come from some heathen realm of primeval sensuality tinged with sorrow. She'd seen unhappiness in his eyes behind all the erotic bravado. She'd felt the curious urge to comfort him, yet another part of her wondered if he used that as his secret weapon to seduce women. He could be a dangerous man, she told herself. Unfortunately, that made him dangerously intriguing.

Arianne knew she couldn't be the first woman he'd tried to seduce. If she was smart, she wouldn't be the next one on his list, either. On the other hand, she thought with a trembling sigh, maybe it would be worth the experience. She'd let other men kiss and touch her, but not within ten minutes of meeting them, not in a public place, and she always had known their names. He certainly was unusual, managing to break all the rules and overcome her inhibitions with one kiss. What would making love with him be like? It made a heart-pounding question for a virgin to contemplate.

No, not him, Arianne told herself. He was way out of her league. She might be wishing she didn't live such a circumscribed life, but she knew better than to get her first experience from an aggressive stranger she'd met on the beach!

She took a last glance at her flushed face in the mirror, turned off the lights and walked out into the empty hall. As she locked the glass door, she grew aware of a strong scent of violets. It overwhelmed the fragrance of her own perfume. Her heart jumped and she began to feel weak with a vague sense of fear. Lately, she'd smelled violets every now and then, and she knew it was the scent Willow used.

Arianne believed ghosts existed. Her mother and a few other people she'd respected over the years had spoken of certain experiences they'd had that they couldn't explain. She didn't think these people she trusted had made up their stories. But just because she believed in ghosts didn't mean she wanted to see one herself, or hear one, or even smell one.

Ever since her father had retired and given her this shop, she often had the feeling that someone or something was with her, observing her at times when she was alone. It was a melancholy presence, and she sometimes found herself growing unaccountably sad and restless. At these moments, she was glad to have a customer come in, for the presence would always seem to go away then, and Arianne could return to her normal, buoyant self.

The sweet, simple violet scent remained very strong, and it seemed to follow her as she walked down the hall. Earlier, on the beach, before she'd met that man, she had felt the ghostly presence, too, though the scent of violets was much more faint. In fact, at first she hadn't been sure who was following her—the presence or the man she'd walked past. And then she'd felt a hand on her shoulder, shoving her so forcefully, it threw her off balance. When she found herself in the man's arms, she'd thought he must have done it. But he was right, she'd been pushed from the other side, toward him.

Why? If it was Willow, what did she want? Arianne knew Willow was her distant aunt. Did she have some message for her, or for their family? Should she contact a psychic? Hold a séance? The very idea seemed farfetched. Besides, the reported ghostly phenomenon at the Aragon had traditionally taken place in and around Room 302, not on the beach or in the perfume shop. Although Room 302 *was* in the same wing of the hotel, three floors up. And Arianne's mother always insisted she'd seen Willow's ghost

in the shop one evening after hours, when her husband had
gone out and left her there alone for a few minutes.

As Arianne reached the lobby, the scent and the presence were fading. Thank God. All she wanted to do now
was go home, eat supper and watch a *Cheers* rerun. She
wouldn't think any more about Willow tonight.

The man on the beach, however, was another matter.

CHAPTER TWO

As Arianne polished crystal atomizers with window cleaner and a cloth the next morning, she wondered again if she should go to the beach that evening at sunset. She'd lain awake half the night thinking of the well-dressed stranger she'd met, his black straight hair that fell over his forehead when he bent to kiss her, his strong features that looked almost stern until he smiled, and his sad, translucent eyes that were either gray or blue. The sunlight had faded too much to tell which color they were. The way he'd kissed her was scandalous, and she was rightly outraged, but ... a wayward part of her she didn't know existed until now longed to experience that kiss again.

Should she go to the beach after work tonight? She often did anyway, for exercise and to inhale some fresh air and clear her head. The perfumery was poorly ventilated. After breathing the potato alcohol that got into the shop's atmosphere from spraying customers with perfume all day, she often felt light-headed by the time she closed for the evening. Perhaps that explained her lack of propriety with the stranger yesterday—she was slightly inebriated from perfume. Maybe she'd only imagined the presence following her and the shove on her shoulder, too. She hoped so. She didn't like to think she'd suddenly gotten easy with men, or that she was actually experiencing a ghostly presence.

She arranged the crystal perfume spray bottles on a glass shelf in an attractive display, then set about removing the bottles from the glass shelf below. As she began polishing them, her thoughts returned to the stranger and the heat of his kiss. She closed her eyes as she relived the moment—the smooth, aggressive way he'd overwhelmed her and held her so snugly against him, the way his sensitive hands explored the contours of her body as his insistent lips moved over hers. He'd made her heart beat so, she thought she would faint. The brazen way he caressed her breast... his hot mouth on her skin creating sensations she'd never felt before... the beautiful electricity rushing through her body....

Arianne leaned weakly against the wall, gaily papered with rose bouquets, and told herself not to think about it anymore or she'd never get any work done. Besides, it might be dangerous to let her awakened desire run rampant in her mind like this. She needed to keep herself in check. What would become of her if she didn't use some caution? She couldn't lose her head like this to any man who touched her in just the right way.

On the other hand, maybe it was her pent-up, unexplored desire that made her ripe for an experienced man to pick. And the man on the beach certainly knew his way around a female body. He was definitely a seducer—or worse.

A shiver went through her. What kind of situation might she have gotten herself into if she hadn't managed to make him stop? Maybe... was Willow trying to warn her? Was that why she'd felt the ghostly presence with her on the beach? Was Willow trying to protect her? Or was she haunting her for some other purpose, to frighten or even hurt her? Arianne thought of the shove again, which might have knocked her down if the stranger hadn't caught her in his strong arms. She remembered the solid feel of his broad chest as she fell against him.

Oh, stop thinking about him, she told herself, realizing her mind was going in circles. Customers would be coming in soon. She needed to be alert, not lost in a sensual daydream.

As she finished her polishing, she reminded herself to turn on the tape player for the background piano music. Her father had always played romantic classical music during the twenty years he'd owned and run this shop. He had given the shop to her upon her graduation from college, and he and her mother had moved to Florida in semiretirement. He was still developing new perfumes, however, using procedures he'd also taught her. They often exchanged potential new formulas. It was a small business, but the shop had its regular clients, many of whom liked the idea that the perfumes were made from all natural ingredients instead of synthetics. The shop's mail order service had a worldwide clientele, most of whom had become acquainted with Lacey-created perfumes while staying at the Aragon Hotel.

She put the last of the polished bottles in the mirrored display case, then went behind the oak counter to turn on the tape player. Before she could press the button, however, she heard the glass door open. She looked up to find cold gray eyes staring at her and a hard, male countenance looking frightfully stern. His mouth was compressed so tightly his lips were growing white.

Arianne recognized him immediately. He was the man who had kissed her on the beach. But he seemed so different now.

He looked like he hated her.

Her heart rate began to increase. Hoping she was mis-reading him somehow, she tried to smile. "How did you find me?"

"Are you Arianne Monroe?" he asked in an accusing voice.

Her brows drew together. What was this all about? "I'm Arianne Lacey."

"All right, Lacey, damn it. But you're part of the Mon-roe family."

"Yes."

"I'm Ross Briarcliff."

Arianne experienced a sinking feeling. A Briarcliff? "Oh." He was the first member of the notorious family she'd ever met, though she'd heard about them all her life. Gathering her wits together, she made a little shrug. "The feud between our families is so old. I have no hard feel-ings toward the Briarcliffs." As he approached the counter, she looked at him with hesitance, her eyes widening as she remembered their erotically charged meeting last night. How could this cold, rigid-looking man in his crisp, pin-striped suit have kissed her so passionately?

As if reading the memory in her eyes, he raised his hand and pointed at her. "Don't look at me that way. It'll be best if we both forget last night ever happened."

Forget? Was he out of his mind? "Why?" she asked.

"Because it wouldn't have happened if you had told me who you were."

"So it's all my fault? Just because I didn't want to give my name to a stranger? You had nothing to do with it?"

"Okay, I was the aggressive one," he admitted. "But if I had known—"

"If you'd known I was one of the Monroe family, you wouldn't have been attracted to me?"

The question seemed to make him pause. "I would have known better than to get involved with you."

"Why?" she asked, growing angry at being dismissed simply because of her lineage. "The Peter and Willow business happened three generations ago. Almost a century has passed. Isn't it time to let bygones be bygones?"

"Are *you?*" He walked to the counter and picked up a boxed bottle of perfume on display there. Pointing to the logo on the box he asked, "What about this? You're using the Briarcliff brooch to advertise your perfume!"

Taken by surprise, Arianne thought a moment. "I guess I hadn't connected the brooch to your family anymore. A replica of it is on display in the museum, and Willow is wearing it in the big photo of her. It's gotten to be a part of the Aragon's history. I thought it was pretty, so I had a drawing made and—"

"Without asking for permission?"

"I asked Alex Howatch, the hotel manager."

"I met Alex. He's the one who told me you were a Monroe. But he has no authority concerning your logo. You should have asked *my family* for permission—which, of course, you wouldn't have gotten."

Arianne's head went back. "Why? You don't own the brooch."

"We damn well do!"

"No! Peter gave it to Willow as a gift," she argued. "It belonged to her."

"So the Monroes like to think. It was meant to be passed from generation to generation in the *Briarcliff* family. Even if Peter had married her, after she died it would have stayed in our family. You have no right to use a drawing of it to advertise your perfume."

Arianne shook her head, amazed at his point of view. "How can you claim rights over a *drawing* of a piece of jewelry you don't even have anymore? I don't know law, but that seems a little farfetched to me.''

"I *am* a lawyer," he told her in an intimidating way. "As for my family not having the brooch in our possession anymore—how do you know we don't?" He seemed to be testing her.

Again she was caught off guard. "Well, I can't know for sure. But I've always heard that the brooch disappeared. Or..." A slight chill crept over her back at the thought in her mind, and she looked away from his hard stare.

"Or what? That Peter ripped it off Willow's dress before he drowned her? That's the Monroe version, isn't it? So maybe we Briarcliffs *do* have the brooch you've put on your perfumes.''

Arianne felt herself growing pale. Had Peter murdered Willow? She'd never formed an opinion on the old question, trying to keep an open mind about such an ancient event. But his descendant standing in front of her certainly looked like *he* was capable of murder right now. "Are you threatening me?" she asked, backing away a step, even though the counter was between them.

He glowered at her. "What, are you afraid of me now? Just because I'm Peter's great-grandson? All I'm saying is that if you don't know who owns something, you shouldn't use a drawing of it as your company's logo."

"*Do* you have the brooch?"

"No," he admitted. "Actually, I believe someone in your family must have it. But it's still Briarcliff property."

"My family?" she repeated with astonishment. "Why would you think that?"

"One old report has it that Willow's parents were seen with the brooch after Willow died. It's probably been secretly passed along from family member to family member, or else it's in some old lockbox somewhere. Do you know who might have it?''

"Of course not! I've heard that story, but it's just a piece of old gossip. There's no truth to it.''

"It was a police report," he corrected her. "After Willow's death, the police interviewed people who were at the hotel that night who might have seen or heard something that could give a clue to how she died. A hotel maid told them she saw Willow's mother with the brooch the day they left for Los Angeles with her body.''

Arianne shook her head. "Then clearly the maid was mistaken. If the brooch was in my family, I would have heard.''

"Maybe not." His mouth formed a sardonic half grin. "They'd want to keep it a secret. If the brooch turned up, it would tend to discredit the murder theory. And naturally, your family wants to believe she was murdered rather than know she committed suicide.''

Arianne felt indignant. "Even if she did kill herself, it was because of Peter, because he jilted her to marry someone wealthy.''

Ross's eyes narrowed. "He broke off the engagement because of her poor health.''

"So *your* family says," Arianne replied with spite. She was surprised how strongly she felt about the historic feud, now that her distant ancestor was being maligned by a descendant of Peter.

"Looks like the old animosity between our families hasn't died after all." He seemed to study her closely. She could see his eyes moving over her face, taking in each feature and her hair, which she'd gathered on top of her head today. "I don't know why I didn't guess the moment I saw you that you were related to Willow. You especially resemble her with your hair up like that." He looked down and wet his lips. When he glanced at her again, there was a contrite aspect in his lead-gray eyes. "I'm sorry about what happened on the beach. Obviously, it was a . . . mistake. As I said, if I had known—"

"If you'd known I was a Monroe, you wouldn't have soiled your hands by touching me?" she asked tartly, feeling insulted at being called a mistake.

"You don't have to take offense. I'm just saying that it's obvious we shouldn't—"

"Shouldn't what?" she baited him, just to be annoying.

"Shouldn't have an affair," he replied harshly.

She felt herself flush. The blunt words shook her. Now she knew for certain that he had indeed intended to take her to bed. She drew in a sharp breath as she realized she'd stopped breathing. Her heart began palpitating, fitfully skipping beats. She tapped her hand to her chest, a habit she had to try to steady her heartbeat whenever it went momentarily haywire.

"Are you all right?" he asked, his thick brows drawing together.

"Fine. My heart just skips a beat sometimes."

She was amazed to see him grow pale. His mouth turned downward in a grimace.

"Like Willow?" he accused. "You have a heart problem?"

Arianne felt wounded by his obvious aversion to her similarities to Willow. "It's not a *problem*," she retorted defensively. "My doctor has given me tests, and he assures me it's nothing to worry about. My heart just misses a beat or two now and then, usually when I'm tired or . . . or upset."

He eyed her warily. "And I've upset you."

"Yes."

"Sorry." As if feeling a trifle guilty now, he added, "Look, you probably know we Briarcliff men have a reputation for womanizing. My behavior last night proves I'm no exception. So you're better off not getting involved with me, no matter what our last names are."

"You've got that right!" she exclaimed. "I had no intention of getting involved with you anyway. I would *never* have gone to the beach to meet you again." This, of course, had not been totally settled in her mind, but he didn't need to know that.

His eyes brightened with an inner, knowing light, and he smiled slightly. She realized he was interpreting her as a lady who protested too much, as if he was sure now she would have met him. His self-possession enraged her. Her face felt hot as she strove to maintain her dignity.

"If that's all you have to say to me, then perhaps you should leave," she told him.

His eyes lost their glow and hardened. "What about the logo?" he asked. "I want your agreement to stop using the brooch design. I'll give you six weeks."

Now she was fuming. "I'll give *you* this," she said, reaching under the counter to pick up a packaged bottle. "It's my newest perfume. I named it Willow." She took it out of the box and sprayed some on her wrist.

His expression changed as the exotic fragrance filled the air. "You were wearing that last night."

"I always wear it. It's my favorite. And because I named it Willow, I have no intention of taking *her* brooch off the box. Nor will I take that logo off *any* of the Aragon Perfumery's products." She put the bottle in the box and handed it to him.

He took it from her in a brisk movement. Clearly incensed, yet seeming distracted now, as if other thoughts had entered his mind, he began to step backward toward the door. "Fine," he said, glaring at her. He held up the perfume she'd given him and using a threatening tone, he added, "I have this to use as evidence when I sue you!"

When he'd slammed out the door, Arianne braced herself against the counter, trembling. Her heart continued to beat unsteadily, so she sat down on the chair behind the counter to recover. Ross certainly fit the image of his disreputable family—charming and ruthless. In less than twenty-four hours, she'd seen the extreme of both traits. Not only that, Ross was rude, arrogant and heartless, too. Look at the high-and-mighty way he'd just threatened her! And the way he'd treated her as negligible—a mistake—after the passionate way he'd pursued her last night.

Women were nothing to the Briarcliff men, apparently. Easily pushed out of the way, as Peter had pushed Willow aside when he met an heiress he wanted more. Enduring such disdainful treatment was hard enough for Arianne, who had merely had a fleeting encounter on the beach with Ross. But Willow had been deeply in love when she'd been forsaken by Peter. Arianne could understand how his rejection had destroyed Willow.

"Poor Willow," Arianne murmured, feeling a strong new affinity for her long-dead relative. Tears filled her eyes.

Suddenly the sound of incredibly sad weeping echoed softly all around her. Arianne glanced up, wondering for a split second if she'd made the sound herself. She looked through the glass door into the hall. Some people were passing by, but no one was crying. They didn't seem to be aware of any sound.

Arianne realized then that the weeping noises were coming from inside her shop. Suddenly she grew aware of a presence right behind her. She turned quickly, but saw nothing. She began to feel a chill.

Fright took hold of her as the weeping continued, despite the fact that the crying sounds seemed to be in sympathy with her own feelings. Even if the spirit meant her no harm, Arianne still felt a sense of dread. What did the ghost of her long-dead relative want from her? Why did she keep returning, more and more often lately?

The weeping sound gradually faded and the sweet smell of violets pervaded the air, overcoming even the strong scent of the Willow perfume she'd just applied. The perfume contained the scent of violets as a main ingredient— the reason she'd named it Willow—mixed with other floral scents and spices. But now she could smell only the pure essence of violets.

And then the ghostly fragrance vanished and Arianne could smell her own perfume again, as if the other scent had never invaded the room. Arianne also felt alone in the small shop now, truly alone. The sense of an invisible presence just behind her, watching, was gone now, too.

She began to cry, feeling just slightly hysterical, and she didn't know why. Was it because she feared the ghost that seemed to have attached itself to her? Or was it because she *was* so alone?

All at once, Arianne felt quite forsaken. Her parents were off in Florida, happy in their new life. Her older brother, a CPA who had no interest in the perfume business, had moved to Seattle where his wife's family lived. Arianne's grandmother, who lived in Los Angeles, was the only relative in California she was close to. There were a number of cousins, most of them in Los Angeles, but Arianne only saw them at Christmas.

She still had friends from school, but most of them were married or about to get married. Being her girlfriends' bridesmaid at one wedding after another was getting to be a chore. She didn't like being single anymore, now that she was beginning to feel left behind.

Her friends had often told her she was too fussy about men. Perhaps they were right. She dated, but no one had impressed her or taken her interest lately. Actually, not many men ever had, even in college, where the selection had been vast. Those few men she found really attractive unfortunately had not taken an interest in her. It was the main reason she was still a virgin. She didn't like the idea of sleeping with a man if she wasn't at least halfway in love with him and there wasn't some prospect of a promising relationship that could lead to marriage. Maybe she was too old-fashioned, but she had to be true to her own feelings and instincts.

Letting out a long sigh as she wiped her eyes, Arianne thought how ironic it was that the one man who had stirred her to the marrow had turned out to be a Briarcliff. And he had not only dumped her already, but he was even threatening her with a lawsuit.

Arianne wished she had someone close by to confide in about this hurtful, unpleasant situation. She'd never been sued before. She needed someone to care about her, tell her she was okay and give her reassurance.

Someone still living, that is.

CHAPTER THREE

Late in the afternoon the following day, Ross mentally braced himself before opening the perfumery's glass door. He'd been thinking about his new plan of action all day and had finally decided to go ahead with it. As he entered the shop, two female customers were walking out, purchases in their hands. The fresh scents of perfumes invaded his nostrils. Again he experienced that feeling of entering another world of sensual pleasures and fantasy.

Arianne looked toward the door as he walked in. She had just begun polishing a wall mirror behind the counter, and when she saw him, she almost dropped the cloth in her hand. Her brown eyes widened, then grew alive with angry sparks. Ross tried not to notice how beautiful she was. Her hair was unclipped and worn down today, reaching almost the middle of her back. She had on a long white gauzy skirt with a sleeveless lavender blouse that had overlapping frills running down its front. Though the neckline plunged, the bouncy frill covered everything, but made a man think if he looked hard enough he might catch a peek. Arianne had the uncanny ability to look proper and seductive at the same time. Like Willow in the photo.

"Here to sue me already?" she asked.

"No. I'm hoping we can come to an amicable agreement about that." Ross had calmed down since he saw her yesterday. He'd realized that it wouldn't help his purposes to further alienate anyone from the Monroe family. If he was going to help William run for the Senate, he ought to do his best to heal old wounds instead of pouring more salt on them.

She looked suspicious. "You think an amicable agreement is possible between a Monroe and a Briarcliff?"

"We can try. I want to show you something," he said, walking up to the counter. He set the leather briefcase he was carrying on it and opened the case, carefully removing the items he'd brought.

Arianne put down her polishing cloth and came around the counter to watch as he took out an old leather-bound journal. As she stood quietly beside him, he noted that the top of her head came only to his chin, and her silky hair tumbled forward over her slim shoulders, innocently brushing the swell of her breasts. She folded her hands in front of her, and her face formed a pensive expression as she looked at the stack of old letters tied with a black ribbon that he was placing on the counter. She reminded him of a good child who had been taught to look but not touch.

Glancing at her, his senses already enveloped with perfume, Ross had the peculiar inner sensation of buoyancy, as if he was in an elevator. An odd feeling began to form in the pit of his stomach that was different from his usual experience of sexual attraction, though desire was certainly present inside him, too. The desire he could keep in its place for now, but this other thing, this curious new ache inside him, he didn't know how to interpret. He decided to ignore it.

"This is Peter Briarcliff's journal," he told her, keeping his voice and manner businesslike so as not to reveal his inner discomposure. "He kept journals during his twenties, until he married. This one covers the time he was involved with Willow. I was reading it last night and came across some information you might find interesting." He opened the book to a page he'd marked with a scrap of paper. "The pages are old and fragile, and his handwriting's not always easy to decipher. But read this page." He handed the open book to her.

Ross had expected her to read it silently, but she read it aloud. It gave him a disquieting feeling to hear his ancestor's words read in Arianne's high, soft voice, which might very well have resembled Willow's.

"'Los Angeles, May 16, 1901. I spoke with Dr. Mott today, which was my main purpose in making this trip to Los Angeles. He gave me the upsetting report that Willow's heart is so weak, she should not have children. He went so far as to say she would not survive a childbirth. Dr. Mott also told me he does not expect her to live past the age of thirty, a prediction he asked me not to relay to her, for he has not told her this himself.

"'I am in shock, though I ought to have guessed. There is no choice for me but to break my engagement to her. If we married, I could not live with her in a platonic manner. My overwhelming desire for her, and her eagerness to please me, would make a marriage in name only impossible. The events of my last visit to Los Angeles only prove this to be true.'"

Arianne looked up from the journal. "What does he mean by that?"

Ross hesitated, unsure how Arianne would take this revelation. "Peter and Willow had begun a sexual relationship. They'd made love on his previous trip to Los Angeles, when he came to visit her."

"But this was in 1901. Proper women didn't..." Arianne looked away from his eyes.

"They weren't supposed to, but that doesn't mean that all women followed the old moral standard."

"But she was beautiful and only twenty," Arianne argued. "She shouldn't have felt it necessary to give in to a man in order to try to keep him."

"Why do you say 'give in'? Maybe she wanted to. Maybe she was in love. Or maybe she was seducing him into marriage for his money."

Arianne's eyes flared. "She was in love! I've never heard that she was ambitious or greedy. Besides, how do you know this reference really means that she slept with Peter?"

Ross took the book from her and paged back to an entry written two months before. When he found the paragraph he was looking for, he began reading, holding the book so Arianne could see it, too. "'When I arrived at her house, her parents were away due to the sudden illness of a relative. Willow had stayed home to greet me. To my shame and guilty pleasure, I took advantage of the situation. Willow sweetly trembled, but became quite willing when my desire for her grew all too apparent. She was a virgin. Of course, I promised to marry her.

"'Perhaps this was hasty, but I think not. Marriage is the only remedy for my wild obsession for her; I can think of nothing else but being with her. My parents will not be pleased with my choice, but I shall ask them for the opal to give her.'"

Ross looked up from the book. "You see, it's quite clear they'd made love. It's hard to tell by this if it was mutual consent, or if he seduced her, or if he only thought he was seducing her. Maybe she actually seduced him and got a marriage proposal out of it."

Arianne looked indignant. "If she was a virgin, then obviously she wasn't experienced at seduction."

"But he mentions his wild obsession for her," Ross said. "It shows she had some . . . some hold over him." He felt uneasy at this thought, as he had when he'd looked at Willow's photo. If it could happen to Peter, it could happen to him.

"His obsession was *his* problem," Arianne said. "Why blame Willow?"

"That's an interesting take on it," Ross muttered in a sardonic tone. Women could twist men into knots and never feel they were to blame for anything, he thought. Somehow they always made it out to be the man's fault. Exhaling as he determined to drop this argument, he said, "Let's go back to May 16. I want you to finish reading that entry." He turned to the page and handed the book to Arianne.

With a sigh of displeasure, she began reading where she'd left off. " 'I shall have to ask her to give me back the brooch. My parents would never forgive me if I do not. I despair at the pain I will cause Willow. In fact, I do not feel able to tell her these things in person. Her beauty and her tears would cloud my resolve. Yet I must break this engagement of marriage for her sake, or else she might very well die one day giving birth to my child.

" 'There is a possibility that Willow could be carrying my child at this moment. We were together only once, so this is, fortunately, quite unlikely. She wrote of no such fear in her recent letter when she made reference to our shared moments of passion. Thus I believe I can rest easy that she is not with child, which would have made my present dilemma catastrophic.

" 'Breaking my engagement to her by letter is not an admirable way to handle the situation, but it is the only method by which I can be sure I will not weaken and that my intent will be made clear to her. I must marry someone else, to ensure that my break with Willow is final and incontrovertible. Miss Isabelle Hastings continues to pursue me. She has never held my interest for more than a quarter of an hour, but my parents would approve of the match. She comes from a prominent San Diego family, which Mother feels is important, and she is due to inherit a great deal, a fact which my father advises me is worthy of my consideration. I had thought the Briarcliffs had enough money already without the necessity of marrying into it.

" 'But Willow's health is such that if I can save her by making myself unavailable to her, and give my parents contentment in the process, then I cannot consider my own feelings. Perhaps I will grow to like Isabelle more over time.' "

Arianne set the book on the counter, her expression grave. Ross studied her a moment and said, "I brought this to you because I wanted you to see that Peter broke off with Willow because he wanted to save her. He didn't marry Isabelle for her money—it's clear he didn't particularly *want* her money. He didn't even care for her. He married her to cut himself off from Willow, for Willow's own sake."

Arianne quietly nodded. "He was certainly relieved that he hadn't gotten Willow pregnant," she muttered.

"And as for the brooch," Ross continued, "he needed to get it back because his parents wouldn't forgive him if he didn't."

Arianne nodded again. "Yes, he seemed most concerned about pleasing his parents," she said. "Maybe he accidentally killed Willow while struggling to get the brooch back from her. Maybe she absolutely refused to give it to him, and so he resorted to violence—all because of his fear of his parents' wrath."

This angered Ross. "But he never *got* the brooch. What I'm trying to show you here is that these entries prove he cared deeply for Willow. If he was trying to save her from himself, how could he have harmed her?''

"I don't get the impression he cared deeply for her," Arianne said, looking squarely at Ross. "He never uses the word *love* in either of these entries. Obsession and lust seem to be what drew him to Willow.''

Ross would have liked to have argued this point, but he had no ammunition. It was true that in the entries he'd read so far, Peter had never used the word *love* regarding Willow or anyone else. But perhaps men of that day didn't write their journals using such terms. Or perhaps Peter wasn't sure what love was. Ross himself had no experience with the emotion, probably wouldn't recognize it if it rose up and hit him in the face.

"What are these?" Arianne asked, pointing to the pile of letters tied with a ribbon.

"Those are Willow's letters to Peter. After they met when she was on a weekend outing with her family here at the Aragon, they wrote to one another.''

"I'd heard that, but I never saw any of the letters," she said. "Peter wrote to her in return?''

"He must have. Her letters include responses to things he'd written to her.''

"I wonder what happened to his letters," Arianne pondered.

Ross put the journal in his briefcase. He began untying the black ribbon that held the half dozen letters together. "Would you like to look at these?''

"Yes," she replied, her tone brightening. "Where did you find them?''

"They're in our family archives, along with Peter's journals.''

"Family archives? Like a library?''

"That's right. The Briarcliff mansion has a library in which all family legal documents, historic papers and so on are kept."

Her ingenuous brown eyes lifted to his. "You live on a big estate?"

"No, *I* don't. I have a condo on the beach."

"Who lives in the mansion?"

Ross felt self-conscious somehow about telling her, though he didn't know why he should. "My father lives there. He was the eldest of his generation and he inherited it from his father, who was Peter's eldest son. I . . . I grew up there."

"You grew up in a mansion?" she repeated in a tone of wary awe. "And you'll inherit it someday?"

"No, my brother, William, is the eldest. He'll inherit it."

"William Briarcliff? The one running for office?"

Ross nodded. "That's why I'm here at the hotel investigating this old tale about Willow being murdered. I'm trying to set the record straight about our family skeletons. If I can throw a clearer light on the Briarcliff name, it may help my brother's bid to become a senator."

Arianne smiled. "Don't they call that damage control?"

"I'm just trying to get at the truth," Ross responded in a testy voice.

"And how did threatening me with a lawsuit have anything to do with the truth or your brother's running for office?"

Ross took in a long breath. "Look, as I said when I came in, I've changed my mind about that. Maybe if we can talk things over in a friendly way—"

"Friendly? You molest me on the beach and then storm in here angry because you found out I'm a Monroe, and now you talk about being friendly?"

"I didn't molest you—"

"You fondled me!"

"We were kissing!" Ross retorted. "You cooperated—kissed me back. So I—" He stopped short. "Why are we talking about that? I told you, we ought to forget it ever happened."

"Forget an experience like that? How?" she asked. "You expect me to have a lobotomy?"

He leaned against the counter, taking a new tack. Looking her up and down, he smiled slightly. "Did I make that much of an impression on you? Do you wish it would happen again?"

Her face colored. "No!"

"Good. Then let's drop it. Agreed?"

Her lips pressed together in consternation. "It's just that you can't do things to people, threaten to sue them, or...or kiss them, and then expect them to just forget it ever happened because *you* changed your mind."

Ross bowed his head for a moment. "High-handedness is in my genes. There's not much I can do about heredity."

"Well, that's an easy way out! I can't help that I'm this way, because my family is like this? As if you have no judgment or willpower of your own?"

"What is this, a psychology session?" he snapped. "Can we get back to the subject at hand?"

She tossed her head as if to throw off her anger. The movement made her hair lift and then fall lightly over her shoulders and breasts. Her eyes sparked with stubborn lights as she asked, "What *is* the subject at hand? I still have no idea why you're here."

She could certainly lay things on the line when she wanted to, Ross thought. He couldn't help but admire her. She would have made a good lawyer.

"I'm here to make amends," he said.

"Could have fooled me."

"Maybe my talents don't lie in peacemaking," he told her with all the patience he could find, "but would you give me a chance?"

She shut her eyes and nodded her agreement. When she closed her eyes, he felt the sudden urge to take advantage of it and kiss her. He quelled the impulse, angry at himself. No, not angry—shaken. Why was he still so attracted to her? His mutinous desire for her would be his undoing if he wasn't careful. She was a Monroe, for God's sake. She even looked like Willow. What happened to his usual rational thinking? Was he going to make Peter's mistake all over again?

"I'm trying to smooth things out with you," he explained. "I regard you as a representative of the Monroes. Our families have never really talked to each other. I thought it's time we did, and meeting you has given me this opportunity. I brought the journal and the letters so you would see for yourself that Peter cared for Willow. He was actually trying to protect her, so I think it's unlikely that he murdered her. Maybe you and I can help stop this old feud."

"How do her letters show that he cared?" Arianne asked.

Ross selected two of the letters and began carefully opening them, for the aged paper had grown brittle. He spread them on the counter. Again, Arianne stepped closer to him to look at them, her bare arm brushing the sleeve of his suit jacket. He was stunned to find that her nearness almost made him tremble. Struggling to ignore his inexplicable inner state, he managed to keep his voice aloof.

"Here," he said, pointing to one letter, "she says that the words he wrote in his last letter moved her to tears. She says she'd never received such a tribute before."

"What had he said to her?" Arianne looked up at him, her eyes alive with curiosity, their warm brown mesmerizing Ross for a moment until he came to his senses.

He made an impatient shrug. "How should I know? We don't have his letters," he reminded her.

"I sure wish we did."

"And here," Ross said, pointing to the other letter, "she writes, 'Don't worry so about my heart. As long as it beats for you, it will remain strong.' So, you see," he said as he glanced at Arianne, "he must have shown concern about her, or she wouldn't have felt the need to reassure him. And then she goes on to thank him for his proposal of marriage, and says she regrets nothing that has happened between them, and that she longs for the day she will be his wife."

He found Arianne blinking hard and avoiding his eyes. Ross realized with a slight jolt that she was crying. "Are you okay?" he asked with hesitance, for he never had known what to do with a weeping female. "Do these letters upset you?"

She shook her head, making her shining brown hair swish, making him long to stroke it. "It's just that you can see how much Willow loved Peter. It's so sad," Arianne said, wiping the corner of one eye with her fingertips. She seemed slightly embarrassed. "Sorry. I'm one of those people who cries easily."

Ross stood beside her for a moment, silent and at a loss. This had all taken a somewhat different turn than he'd anticipated. Feeling edgy, he began to gather up the letters. "Maybe we've looked at these enough for now."

"No, wait." Arianne reached out to stop him, brushing his hands with hers as she took hold of the letters. Her warm touch made him immobile for a tense moment as a quake of desire tremored inside him. With a frightening thud he realized the depth of his own weakness for her. The impulsive part of his brain asked, *Why are you fighting it?* The sensible part of him, which he tried to foster, told him to stay away from Arianne if he knew what was good for him.

And then an image, sudden and vivid, formed in his mind's eye. He saw a clear vision of Arianne wearing the missing Briarcliff brooch. She looked proud and secure with the fiery opal pinned to her dress—like Willow in the photo, only he was certain he was seeing Arianne and not her ancestor. Arianne looked far more radiant, her warm eyes aglow with feeling, appreciation...and unshed tears. Not tears of sadness, as he'd just seen her wipe away, but of happiness. In the vision she looked fulfilled.

The unbidden image stunned Ross. He'd never had any such visions before. It seemed to him like a premonition, and a very disturbing one, too. Yet, how could he *know* it was a premonition? he asked himself. He had no experience with such things, nor did he believe in them. Still he had to ask, why had he seen *Arianne* wearing the brooch? Did it mean that she or someone in her family had the Briarcliff jewel, even though she denied it? Was this perhaps ESP at work? Or was his imagination playing tricks? Was he going to put stock in a split second image that had mysteriously come to him? Or was he going crazy?

Concerned for the moment about his sanity, he grasped the letters tightly and fought to pull them out of Arianne's hands. As a result, one of the old envelopes began to tear. "What are you doing?" he asked sharply.

"I want to read them *all,*" she pleaded.

"Another time," he said, feeling more and more agitated. "I have to leave."

But before he could put the letters into his briefcase, Arianne made another effort to grab them away, saying, "They're Willow's letters. I have a right to see them. Let me borrow them."

"They belong in our archives," Ross said with finality as he quickly avoided her grasp.

"How can you be so unfeeling?" she asked, tears rising in her eyes again. It reminded him of his premonition, only she looked angry now and in the vision she'd looked so happy. "Willow was *my* relative and I have a right to read them!"

What was going on here? Ross wondered as he dropped the letters safely into his briefcase and shut it. The energy level in the room seemed heightened, and their emotions were definitely escalating.

All at once a bottle of perfume on the counter, not far from his briefcase, tipped over. Ross would have taken little notice of it, but Arianne stared at the bottle and immediately turned ashen. He looked at the bottle again and noticed it was a tester bottle of Willow perfume.

"She's here," Arianne whispered on a tremulous breath. "She's never come before when there was someone with me. Maybe she's angry."

"Who's here?" Ross asked, looking around him. The shop was still empty, other than the two of them.

"Willow."

"Willow? Oh, not you, too!" Ross said in a tone that was more harsh than he meant. "For God's sake, you don't believe Willow is here hovering next to us, do you?"

"I *know* she's here. How do you explain the bottle falling over?" Arianne asked, pointing to it. "All by itself."

"I was shutting my briefcase. Probably the vibration on the counter knocked it over."

"But the bottle has a wider bottom than its top. It couldn't fall from a vibration. It was knocked over."

"Calm down," Ross said, alarmed now because Arianne was visibly shaking. Her fingertips were at her heart, as if she felt it beating unsteadily. "There's a logical explanation. Why jump to the conclusion it's a ghost?"

"Because she's been here before," Arianne told him. "She . . . she haunts me."

Ross shook his head and automatically began to reassure her, settling his hand gently upon her shoulder as if she was a child. "Ghosts don't exist, Arianne."

She gave him an impatient look and moved out from under his hand. "What do *you* know? You've only been at the hotel a few days."

He exhaled. "Have you ever *seen* a ghost here?"

"I haven't yet, but some guests have said they've seen a mist that took the shape of a woman. And my mother said Willow appeared to her once when she was here in the shop. After that, my mom never wanted to come here anymore, even though my father worked here. Mom was so frightened, she never would even talk about it. She never told me exactly what she saw, maybe because I was little then, and she didn't want to scare me."

"Did your father ever see the ghost?" Ross asked out of curiosity.

"No," Arianne replied, shaking her head. "He worked here for over twenty years and said he never saw, felt or heard anything. He thought my mother was imagining things." She looked at Ross, an innocent earnestness in her eyes. "But my father wasn't a Monroe. My mother's the granddaughter of Katy, Willow's sister. So, it stands to reason Willow would appear to her and not to my father. Just as she . . . comes to *me,* now. But I don't know why."

Ross made a patient nod. "I think your father was right. You're imagining things."

Arianne's huge eyes turned against him. "How would *you* know? I trust my instincts. I know what I've felt and heard."

"Heard?"

"She was crying yesterday, after you stormed out threatening to sue me. Maybe she's upset with you—maybe that's why she knocked down that bottle, because you wouldn't let me have her letters."

Ross couldn't help but think again of the odd charge he'd felt in the atmosphere a few moments ago. But he began to think now that perhaps he'd been confused by his own reactions to Arianne. It was undoubtedly Arianne who had altered his energy level by inciting his desire and making him tense. . . .

Never mind that, Ross told himself. The thing was, his inner agitation, perhaps even the vision he'd had, may have been caused by the sudden, unexpected longing he'd felt, which had thrown him momentarily off balance.

Whatever had happened, it was over. Everything seemed calm now. Ross felt back in control of himself and the situation. In fact, he found himself feeling rather protective of Arianne, which he perceived to be a much safer state of mind. Like a big brother, he felt strong and in charge. She was frightened, afraid of an imagined specter, and he wished to reassure her. He'd left her upset yesterday, and he didn't want to leave her in distress again today. Especially if she was blaming *him* for disturbing the "ghost."

"Do you think she's still here?" he asked, humoring her.

"No," she said, alert and standing very still, as if testing the air, "I don't feel her presence anymore."

"Good. Isn't it time for you to close up shop?" he asked, glancing at his watch. "It's almost six. You need some fresh air. Maybe some supper. You'll feel better."

Arianne nodded. "You're probably right."

"Doesn't breathing this perfume all day get to you?"

Arianne smiled sheepishly, the most charming expression he'd seen her make yet. She appeared innocent and artless, certainly not a young woman to be wary of. "The alcohol does make me light-headed by the end of the day," she admitted, "if I've had a lot of customers. I give them perfume tests, and the potato alcohol gets sprayed into the air all day long. The hotel is old and the ventilation system isn't very good."

"Is that when you usually get a visit from Willow, at the end of the day when you're light-headed?" he asked with amusement.

"No," she said in a grave tone, losing her smile. "I've felt her presence at all times of the day. Even on the beach, just before I met you. Remember I asked if you pushed me?"

Ross nodded, narrowing his eyes in disbelief. "You mean you think the ghost—"

"I felt a hand on my upper arm," she insisted, "pushing me toward the beach. It knocked me off balance. That's when you caught me."

He shook his head. "You must have imagined it. Maybe it was a gust of wind."

"I'm not so frail that a breeze would knock me over."

"You look like you are," he said softly.

She studied him with a sober expression, as if wondering what he'd meant by that.

Ross ignored her look, not wanting to deal with the question implied in her eyes. "Why don't we grab a bite to eat?'' he suggested in a new tone of voice. ''I think you'll feel better.''

''*We?*''

''I'm . . . asking you to have dinner with me,'' he said, justifying his action in his own mind as he explained it to her. ''Consider it a historic occasion—a Monroe breaking bread with a Briarcliff.'' It was part of his mission to try to heal old wounds on behalf of his family.

''I don't think we have to go to that extreme,'' she said with doubt in her eyes, as if remembering their encounter on the beach.

''Can't we just try to be friendly? You don't have to read anything into it,'' he said with annoyance. ''Besides, I want to be sure you're all right. You seem so shaken.''

''I'll be all right,'' she assured him in no uncertain voice.

The idea that she might actually refuse to have dinner with him made him try all the harder to convince her. His Briarcliff pride was rearing its head. ''We can look over the rest of Willow's letters,'' he offered.

Her expression changed, as if she was considering taking the bait, but she still seemed doubtful. Ross felt his insides knotting. He wasn't used to a woman keeping him on tenterhooks.

Finally she said, ''Well . . . all right. But let's go to one of the restaurants here at the hotel.''

The stipulation intrigued him. She must be afraid to go off to some other place alone with him. He had to admit, she had reason to be. Here at the hotel, they were more or less on her territory. Including the beach. Perhaps that was why she'd felt safe enough to give in to his kiss.

''That's fine with me,'' he said, relieved that she'd agreed to have dinner.

But as they walked out of the perfume shop and into the stale air of the hallway, Ross began to feel confused again.

He asked himself, *Why are you doing this? We'll probably just argue some more. Either that, or those dark Willow eyes of hers will be your undoing. You've got to be careful.* He remembered his fleeting premonition. Did it foretell Arianne's coming triumph over the Briarcliffs, and over him?

And then Ross realized there might be another explanation for the vision—it might have been the effect of the perfume alcohol on *his* brain. If Arianne could imagine ghosts, he could have visions, he supposed.

That must be what happened, he thought, relaxing, feeling a definite release of tension in his body. Thank God, he'd managed to think through and analyze the situation. It just showed that if a person used logic and reason, he could find a rational explanation for any unusual phenomenon.

In the same way, if Ross simply used common sense, he could keep his unruly physical attraction to Arianne from turning him into a fool. Peter may have lacked such common sense, but Ross had the advantage of knowing family history. He reminded himself of the old platitude—if he didn't learn from the past, he was doomed to make the same mistakes. It was all a matter of being on guard.

And staying away from perfume.

CHAPTER FOUR

Arianne sat down at the table with Ross. They were in the elegant main dining room of the Aragon Hotel, noted for its high ceiling made entirely of carved wood. The waiter had led them to a small table set in front of an upholstered booth seat built into the wood-paneled wall. There were no chairs set opposite the booth seat, so Arianne had to sit next to Ross. The close proximity made her wary, but she decided she was safe in a huge dining room filled with people. Still, when she felt his body heat as he slid in next to her, she grew tense and too aware of his masculine presence. After they'd ordered from the menu, she glanced at him.

"You promised I could see the letters," she reminded him. Whatever he'd had in mind for this dinner, she planned to keep him to his word.

Ross appeared to be distracted. "You're wearing your Willow perfume, aren't you?"

"Yes. Why, don't you like it?" she asked, wondering what was bothering him.

His mouth quirked and he seemed uneasy, even slightly restless. "You need to advertise your product, I suppose," he muttered.

Now she knew why he was annoyed. "It reminds you of our dispute over my logo, doesn't it? You threatened to use the bottle I gave you as evidence."

He vigorously shook his head. "Not at all. I think we can settle that amicably."

Arianne was doubtful. "Really? How?"

Ross took in a breath, making his broad chest expand, as if he was still pulling his thoughts together. "If you'll agree to stop using the brooch design out of consideration for my family, I'll agree to pay the cost of creating a new logo and printing your first batch of new boxes and labels."

The generous offer surprised Arianne. But coming from a fabulously wealthy family as Ross did, such an offer probably cost him relatively little. Arianne kept her expression impassive and told him, "I'll think about it and let you know."

He seemed taken aback, as if he'd expected her to jump at it. "When?"

"When I've thought it over," she replied. She wasn't going to let herself be intimidated by him just because he was rich and influential. "Now, can I see the letters?"

He pressed his lips together in consternation, but made no verbal objection. Leaning to one side, he brought up his briefcase. He took out the letters, still in disorder from their fracas earlier, and handed them to her.

Arianne put them in order according to their postmarked dates, then read them one by one. They were short letters, most no more than a page long, written in Willow's graceful, flowing hand. The first ones were quite formal and proper. The couple apparently had gotten to know each other only briefly before Willow and her family went back to Los Angeles after their weekend holiday at the Aragon. Peter, who lived in San Diego, had gone to the hotel to participate in a local charity event. From the letters, Arianne gathered that Willow met Peter on the beach on Saturday afternoon, when a wave took her off balance while she was wading and Peter came to her rescue. They spent a few hours talking after she'd gone to her room to change out of her wet clothes. Peter came again the next day, Sunday, to see her once more before she left for Los Angeles.

Their letters, which grew increasingly friendly, even intimate, judging by Willow's, kept the romance going until Peter began coming to Los Angeles to visit her. One of the letters was written after his first visit to her home. Willow wrote:

I so appreciated your brief stay with us. Merely being with you, enjoying your humor and your tender courtesies, makes me feel entirely well and whole. My parents are quite impressed with you, too. How could they not be? You are the kindest, most considerate, most handsome gentleman any of us have met. Speaking for myself, I know I will never find your equal in another. So I must selfishly hope and pray that you will continue to be my friend, my good confidant, my splendid knight in shining armor. You rescued me from the sea and rescued my lonely heart, as well.

Arianne found moisture welling in her eyes as she read these words. A tear dropped onto the letter and she quickly reached for her napkin to blot it before it could smear the aged ink. The waiter had brought their salads, so Arianne gathered up the letters and handed them to Ross.

"Can you make me copies of these?" she asked with a sniff.

Ross studied her eyes as he took the letters. "Sure. They made you cry again?"

"Willow thought so highly of Peter," she said, blotting her eyes with the napkin. "She calls him her knight in shining armor. *I've* never felt that way about anybody, except maybe my father. She was fortunate enough to find someone she really loved and admired, and...and then he betrayed her."

"He *didn't,*" Ross insisted. "He left her to save her life."

Arianne adamantly shook her head. She'd come to another conclusion. "If he really loved her, he would have stayed with her and kept their relationship platonic."

Ross looked askance. "You have to be realistic, Arianne. People are people. They have drives and needs. A platonic relationship between a man and woman who have a strong physical attraction is just about impossible."

"Love doesn't have to be physical," Arianne argued.

His head went back and his brows drew together. "Were you raised in a convent or something?"

She gave him a look. "No."

"You seem to have some idealized notion of what male-female relationships are like. You're beginning to look upon Willow as a saint. And you expect Peter to have behaved like some Prince Valiant on a white charger, which is apparently what she thought he was. Well, people aren't like that in real life. They're human. They always fall short of perfection."

"All I'm saying," Arianne reiterated with impatience, "is that she clearly loved him. I feel sad that she was so disappointed in that love."

Ross's shoulders lifted in what appeared to be an indifferent shrug. "Well—too bad she wasn't healthier. Peter probably would have married her, and we would all be happier today."

Arianne had picked up her salad fork, but his state-ment made her pause. "We would?"

"At least we wouldn't have this feud between our fam-ilies."

A new thought came into Arianne's mind. "What if her doctor was wrong, and she could have married Peter and had children? Then you and I would be cousins. I would be distantly related to the wealthy Briarcliff family now instead of a middle-class citizen with no important con-nections to brag about." The notion amused her.

"Must be nice," Ross muttered.

"What?"

"I wish I had been born into an average family. You think it's easy to be a Briarcliff?" he asked rhetorically. "Money might bring material security, but not emotional security. My family seems terminally tainted and scandal-ridden." He studied Arianne. "What were your parents like?" he asked as if genuinely interested. "Did they have a good marriage?"

"Oh, yes," Arianne said with a smile. "Still do. They've moved to Florida now, and I've stayed here because my friends are all here. But I miss them."

"What's your father like?"

"He's a quiet, steady sort of man. But also romantic. It stands to reason—he made a career out of developing perfumes. That's what my mother liked about him. Al-though she sometimes complained he was too romantic and spent too much money on flowers and things for her. He named a perfume for her. It's Nanette, one of our more popular scents."

"Did he name one for you?" Ross asked.

"He's still working on it," she said with a laugh. "He tried a few formulas, but complained that I kept changing as I grew up, as every child does. Said he hadn't yet been able to pin down my essence. He never knew whether to emphasize floral or spice, because I was one way one day, and another the next. He says he's waiting for my personality to gel. I just turned twenty-four. You'd think I'd have gelled enough by now.''

Ross scrutinized her, smiling as he took in her features. Arianne felt unsteady under his close gaze, especially when he looked as handsome as he did now. When he smiled, creases formed in his cheeks and near his eyes, and he looked . . . well, wonderful.

"A tad more experience in the real world is all you need,'' he said, an unexpected light coming into his gray eyes, making them shine like silver. "A little less time spent breathing in perfume ethers and communing with ghosts. You should be out with people more worldly than you are.''

She raised her eyebrows in a knowing way. "Like I am now, with you?''

His smile grew sad and he lowered his eyes. She'd noticed that when he wasn't angry or agitated about something, he usually looked melancholy. "No, not me. Even if we didn't have this historic problem between our families, I wouldn't be a good example for you to learn from.''

"On the beach, you seemed to think you'd be good for me,'' she pointed out. Something inside prodded her to bring up the episode he kept wanting her to forget.

"Arianne,'' he said with patience, as if she was very naive, "that was just sex, pure and simple. Sparks from the wrong chemical experiment. That's not what I mean.''

Just sex? Sparks from the wrong experiment? Arianne couldn't help but feel shocked at his clinical assessment of what had happened between them, though she ought to have guessed that he'd look upon it that way. Maybe she *was* idealistic and inexperienced. "What do you mean, then?"

"I didn't know you as a person when I met you on the beach," he said. "You were just a beautiful woman I wanted. Now, I see you more as an individual and..." He seemed to hesitate.

"What?"

"You're a nice, well brought up young woman. You don't deserve a man like me in your life. You know how notorious Briarcliff men are. It's probably because we didn't have a good home life, such as you were brought up in. You have parents who seem to adore each other. And they apparently gave you lots of attention. My parents— well, they got along better domestically than most Briarcliff matches have, but they certainly didn't have a marriage I'd want to emulate. They were often abrasive toward each other, then sometimes went for days without speaking to each other. It probably was better than shouting and throwing things, but it wasn't a happy household. My father was critical, when he noticed us at all. My mother was... subdued and just seemed to cope day by day. She was too involved in her own problems and deficiencies to be able to give much attention to my brother and me. We never even expected affection from my father. My brother is the only one who made our family life tolerable. He's gifted with humor and an innate optimism. But I'm pessimistic and selfish—like my father. I sometimes wonder what I might have been if I'd been born into a different family, one that was warm and loving, like yours. I envy you your parents."

Ross finished his surprising burst of words on a bitter note. Then, for a moment, he stared mutely at his uneaten salad, as if wondering what had happened. "Sorry," he muttered in a self-conscious tone, "I don't usually talk so much."

"That's okay," Arianne said, feeling strange and yet glad that he had felt like confiding in her. "It's good to get things off your chest."

"Why?" he said, his voice very cold now. "It doesn't change anything." He picked up his salad fork and began eating.

Arianne guessed that he was either embarrassed at having revealed so much about himself, or reminding himself of his life problems had put him in a sullen mood.

"But it's still good to talk about things," Arianne said. "Sharing your story with someone else makes you feel better, even if it doesn't change anything."

Ross ruthlessly speared a tomato with his fork. "Doesn't seem to work for me."

His sudden change of mood disconcerted Arianne. The anger in him was so formidable, she didn't know how to react to it, even if it wasn't directed at her. She'd always been a little afraid of moody men who seemed to have tightly wound springs. Her father and brother were never like that. While she had little experience with such intense men, they seemed romantic to her, because they were so emotionally charged. She'd been drawn to a few such young men in her college years, but they had never returned her interest. Perhaps they also had thought she was too inexperienced. And yet they continually intrigued her. Maybe it was because she hoped their dark emotions could be rechanneled. If they could feel such deep hurt or anger, perhaps they were also capable of deep love.

Though she would have liked to draw Ross out more, she didn't know how to go about it without risking making him more morose. So she ate in silence next to him until she'd finished her salad.

The waiter appeared with their main course and, with a thick slice of prime rib in front of him, Ross seemed to slowly come out of his dark mood.

"Tell me more about your family," he said after a while.

"Really?" She wondered if that was wise.

"I'd like to know how the other half lives, what a normal American family is like."

"Well, I'm not sure if we were normal," she joked, "but we did have fun together."

"You had brothers and sisters?"

"An older brother. He's married and lives in Seattle now. Everyone's left me," she said wistfully.

As he cut his meat, he asked, "By the way, how did you wind up here at the hotel? It seems like quite a coincidence. I didn't know anyone from the Monroe family lived in San Diego, much less worked at the Aragon."

"I know. It's like fate or something," Arianne said, feeling a little shiver. She'd often thought she was destined to be here, especially now that Willow had begun to haunt her, as though something was happening in the cosmos beyond her control. "My father was from Florida, but he moved to San Diego with his parents when he was a teenager. When he was grown, he studied perfume making in France, because it had always interested him. He came back to San Diego and started up his own business making perfumes in his home. Eventually, he arranged with the hotel to open the Aragon Perfumery. My mother was from Los Angeles, like most of the Monroes. They met when he was attending a fragrance convention in Los Angeles. She was a model hired to demonstrate perfume products for a well-known manufacturer. Eventually they married and she moved down here with him. She had heard the story about Willow's drowning, of course, but she hadn't paid much attention to the reports that the ho-

tel was haunted. Once my mother found out the importance the hotel seemed to place on the Willow legend, she
asked my father to ask Alex to keep quiet that she was a
Monroe. And Alex did, until my father gave the business
to me. I was the one who began to take an interest in Willow and named a perfume for her.''

Arianne paused and smiled at Ross. ''Some of our
family are embarrassed, and others are intrigued by the
idea that Willow still haunts the hotel. Some think it's a lot
of hogwash. My mother said she used to think it was a silly
story the hotel made up to get publicity.''

''That's exactly what it is,'' Ross interrupted.

Arianne lost her smile. ''But she saw the ghost. That's
my point. She didn't believe the story, but then she actually saw the ghost, got scared to death and has believed in
ghosts ever since.''

''What scared her?''

''I don't know. Maybe just seeing an apparition frightened her. It would sure scare me.''

''But you haven't seen—''

''No. No, I . . . I hope I don't, either. The scent of violets and the weeping are enough. And that bottle getting
knocked over—''

''*I* probably knocked it over accidentally without realizing,'' Ross said.

''No, you didn't. I was right next to you. Your hand
wasn't near the bottle. You were grabbing the letters.''

He cut another piece of meat. ''Even if there is something supernatural going on—which I don't believe for a
moment—but for the sake of argument, why are you so
afraid? Scents and weeping can't hurt you. Neither can a
knocked over perfume bottle. Seems to me it's more
amusing than scary.''

"But the weeping sounds so tragic," she told him with feeling. "When I sense her presence, I grow inexplicably sad, too. For no reason. And besides that…" She drew in a breath, anticipating what Ross would think of what she was about to tell him. "I met a psychic at a party recently. I told her about my experiences and said I believed the ghost was my relative, Willow. I was looking for advice and asked, Should I try to contact the spirit? You know, through a séance or one of those ouija boards. Not that I know how to use such methods, but I figured I could read up on it."

She paused when she saw Ross roll his eyes. "I know you think it's all ridiculous," she told him, "but it's real to me."

"Why would you want to contact Willow?" he asked. "To be sure it's your relative and not some other stray ghost?"

"Yes. And to find out what she wants. She must be haunting me for some reason. I think she may have some message for our family, and she's trying to make contact."

"What did the psychic say?" Ross asked in an indulgent tone.

"She grew quite concerned and warned that I should absolutely not try a séance or use a ouija board. She said it could be very dangerous. Some spirits are evil. If you invite them in, you can leave yourself open to great harm, she told me. The best thing, she said, is to have an expert come in and make contact."

"An expert? Like her?"

"Yes."

"Sounds like she's trying to drum up business." Ross threw his napkin on the table after finishing his plate. "She's probably one of those professional ghost busters.

She'll charge you some hefty sum and use some mumbo jumbo to convince you she's gotten rid of your imagined ghost."

"It's *not* imagined!"

"All right," he said in a soothing tone. "Finish your chicken. You're not eating."

He reminded her of her father now. She said no more and resumed eating. Let him talk about whatever *he* wants to, she decided. She hoped he'd choose some subject other than ghosts or family, since these topics inevitably led to tiffs between them.

"So it was just coincidence that your father worked at the hotel and then married a Monroe?" Ross said, apparently wanting to settle the question he'd asked earlier.

"Just coincidence," she confirmed, when she'd swallowed a bite. "Or maybe it was fate."

"You believe in fate, too?"

She smiled. "I don't know. Do you?"

"No. I don't believe in much of anything," he said dourly. "Want some dessert?"

She shook her head.

They were silent for a while. As Arianne finished her plate, she hoped they were finally done with the topic of family. All at once Ross asked, "Do you believe in love?"

This question, out of the blue, threw her. "Sure."

"I suppose you would," he said philosophically. "You had your parents' example to learn from. That's the problem with the Briarcliffs. None of them ever loved their spouses. They always married for lust or money. They don't seem to know how to marry for the right reason." He paused. "Except my brother. He's happily married. Somehow he just knew."

"What about you?" she asked, curious.

"Me? I'm like the rest of my family. But I don't intend to follow in their footsteps, at least not when it comes to making bad marriages."

Arianne grew interested. "How will you make a good marriage?"

"I won't," he said. When she drew her brows together in puzzlement, he explained, "I don't intend to marry at all."

"Oh." She felt cold all of a sudden. "I see. So that's why you follow women on the beach. Sex, pure and simple, as you said before."

"'Fraid so. Though, *you* don't have to worry about that any more. I won't..." He seemed to think better of what he was about to say. "No, I can't promise it won't happen again. Not if you keep wearing that perfume. You'd better stay on guard."

Her eyes widened in astonishment. "Thanks for the warning."

He stared at her, the pupils of his eyes growing large. "Look, I don't want to get involved with you. It wouldn't be good for either of us. But...I *am* attracted. I'm trying to be honest about it, so you know. I'm attracted to you, and I don't *want* to be. And I know you'd prefer me not to be." He tilted his chin. "So you're very smart to avoid me. But I'm a born skirt chaser, and there may be times when my basic instincts will get in the way of my good intentions. Just so you understand—it's nothing personal. You're beautiful and you're feminine, and I find myself...responding, that's all. Keep on avoiding me, as you have been. That's my advice."

This was the most peculiar piece of advice Arianne had ever received. "Why, will we be seeing each other after tonight?"

The question seemed to take him off guard. "I'll ... be doing more research here at the hotel. I'll probably run into you. And there's the logo issue that has to be resolved between us."

"Oh. Yes, I forgot. I'll let you know what I decide. Do you have a business card? I can leave a message with your secretary, and that way we won't have to see each other."

His eyes darkened beneath his thick black eyebrows, giving her a start. She wondered if she'd said something to spark his anger. Yet she was trying to be cooperative and follow his advice.

He pulled out his wallet and gave her a card. He seemed restless now. Arianne didn't know why—whether he was put out with her, or himself, or what. She didn't know what sort of response he wanted from her, and she was beginning to suspect he didn't know, either.

Though Arianne objected, Ross paid the check and they left. As they walked though the hotel lobby, Arianne reluctantly said, "Thank you for dinner." She had wanted to pay her share.

"My pleasure," he said. "Can I take you home?"

The offer surprised her, coming from a man who had just finished telling her he didn't want to get involved. Maybe he was being polite. She quickly said, "Thanks, but I have my car."

"I'll walk you to your car, then."

She purposely gave him a gracious smile. "That's really not necessary." Extending her hand to shake his, she said, "Thanks again for dinner, and I'll let your secretary know my decision about the logo."

He didn't take her hand. "I have to go to the parking lot to get my car, too. So we might as well walk together. Besides, it's after dark, and you shouldn't go out there alone."

She reluctantly nodded her agreement, since he'd demolished any arguments she could come up with. "You know," she said, taking a tone of teasing irony, "I never know from one minute to the next if you're going to threaten me, be a rogue or a gentleman. You're hard to figure out."

"You have no idea," he said in a sardonic tone, casting his gaze to the carpeted floor as they walked. "*I* have to *live* with me."

She chuckled at his unexpected, self-effacing humor, which she rather liked.

He quietly added, "I wish I could laugh, but it's not funny."

Her humor checked by his comment, she walked in silence alongside him out to the south parking lot. It had indeed grown quite dark. Dinner must have taken longer than she'd thought. The hotel, illuminated by floodlights, took on the surreal dimension of a large, white, gothic fantasy, with its pointed towers and multilevel eaves outlined with strings of lights. They were at the backside of the south wing, and she glanced up at the third floor. Long ago she'd figured out which window belonged to Room 302. When she found the correct double-paned window, she thought she saw a wispy figure in white there. A sudden tremor ran through her as she wondered if it was Willow, watching them. But she blinked and looked again, and the window was black and empty. She'd imagined it, she told herself.

Shaken, she pointed out her blue Camry to Ross and nervously got out her keys. He walked beside her, quiet, yet aware, with a sense of power in his stride. His superior height and robust frame made her seem diminutive by comparison, though she was of average height. No one was around, and she began to feel vulnerable being alone with him. The fact that he'd admitted he was attracted to her, and didn't want to be, kept her on edge. It made him altogether unpredictable.

When they reached the car, she immediately unlocked the door, eager to separate from him as quickly as possible. In the silence and the darkness, she'd grown so aware, once again, of his masculine presence, that her pulse was beginning to race. She wasn't sure if she could predict *herself,* either. The night atmosphere vividly reminded her of what had happened on the beach. She certainly didn't want a repeat of that scene.

Again, she extended her hand. "Good night."

He took her hand and kept it in his, stepping close to her. "You look jittery. What's wrong? Is it being with me?"

"No," she prevaricated, not wanting to get into another conversation about their odd relationship. "I...I looked up at the window of Room 302," she said, pointing to the south wing, "and for a second I thought I saw a face there. I'm sure I imagined it. But it's shaken me a little."

He turned to look where she'd pointed. "Which window?"

"Third floor up, fifth one over from where the west wing intersects the building."

"Fifth room? Isn't it 302?"

"There's a linen closet that's not numbered, and a larger suite, called the executive suite, which isn't numbered and has two windows."

Ross seemed to look at the windows, which were all unlit and still. He turned to her with a slight grin. "You've apparently checked it all out. Have you ever been in 302?"

"No. Just passed by it—fast." She smiled. "I felt a chill when I went by, but it may have been my own fright.

Sometimes I wonder if I do imagine things," she admitted.

"It's that perfume alcohol," he said, bringing her wrist to his nose to sniff the fragrance she'd applied there. He paused, and his body seemed to tense. Yet he didn't let go of her hand; in fact, his grasp grew more possessive. "It's playing havoc with your emotions," he said in a low, whispery voice that gave her goose bumps. He shifted his shining eyes and looked directly at her. "With our emotions."

"Ross—" she said, trying to pull her hand away, feeling wary. The acquisitive way he was looking at her was all too familiar. She'd seen the same inner lights in his eyes on the beach. This shouldn't be happening. And yet, she felt powerless—didn't want it to stop. His masculine presence and confident bearing, his squared shoulders and deep chest, overwhelmed her. Yet his whispered low voice seemed to carry so much tenderness. Being swept away by him again was too tantalizing. Her desires, awakened a few days ago by this same aggressive, sensual man, were crying out inside her. She longed to be in his arms again. What was wrong with her? Where was her usual caution?

He moved his head downward toward hers in a deliberate manner. She could see his intent face growing closer, larger, feel his breath on her cheek.

"No," she said weakly, but the word was smothered by his seeking mouth. His strong arms enveloped her and pulled her tightly against him. She could feel his heart beating fast as her chest met his, and soon it seemed to beat in unison with her own heart. The sensitivity in his warm hands roving over her back lulled her into relaxing against him as he deepened the kiss. His seeking hand found the side of her breast and caressed its curve. She yearned for even more intimate fondling, and her nipples hardened with sweet anticipation.

But he slid his hands downward to her hips and then over her derriere, pulling her provocatively against him. All at once she became aware of his all too ready and potent male desire for her. Her instincts told her he harbored every intention of finishing what he'd begun. Her car was unlocked. All he'd have to do was push her into the back seat. However much her own unexplored, yearning desires pulled on her wisdom, she realized she wasn't ready for this.

Arianne began pushing with her hands on his chest, trying to wrench her mouth away from his. She managed to cry, "Stop it!"

His arms keeping her snugly against him, he stared at her with heated, incensed eyes. "Why?"

"Why! You told me that a relationship between us was no good."

"I was wrong." His voice grew urgent as he inclined his face toward hers. "This is just what we need," he whispered, brushing her bruised lips with his. "There's an easy way to settle this old feud. Why not make love?"

She twisted away from his mouth. "Because it wouldn't be making *love*. It would just be sex. You said it yourself."

"There's nothing wrong with sex," he argued, nuzzling the side of her head, biting her ear. "I could feel you responding. I can tell you're attracted to me. Why not explore our desires? This could be the best romance either of us will ever have."

She pushed hard on his shoulders, angry at the way he ignored her protest. "It's lust, not romance! I don't want to be your newest toy, the latest piece of gossip connected with your family."

He drew his head back, his eyes cold and hard as they pinned hers in a stare. "You're refusing me because you're afraid of a scandal?"

"Ross, you told me yourself that you're like all the men in your family. You advised me to stay away from you. It was your intention to stay away from *me*. You're going against—"

"Because I *can't* stay away from you!" He almost shouted this, but his voice broke as he did. "Sure, I know better, when I stop to think. But it won't work." He seemed beside himself, as if tormented by his need and frustration. "You put on that damn perfume, and look at me with those brown eyes, and I'm . . . I'm Peter coming under Willow's spell all over again. He couldn't resist her sorcery, and I'm no better. I don't care what happens. I want you!"

Arianne's hands grew icy as she drew them away from his shoulders. "You compare us to Willow and Peter? You think Willow seduced Peter through sorcery, and that *I'm* putting a spell on *you?*" She swallowed convulsively. "And then what? Are you going to drown me like a witch, if I'm in the way once you're finished with me?"

His eyes became round. He stepped back suddenly, letting her go. "How can you accuse me of being capable of murder?" he asked, looking at her as if she was a danger to him. "You must be like Willow was—bewitching and treacherous! Accusing me of things before we've even . . . She must have driven Peter wild with desire, and then when he'd given in, she drove him mad with accusations."

"So you're saying he *did* drown her, because she'd driven him *mad?*"

"Who knows? But I do understand his predicament a lot better after meeting you. I can see why he was obsessed with her. And when he broke it off for her sake, instead of understanding, all he got from her was blame. That must be why they argued on the beach that night. Maybe she did drive him to murder.''

Arianne turned away from him and opened the door to the driver's seat. She quickly got in, shut and locked the car door and rolled down the window an inch. ''Look, *Mr. Briarcliff*, I think you and I had better stay away from each other,'' she told him through the glass. ''Otherwise, it's only going to get more and more ugly between us. I'll stop using the brooch design for my logo. I don't want anything in return from you, because I don't want to have to deal with you. And from now on, I don't want you to see me or talk to me. If you come near me again, I'll make sure your family has a bigger scandal on its hands than you ever dreamed of!''

With that bold threat, she started the car motor and backed out of the parking space with such speed that he jumped out of the way. She raced off with the satisfying feeling of leaving him in her dust. The last she saw him, he was a lonely, angry figure in her rearview mirror, looking after her.

By the time she drove the mile to her home, she was shaking as the incident kept replaying in her mind. The heated kiss, to which she'd once again succumbed with such unexpected desire; the terrible things they'd said; the threat she'd made, which she knew she could never act out. She wasn't the sort who could make herself the focus of a scandal. And besides, to take on the Briarcliffs was foolhardy. Ross was a lawyer and would turn her to mincemeat. Or worse. He was Peter's descendant. Perhaps he *was* capable of...

Oh, Lord, she thought. What had she done? She shouldn't have threatened him. Not if she valued her life.

CHAPTER FIVE

Late the next morning, Arianne was finishing with a customer when Alex Howatch walked into her shop. He smiled at her and waited patiently, looking dapper as he leaned on his walking stick, until the customer had paid for a bottle of Willow perfume. "I wonder if I'll see the ghost now," the elderly lady joked as she dropped her wallet into her handbag. Arianne smiled to humor her. When the customer had left, she turned to the Aragon's manager.

"Hi, Alex. Haven't seen you for a few days. You look great. New suit?"

"I bought it for summer. Nice light shade of blue, isn't it?" he said, lifting his stick as he tugged at his lapel. Arianne knew he had arthritis in his knees, but the straight, golden-handled cane he used allowed him to maintain his slow but debonair stride.

"Beautiful," she agreed. Indeed, the pale blue perfectly offset his white hair and gray mustache. He'd finished off the suit with a pastel-yellow club tie worn with a white shirt to *GQ* perfection. She also noticed he was carrying a large, colorful bouquet of flowers in his free hand. He'd been a widower for seven or eight years, and she wondered if he'd found a new lady friend. "Are you meeting someone for lunch?" she asked.

"No. Unless you'd like to join me," he said with a grin.

Surprised by the answer, she said, "Oh, I can't. Doris called and said she can't come in today, so I'm by myself here all day."

"Can't blame me for trying," he said with equanimity.

Arianne supposed the flowers were to be put on display in the lobby or dining room. There was something she'd been meaning to ask Alex. "Has there been any increase in ... you know, ghost complaints by hotel guests?" She'd been wondering if Willow had been generally more active lately, or if the unhappy spirit had been centering her manifestations mainly on her. Alex had once told her he believed the ghostly phenomenon was real, so Arianne felt comfortable asking him such a question.

"No, this past week has been relatively quiet. But then no one has stayed in Room 302 recently. We rent it out only as a last resort. Or if someone requests it and gets my permission."

Arianne nodded. He'd told her before that they didn't like to rent the room, or even the rooms nearby. "I've noticed her scent of violets here in the shop."

Alex's eyebrows lifted. "Really?" He sniffed the perfume-laden air. "How can you tell?"

Arianne smiled. "I know what you mean. But, believe me, when she's present, her scent overwhelms everything else. It's all you can smell. And then, suddenly, it disappears."

"Have you seen her appear?" he asked, growing interested.

"No, but I've heard her weeping."

Alex angled his chin, as if thinking. "Many guests have reported that over the years. But you've actually been aware of her *here?* Not upstairs, on the third floor?"

"Here," Arianne said. "It *is* a change in her pattern, isn't it? I...I think I've even felt her presence on the beach. Maybe she follows me because I'm her relative."

"On the beach! My, that *is* new. No one has ever reported that, to my knowledge. I didn't know she could move about that much. Something has disturbed her, perhaps."

"Ross Briarcliff?"

Alex glanced at the flowers in his hand and then at Arianne. "You may be right," he said in all seriousness. "Briarcliff came to see you, didn't he?"

Arianne felt heat flood her face. "Yes."

"He told me he would a few days ago. He was upset about your logo."

"I know. I'm going to change it, just so I don't have any more trouble from him."

"Trouble?"

Arianne decided she'd better be more careful about what she said. "He can be rather overbearing sometimes."

Alex carefully set the flowers, wrapped in clear cellophane, on the counter between them. His expression showed concern. "I've met with him a few times now, and I don't trust him. He's bent on proving his great-grandfather Peter's innocence. I detect a ruthless energy in him to accomplish that, at all costs. Has he threatened you? Made advances toward you?"

Both, Arianne wanted to say. But she was afraid to. Alex, she knew from experience, could be a well-meaning gossip due to his talkative personality and his natural interest about people. She didn't want her problems with Ross to be known. "I think I have things under control now," she told him.

"Is he falling in love with you?"

Arianne stared at Alex in shock. "Falling in...? Why would you ask that?"

Alex looked thoughtful, his clever eyes studying her. "A few reasons. First, you're the descendants of star-crossed lovers, and you're both single. It's natural you'd have a curiosity about each other, and out of that a romance might develop. Second, he's seemed even more morose and restless the last few days, since he met you, than he was when he first came to the hotel. I wouldn't have thought he could *get* more sullen. And third, when I asked you about him, you blushed. Which leads me to think he has made some advance. And last of all, the most telling reason," he said as he lightly placed his hand on the long stems of the flowers, "is that he came in this morning with this beautiful bouquet and asked me to deliver it to you."

"W-what?"

"Yes, my dear," Alex assured her, "these are for you. He told me that he didn't want to see you in person, but he wanted you to have them. He said the note—" he pointed to a white envelope tucked into the cellophane "—would explain."

"Oh," she said, mystified, wondering if this was meant to be an apology or even a new overture. "What was his mood when you saw him?"

"I noted a touch of humility," Alex said with tart amusement. "He was the most polite to me that he's ever been. But then, he was asking me for a favor, wasn't he?"

Arianne fingered the cellophane, still recovering. "Sounds like you've had some problems with him, too," she said absently, feeling confused about this turn of events.

"Oh, he's just been sharp-tongued and suspicious," Alex said. "Nothing I can't deal with. I've been around long enough to know how to handle rich, overbearing young men. But you haven't. Your father was always protective of you. He and I became good friends over the years, as you know. So I feel I need to look after you a bit, since he's not here to do so himself.''

''Thank you,'' Arianne said, touched. She'd always liked Alex, though she suspected his gracious charm could sometimes be manipulative. But she felt his concern for her now was genuine.

''That's why I'd like to caution you to take care. When Ross handed me these flowers to give to you, it popped into my head that the man was in love. He may not be the sort of fellow you ought to get involved with.''

''What made you think he *loves* me?''

''Well, he appeared so preoccupied. Nervous. The flowers were foremost on his mind. He seemed to have forgotten about his research, his usual reason for snooping around my files and the hotel. And there was a look in his eyes.'' Alex squinted and then fluttered his fingers, as if trying to find the words to describe what he meant to say. ''There was *some* strong emotion present. Maybe it's not love. Now that I think of it, I doubt the Briarcliffs are capable of love, given their reputation. But he may be infatuated with you. Yes, perhaps infatuated is a better word. I had the feeling he's bent on having you.''

Arianne felt shaky. Her heartbeat grew arrhythmic, and she pressed her fingertips to her chest.

''I see you have reason to believe that, too,'' Alex said, watching her reaction closely.

''I'm . . . not sure. But he has said that he's attracted to me, and he doesn't want to be,'' she told him, deciding she needed to confide in someone.

''Oh, dear. Then it's worse than I imagined.'' Alex made a clicking noise with his tongue. ''He sounds quite confused about you, doesn't he? He's obsessed! That's it. Perhaps that's how Peter felt about Willow when he..."

Arianne could feel the blood draining from her face. Ross had used the same word, *obsessed*, regarding Peter. "You think so?" she whispered.

"I didn't mean to alarm you," Alex said, reaching out to pat her hand. "Don't worry, Arianne. You're safe as long as you aren't alone with him. If necessary, we can always ask for a restraining order from the police, to keep him away from the hotel and from you."

She drew a shocked breath. "I don't think *that* will be necessary," she said, surprised at the lengths Alex was ready to go. "I've already decided to stay away from him."

"Good." Alex hesitated, staring at the white envelope beneath the cellophane. "Perhaps we should see what his note says. It might give some indication of his state of mind."

Arianne would have preferred to read the note by herself, but since Alex had taken such an interest in her situation, she decided to let him see it, too. She removed it from the cellophane. As she unsealed it, she noticed it was a standard-size note card, not the small enclosure card usually presented with flowers.

Alex stepped around the counter to look over her shoulder as she pulled the note from the envelope. The card showed a painting of a lone wolf at night, howling at a full moon.

"My God," Alex said, looking at it with distaste. "What a thing to choose to send with flowers."

Arianne thought it might be a nature or wildlife card, however, and she turned it over. On the back was the logo of a well-known environmental organization. "I read in the paper that Ross's brother supports this group," she said. "Ross probably bought some of their cards."

"Couldn't he have chosen something with wildflowers or birds instead of a howling wolf? But it reminds one of their family, doesn't it? The Briarcliffs have often been compared to a pack of wolves. Gives me the shivers."

Troubled and apprehensive, Arianne opened the card. The handwritten note read:

Arianne,
Please accept these flowers as my apology for last night. I'm sure we both said things we later regretted. I'll ask Alex Howatch to find someone to deliver the flowers, so you won't have to see me again so soon. I know you would prefer not to deal with me under any circumstance right now, and I can understand that.

I have decided to forget my objection to your use of the Briarcliff brooch as your logo. The brooch is a part of the hotel's history, as well as my family's, so I hereby agree that it is not inappropriate for you to use it. I have no wish to cause any further animosity or mistrust between our families, and I don't want you to make any concessions to me merely to avoid me.

I hope someday we can be friends. For now, can we at least not be angry with each other? I lost sleep last night, reliving in my mind the things we said. Let's never allow such a scene to happen between us again.

Yours,
Ross

Arianne scanned the letter again, astonished. Ross's words were so generous and conciliatory. She hadn't expected the flowers, much less this. Perhaps she'd been wrong about him.

"Sounds like he wants to see you again," Alex said in an ominous tone.

Arianne paused and reread the last line of the note. Ross's choice of words might indicate that he assumed they would encounter each other again. But she decided not to interpret the line as if he had a plan to see her. She wanted to think the best of him, rather than be suspicious. Suspicion only led to accusations and anger, and, as Ross had written, she wanted no more of that. She hadn't been able to sleep last night, either, replaying in her head all the ugly words they'd exchanged.

"I think he's just trying to smooth things over to avoid any further trouble between our families," Arianne told Alex. "His brother is running for office, and he...doesn't want bad publicity." Her voice dropped as she realized that Ross's motives for being conciliatory might not have had all that much to do with her.

Alex nodded and walked to the other side of the counter. "I'm inclined to think that saving his family's reputation is his main purpose for everything. That's why he wants to put to rest the Willow story, and make it look as if Peter had nothing to do with her death. He as much as told me so. And now he wants to smooth things over with you."

"I did threaten to make a public scene if..." She didn't finish; she was growing depressed now. Perhaps Ross *had* only sent the note and flowers because he believed she might make good on her threat.

"If he didn't leave you alone?" Alex asked, concluding her sentence for her.

"Yes," she said with a sigh.

"Then I was right! He must be obsessed with you." Alex leaned over the counter toward her. "If he gives you any more trouble, Arianne, you must call on me. Any time, day or night. I'll be happy to help you get a restraining order. We'll keep him away from *here,* all right. We can't be intimidated just because of his family's wealth and reputation."

"Really, Alex, I don't think a restraining order will be needed." She wondered why he seemed fixed on the idea of keeping Ross away from the hotel. Did he have some other reason besides protecting her?

"Well, you never know." Alex paused, his eyes scanning her face. His tone softened. "I'm sorry, I don't mean to frighten you. He's done enough of that already, hasn't he?" He patted her hand again in a fatherly way. "But I just want you to know that if he gives you more trouble, you can come to me. All right?"

"Okay," she said, attempting to smile. For some reason, she didn't feel reassured. She sensed Alex was anxious to be rid of Ross, yet he'd said earlier that he knew how to handle men like him. But Alex would probably prefer not to have to handle Ross at all, and he'd found a reason to keep Ross off the hotel grounds. Arianne didn't like the idea of being that reason.

Alex soon left, saying he'd look in on her more often, just to make sure she wasn't being harrassed by Ross. Arianne walked down the hall a few doors to the florist's and borrowed a glass vase to put the flowers in. The bouquet looked beautiful, a mixture of roses, tulips, gladiolas and other flowers in a bright blend of colors. She set the flowers on the counter and worked over them for a few minutes, rearranging them to make the most pleasing display.

As she did, she suddenly heard a quick, gay little laugh. "Hee-ha-ha." High-pitched, it seemed to come from right behind her, near her ear. She turned quickly at the sound. No one was there. The atmosphere was still. At the moment, there wasn't even anyone out in the hall, she noted when she looked through the glass door of her shop.

She felt disconcerted for a moment, then decided she probably imagined it. It couldn't have been Willow. No one had ever reported hearing the ghost laugh. Willow only sobbed and wept. No, she *must* have imagined it. She'd done a lot of perfume testing on customers all morning, breathing in all that potato alcohol. Come to think of it, she did feel a little light-headed.

She decided she'd better eat some lunch to keep herself from getting slightly inebriated, so she went into her storage room and phoned the hotel café to send over a hamburger. Then she went out into the hallway in front of her shop for a while to breathe some unperfumed air. But she found herself wistfully looking through the glass door at the beautiful flowers on her counter.

She ought to thank Ross, she decided. But she wasn't sure how. She wanted only to be polite. He musn't think that she wanted to see him or have anything more to do with him.

Two days later, in the early evening, she hadn't yet decided what to do about responding to Ross's note and flowers. She eyed the still magnificent bouquet on her counter and felt guilty that she hadn't even let him know she'd received the flowers. On the other hand, she told herself it was good she hadn't responded too quickly. She wouldn't want him to misinterpret any reaction from her as interest. But he had seemed to make a sincere attempt toward being conciliatory, even if it may have been for the benefit of his brother's political campaign, and she didn't want to seem rude. Maybe she'd write him a note tonight.

She closed up shop early, at about five-thirty instead of six. It had been a while since she'd walked on the beach. In fact, she hadn't done so since the evening she first met Ross. She thought if she went walking at an earlier time, there was less chance she would run into him. If he had been returning to the beach after six each evening, perhaps hoping to see her again, then she would avoid him. On the other hand, maybe he'd been avoiding the beach, too.

But when she walked out onto the sand, the first person she noticed was Ross, standing at the shoreline in a navy blue suit, looking out to sea. Before she could quietly turn and go back, he pivoted around, almost as if he'd sensed her eyes on him.

Now she was stuck. She'd look weak if she turned and ran away. Besides, she owed him a thank-you. Casting her gaze down to the sand, she began walking toward him in a deliberate manner. When she looked up, she found he'd come halfway across the beach to meet her.

"I didn't think you'd be out till after six. That's why I came early."

She made a hesitant smile. "I had the same plan. We don't seem to be successful at avoiding each other."

"Maybe we try too hard."

Arianne wet her lips. "Thank you for the flowers and the note. I did say things to you that I regret. As for the logo, I'll be happy to change it."

"No, I don't want you to," he insisted.

"But I—"

"Let's not argue about *this* now," he said, smiling gently. The attractive creases formed in his cheeks, making him look charming, almost warm, and engaging. He'd taken off his tie, and his unbuttoned suit jacket and straight black hair blew in the wind off the sea. "I've been in court all day today, defending another Briarcliff lawsuit. I don't need any more disputes. The logo is yours."

"You were in court all day? How did you wind up here, on our beach?" she asked, curious and a bit wary.

"I like to relax by walking on the shore."

"But didn't you tell me that you live in a condo on the beach?"

He nodded. "I like this beach better now. I...have a nice memory of it."

She felt a strange rush and tried to maintain her cool composure. "I thought you said we both should forget that."

His eyes took on an ardent glow as he looked at her. "I told you, I can't."

She began to feel nervous. Was Alex right? Did Ross harbor an obsession for her? Did he look upon them as reincarnations of Peter and Willow? Or was it Arianne who thought of them that way? Maybe *she* was the one who was obsessed.

"I'd better go," she said.

"No, don't," he said softly, as he reached to stop her from turning away. "I've missed you. I can't stop thinking about you. Don't leave."

"Ross," she said, shaking her head. "You know we can't..."

"Why not?"

"Because, you said yourself—"

"I take back what I said. I *need* to see you. I'll go crazy if I can't be with you."

"Aren't you worried," she taunted, "that I'm like Willow, and I'm casting some spell on you?"

His eyes blazed at her. "Yeah, I am. It's working!"

"Then you should avoid me."

"Too late." He took hold of her upper arms and pressed his head against the side of hers, whispering, "I want to drown with you in this sea of passion."

The words made her freeze. He took advantage and kissed her soundly. The heat of his insistent mouth made her limbs grow weak and her knees feel like they were about to give way. She tried to keep herself from succumbing and to twist out of his grasp, but he held her tightly.

He took his mouth from hers and drew her even closer. "Make love with me," he whispered urgently in her ear while his fingers dug into her upper arms. "Let's act on our desires instead of repressing them. We can't ignore this."

With a sharp push on his chest, she managed to put some space between them, though he still gripped her arms. "You'd be disappointed," she told him, her voice strained from struggling.

His brows drew together darkly. "What do you mean?"

"I'm...inexperienced. You must be used to sophisticated women."

He stared at her. "You're saying that you're a virgin?" His gray eyes seemed to grow pale. "Like..."

"Yes, like Willow was! And then she met Peter. Will you promise to marry me, the way he promised her?" she asked, knowing very well that he wouldn't.

Ross let go of her. He looked down at the sand and breathed through his mouth, as if short of breath. When he raised his gaze to her again, his eyes looked harrowed. "What's going on here? Why is everything that happens between us so connected with the past?"

"I don't know, but it scares me, too. Stay away from me, Ross," she pleaded. "Can't you see it's best for both of us? I think we're bad for each other. Maybe Willow is influencing us in some malevolent way."

His eyes grew steely. "That's a cop-out. Don't blame everything on your imagined ghost. Whatever's going on, it's between you and me! You've inherited Willow's spellbinding ways, and I've inherited Peter's weakness for such a woman. *That's* what's happening. That's why history seems to be repeating itself."

She ignored his analysis of Willow. "Then we ought to keep away from each other," she repeated for emphasis.

"Don't you think I want to?" he asked with exasperation. "In court all day, I could hardly keep my mind on the case. All I could think about was when and if I'd hear from you or see you again. At night I lie awake imagining us together."

"Then it's just . . . you're infatuated with me right now. Maybe because of the research you're doing on Willow and Peter. Tomorrow you may meet someone new and—"

"No!" He stepped closer. "I'm not even aware of other women anymore. For me, that's unheard of."

"Maybe you should see a psychologist."

He glared at her. "Are you saying this is all *my* problem—that you aren't as drawn to me as I am to you?"

"Y-yes," she said as forthrightly as she could, though she was not being truthful.

"I don't believe you. When I take you in my arms, I can feel you respond." He drew her to him again as if to prove his point. His hand at her back, he pressed her chest to his, crushing her against him. She felt the heat and strength of his body and began to tremble in his arms. He glided his other hand upward along her neck, beneath her hair, with a caressing intimacy, then slowly pulled her head to his until their lips met.

His kiss was thorough as he held her tightly in his arms. The breath from his nose scorched her cheek. Soon she was growing quite weak, as if locked in a heated vise and forced to absorb sensations too rich to endure. Her knees buckled, and she began to feel limp.

Ross broke the kiss and kept her from sinking to the sand by maintaining his hold on her slender frame. "Tell me you didn't feel anything!'' he whispered harshly. ''Tell me you don't want me, too.''

''I'm afraid, Ross.'' Her voice came out strained and thin as she held on to him to steady herself. ''What I feel is *too* strong. Willow gave in to it, but I mustn't. She gave herself to Peter, and she died because of him. I don't want to...follow in her footsteps.''

''You think I would harm you?''

''We're so volatile when we're together. I don't know what might happen. I don't want to find out.''

''And what am I supposed to do? Go on trying not to want you?''

''Yes,'' she said. ''It's sensible to avoid potential danger for both of us, isn't it?''

He vigorously shook his head. ''How can you talk about being sensible? We passed that mark the night we met. We're in this together, and we need to find our way out together. Staying apart only prolongs the chaos. Come home with me tonight,'' he insisted. He raised the palm of his hand to her cheek and caressed her skin. ''We need to play this thing through to the end, not ignore it.'' He pressed his forehead to hers. ''Let's make love!''

She pushed on his chest. ''Let me go!''

''Arianne—'' he protested, taking her by the shoulders again to try to keep her from running away.

''Let me go!'' she insisted with fiery determination, keeping up the pressure of her hands against his lapels. ''If you don't, I'll scream. There are still enough people on this beach to hear me.''

Reluctantly, he let go. As she turned to rush to the hotel, he called, ''Will I see you again?''

She'd taken a few steps but turned to look at him. His face and eyes carried a bleak, lonely pride. She intended to reply no, but found herself saying, ''I don't know.''

His eyes seemed to ignite with silver fire. "That's not good enough. Don't leave me hanging!"

The tug-of-war inside her between what she knew she should say and what she wanted brought tears to her eyes. "I can't give you any other answer," she told him.

"See me just to talk, then. I won't even touch you. See me tomorrow," he said, taking a step closer.

She backed away. "No."

"Arianne—" he said with desperation, coming toward her.

"No!" She turned and ran as fast as she could.

Later that night, Ross reluctantly drove to the Briarcliff mansion to see his father, Norman, who had been complaining lately that Ross didn't visit him enough. Might as well end a miserable day with a miserable evening, Ross had decided. But when he arrived, he found to his pleasant surprise that William's car was in the circular driveway, too. His brother had probably stopped by to discuss the financing of his campaign, which was paid for largely by the Briarcliff foundation Norman had created for this purpose.

After being admitted by his father's butler, Ross walked to the library, where he was told they were. William, who had sandy hair and was shorter than Ross, grinned when he saw Ross come in. He'd been standing in front of the Italian marble fireplace, and he quickly walked over to embrace Ross.

"This is a nice surprise," William said. "Dad was just asking if I'd seen you lately."

Ross stepped over to where his father sat in a high-backed leather chair. Norman looked thin and his face was weathered. A liver condition from days gone by when he'd been a hard drinker was taking its toll. Ross extended his hand and Norman took it in a weak grip.

"Sit down," Norman said in his usual growling manner. "Drink? Smoke?"

"No," Ross replied as he took a seat in a leather chair opposite his father. William sat down on a couch at right angles to them both. A large square glass-topped coffee table lay in front of them.

"What have you been up to?" Norman asked Ross. "I can read in the papers what William's doing. Can't keep track of you. You don't phone. You don't stop by."

"I'm here now," Ross pointed out. "I was in court all day today." He mentioned the cousin whose lawsuit he'd defended.

"Win?"

"Sure," Ross said. "Piece of cake." He noticed that he took on a different demeanor around his father. Norman spoke in a brusque manner and seemed most impressed with those who responded in kind. The main reason Ross didn't like visiting his father was that he never felt he could be himself. Norman always had expectations of his sons, and he was always ready to criticize if they fell short. William, however, had never used the self-protection of taking on a strong persona around Norman. He was always his easygoing self with a ready smile, even when Norman found fault with him. Ross envied his brother's ability to take their gruff parent with such equanimity. William had possessed that skill since childhood.

"Good," Norman replied, apparently satisfied at the outcome of Ross's day in court. "What about that old Willow nonsense? Clear that up yet?"

"I'm working on it," Ross said, bowing his head. Arianne's rejection was still fresh in his mind.

"When are you going to start putting your articles in the paper? William needs some good publicity."

"Dad," William admonished, "research takes time. The election's not till November."

"It's summer already. Can't wait too long."

"My first article is due in three weeks," Ross said. "Problem is, so far I haven't come up with anything. Though I've..." He hesitated to bring Arianne into the conversation. But she was on his mind.

"What?" Norman said with irritation. "I hate it when you leave off mid-sentence. Am I supposed to be a mind reader?"

Ross clenched his jaw, then said, "I met someone from the Monroe family."

"Really?" William said with interest.

"Saints preserve us!" Norman exclaimed with distaste. "Where? Who?"

"She runs the Aragon Perfumery," Ross explained. "One of the shops at the hotel." The scented atmosphere of the perfumery seemed to fill his nostrils as he spoke about it. "She...sells fragrances all day long."

"Young? Old?" Norman prompted. "What's she look like?"

Ross hesitated. "Willow. She looks a lot like the photo of Willow."

There was silence for a long moment. Norman appeared aghast.

"She's pretty, then?" William said, studying his brother with curious eyes.

"Beautiful."

"So what does she want?" Norman asked.

"Nothing," Ross answered, put off by the question.

"Oh, come on. Everybody wants something from us—either money or a piece of our hides. There must be some reason a Monroe came to talk to you."

"I went to her."

"What the hell for?" Norman asked. "She have some historical documents on Willow? Why would she show them to you?"

Ross didn't want to mention the fact that Arianne was using the Briarcliff brooch as her logo, the initial reason he had gone to see her. He'd decided to let that matter go, and he didn't want his father learning about it, because Norman would certainly pursue the issue himself.

"I thought it would be a good thing for one of us to meet someone from their family. The whole idea is to put a better face on our past and heal old wounds for the sake of William's campaign. So, when the hotel manager mentioned Arianne was a member of the Monroe family, I decided to introduce myself." Ross figured that rendition of the facts was accurate enough for Norman's purposes.

"Arianne?" William said with a smile. "That's her name?"

Ross nodded.

"What's she like?" William asked.

Ross felt at a loss. How could he describe Arianne? "She's frail and feminine. Twenty-four, but she looks younger—kind of...well, very...innocent. Big eyes. Long, dark brown hair...." In his mind's eye, Ross visualized her shining hair tumbling over her shoulders and breasts.

"You have the hots for this Monroe broad?" Norman asked with suspicious displeasure.

The cranky, sharp voice shattered the portrait in Ross's mind. "Come off it," Ross retorted, angry at the coarse remark and self-conscious about the truth in it.

"That's all we need," Norman joked to William, "for a Briarcliff to fall for a Monroe again. We don't have to go that far to make peace with the damn Monroes."

"I don't see anything wrong with it," William said with a shrug and a smile.

"Well, *you,*" Norman chided his eldest son, "you think Christmas lasts all year long!"

William laughed, while Ross merely felt relieved the subject had veered off track. Perhaps sensing Ross's discomfiture, William began talking about his campaign plans and the combined subjects of Willow and Arianne were dropped.

An hour later, when Ross had had enough and he could detect even William's patience was waning, the two brothers bid their father good-night. They walked out to the elegant oval driveway together. The night air felt cool and cleansing. The mansion was set on a hill and featured a panoramic view of the ocean and San Diego, now a complex pattern of lights spread below them and gleaming in the darkness. Out in the distance, beside the black sea, Ross could pick out the Aragon Hotel, its unique tapered rooftops and pointed towers outlined with lights.

"I know it's blasphemy," William said in a conspiratorial tone, "but I always liked the Aragon."

Ross hadn't realized how obvious he'd been about staring at the resort as they strolled toward their cars. "Yeah," he muttered. "Nice architecture."

William tossed his car keys in his hand. In an affable manner, he asked, "So what about this Arianne?"

Ross glanced at his brother. "What about her?"

"Are you seeing her?"

"No, not . . . No."

"Don't sound quite sure," William teased.

Ross never could sidestep his irrepressible brother. "I'm not sure of anything lately," Ross admitted quietly. "Something's wrong. Sometimes I think I'm losing it. My stability, I mean. My mind."

William looked concerned. "Why?"

Ross ignored the question for the moment. "Do you think Willow had some power over Peter? In his journal, he writes how transfixed with her he was."

"You know me, Ross. I never could get into family history all that much. I never even opened Peter's journals."

"Well, the reason Peter wanted to marry Willow was because they apparently had an overwhelming sexual attraction. She wasn't from an affluent family and she was in poor health, yet he overlooked all the obstacles, had an affair with her—highly unusual for those days—and he decided to marry her because he couldn't leave her alone. It was only when he found out she wouldn't survive a pregnancy that he broke the engagement. And even you must remember what happened then."

His brother nodded. "What's this got to do with your losing your stability?" William always was a bottom-line man. "You think you're reacting like Peter did to Willow?"

Ross took a long breath and released it uneasily. "It's crossed my mind."

"But you're not having an affair with Arianne."

"It's not because I wouldn't like to," Ross said.

William stared at him. "You've always pursued women. Apparently Arianne's attractive. What's the big deal?"

"She's a Monroe."

"You aren't seriously holding the old family feud against her," William said.

His brother's open-mindedness made Ross feel ashamed. "It's hard *not* to. Whenever I see her, we wind up arguing about Peter's guilt or innocence in Willow's death. But worse than that, it seems like the old story is repeating itself. Willow had some *hold* over Peter. He was...trapped."

"And?"

Ross didn't continue.

William said, "You think Arianne has some hold over you?"

Ross spread his hands in a helpless gesture. "All I can think about is her. She's on my mind every minute. And when we're together, there's always fireworks. Even when we met. I didn't know who she was. I saw her on the beach, and she was so beautiful, I had to meet her. I admit I looked upon her as my next conquest, but now it seems like I'm the one who's been conquered."

"About time," William said.

"Huh?"

"About time some woman got the better of you. I stand for women's rights, you know," William said with a smile, "and it's time one of them gave you some of your own medicine."

"It's not like that. She doesn't want to get involved with me. She avoids me."

"So she's got brains, too."

"Look, Will—"

"And she's obviously not after your money," William continued, ignoring Ross. "She sounds just right to me."

"Right for what?" Ross retorted. "Don't start on me about marriage again. She'd never marry me, anyway. She thinks I'm dangerous because I'm Peter's great-grandson. She adheres to the Monroe party line about how Peter did Willow in."

William nodded, as if piecing things together. "I see. And the fact that you've been pursuing her the way Peter pursued Willow only convinces her that she's right."

"It convinces *me*, too."

William looked up. "What do you mean?"

"I haven't been myself since I met her. Just as Peter's life changed the day he met Willow."

"Peter must have fallen head over heels."

"Exactly," Ross agreed. "He was under her spell."

William's forehead creased in amusement. "What's this talk about a spell? *You* believe in spells? You, the classic cynic?"

William's reaction threw Ross. "I'm just saying that something happened that changed Peter forever, and changed history, too, the day he met her."

"Love at first sight," William said, as if the answer was obvious.

"*You* believe in love at first sight?" Ross countered.

"Sure. It happened to me."

Ross stared at his smiling elder brother. "Marlene? But you dated her for years before you married her."

"We were young, and we needed to finish our education," William explained. "But I knew she was the one on our first date."

Ross stood silent for a while, his eyes straying to the distant Aragon Hotel. Finally, he said, "So you think Peter actually loved Willow? It wasn't just a sexual attraction?"

William shrugged. "How can *I* say? You're the family historian. But I know from experience that meeting the right woman can hit you like a ton of bricks. It can change your life plans. It can make you a better person. Or, if things don't work out, it can destroy your happiness."

"Then maybe that's why our family is so messed up," Ross muttered.

"How do you mean?"

Ross turned to William. "See if this makes sense. Peter couldn't marry the woman he loved, so he married someone he didn't love. In fact, he grew to despise her. That bad marriage set the example for all the generations that followed. Peter's children grew up maladjusted from living in such an unhappy home. They had no idea what a good marriage was like, or what was required of them to make a sound marriage. So when they wed, they were bound to make the same mistakes. And they, in turn, were a bad example for their offspring, and so on. That's why no one in our family ever seems to have experienced marital bliss." He looked at William. "Except for you. Somehow you managed to break out of the mold."

William nodded. "Your theory makes sense. And you can break the mold, too."

Ross shook his head. "I have all the wrong family traits. I'm a lot like our father. I'll probably *become* him when I'm his age. Except I won't have gotten married."

"Ross," William said, clapping him on the shoulder, "I don't think you're like Dad at all. And you take him too seriously."

Ross faced William squarely. "Tell me, how do you deal with him so easily? Like tonight—you didn't let him get to you. He's our parent. How can you *not* take him seriously? All his criticism. The negative example he sets."

"I never paid any attention to it," William said.

Ross studied his face, feeling a little dumbfounded. "How can you not pay attention? He's our father."

"I heard his criticism, but I didn't buy into it. I never believed you or I deserved to be treated that way. I figured that's just how he is. It's *his* failing. No reason you or I should believe him."

"That's incredible! How did you know that? Even when you were a kid?"

William thought a moment. "I don't know. I just had a natural faith in myself. There were some teachers at school who made me feel good about myself, too. And you and I both knew—we used to talk about it—that we didn't come from a normal family. We knew we'd inherited problems."

"We both knew, but you overcame it. I'm still enmeshed in it."

"People are different, Ross. Even brothers. You always were more serious and sensitive to Dad's criticism and our mother's indifference. You always looked for their affirmation and love. I wanted that, too. But I knew they weren't capable of showing affection. So I ignored them—learned to counter their criticism with humor. I knew I deserved better, and eventually I got what I deserved. I have a great family of my own now. I've always tried to get you to see things the way I do, but..." William shrugged and bowed his head, as if feeling he'd failed.

"I inherited the Briarcliff pessimism about life. How could I learn your positive outlook? It's not in my genes."

"We share the same genes," William pointed out.

Ross eyed him with humor. "I don't know. Maybe our mother had an affair with a cockeyed optimist before you were born."

William laughed. "I almost wish that was true, but my Briarcliff chin proves otherwise," he said, pointing to the cleft in his chin, which many members of the family inherited. Ross had one, too, though not so pronounced.

"That's true," Ross agreed with a smile. "I'm glad you're in the family, however you got here."

"Let's go back to your theory about Peter," William said. "I think you've found the crux of it. If Peter had married Willow, he might never have developed the negative qualities he did. The problem didn't come from his genes. It probably came out of his lifelong despair, because he'd lost the woman he wanted to be with and instead wound up with a wife who was totally unsuitable for him. And that despair carried on from generation to generation, because the family didn't know how to live any other way."

Ross slowly let out a long breath, releasing pent-up energy. He felt tired now. "Well, we may have solved the mystery of how we inherited all this agony, but what do we do?"

"Step out of it," William said. "Make a family of your own. My wife and kids give me the love and support I never got growing up. Except from you."

Ross shook his head. "It wouldn't turn out the same for me."

"It won't if you take a defeatist attitude!" William admonished.

"You said it yourself," Ross argued. "We're different. I'm glad for your happiness, but I can't *be* you."

"Of course not. Be yourself. Be the best of yourself. Don't let the past bog you down."

"That's difficult, because I'm faced with the past every day lately, doing my research and..."

"And meeting Arianne, who compares you to Peter?"

"Exactly," Ross said, feeling burdened and old.

"Face the dragon and slay it," William said. "Or the past will haunt you forever."

Ross raised his eyebrows at the advice. "Funny you should mention haunting. Arianne believes Willow haunts her. You know the ghost story at the Aragon."

William made a half smile. "She does? I've never believed in ghosts. What do you think?"

Ross looked out at the Aragon Hotel again, feeling wistful and something more he couldn't discern. "Arianne is ... she's sort of a fairy-tale character," he said, his ideas forming as he spoke. "She's very feminine and ... willowy—if I dare to use that word," he added with irony.

William grinned and listened, fascinated, as Ross continued.

"She works in a poorly ventilated little shop spraying people with perfume all day, breathing in all the fragrant ethers. Whenever I go in there, I feel like I've stepped into some otherworld atmosphere. After a while, I can barely think straight. But then, that happens whenever I'm with her. Anyway, she admits that sometimes the perfume alcohol makes her light-headed. I think maybe it affects her imagination, though she denies it."

"So you think she's imagining that Willow haunts her?"

"It's the only explanation," Ross said. "She's heard the Aragon ghost story all her life, and she's young and a little gullible. Though she knows how to stand up to me well enough."

"Sounds like you're pretty taken with her. You never talked like this about any other woman, including that one you almost married."

"Like what?"

"There's a respect and an uncertainty in your voice I haven't heard before."

Ross exhaled. "But it won't work. The past is strangling the future. She's haunted by Willow, if only in her mind, and she's afraid of getting involved with me. *I'm* afraid of behaving like Peter. I haven't been able to disprove the theory that he murdered her. And..." Ross took a harrowed breath. "Sometimes my emotions run so strong when I'm around Arianne, I can understand how Peter may have felt—how much he wanted Willow, and how not being able to have her may have...put him over the edge of sanity."

"Ross," William admonished in a light and reassuring tone, "you're getting carried away."

"I'm afraid I *am* being swept away," Ross told him, feeling an ominous sense of foreboding, "by something stronger than I knew existed. Passion is a dangerous thing."

At his condo, later that night, Ross got ready for bed. He opened his bedroom window and could hear the sound of the waves on the beach below as he sat on the edge of his bed to adjust his radio alarm. The radio was beneath the lamp on the bed stand next to his pillow. His gaze came across the Willow perfume Arianne had given him. He'd set it on the bed stand when he brought it home the night she'd given it to him.

He picked up the white box, embossed in gold with the Briarcliff brooch, and ran his thumb over the logo. Whatever happened to the damn brooch? Ross wondered. If he knew that, it would be a clue as to what happened that fateful night on the beach between Willow and Peter.

Ross opened up the box and took out the bottle of perfume, whose label also featured the brooch emblem above the word *Willow*. He took off the cap and sniffed the bottle. The floral and spice fragrance he'd come to associate with Arianne filled his nostrils. He quickly capped the bottle and put it in its box. If he wanted a good night's sleep, he'd better not remind himself of her in such a sensual way.

After turning off the lamp, Ross tossed aside the sheet and blanket, too hot in summer, and stretched out to go to sleep. He lay awake for a while, thinking over his conversation with his brother. Gradually he dozed off, and William faded from his mind.

All at once, in the darkness, he heard crashing waves. He saw Arianne running, dazed, bathed in moonlight, as if she was in a panic. She wore a long, filmy dress and tears streamed from her huge, dark eyes. In her hand, she was clutching the Briarcliff brooch. He recognized where they were—on the beach at the Aragon Hotel.

Arianne ran past him, headlong toward the shore and the ocean's high waves. Ross instantly feared that she intended to drown herself in the angry sea. He ran after her with all the speed he could muster. He reached her as she stepped into a wave lapping up on the shore and caught her around the waist. As he pulled her farther back onto dry sand, she struggled against him, her gown coming off her shoulders as she did. Soon it had slipped down, revealing her exquisite breasts.

Stunned by an overwhelming desire, he began to kiss her with consuming need. They fell together onto a bed. Somehow the sand and sea had disappeared and now they were indoors. He caressed her soft breasts and she closed her eyes sensuously, tears still streaming from her lashes. She moaned when he suckled her nipple and she rustled her fingers through his hair. He cradled her in his arms and kissed her body and her face until she breathed in short, whimpering gasps. Sensing that she wanted what he did, he ripped away her thin dress and pressed her down onto the bed. Her arms fell back over her head, and she smiled in sweet delirium. Never had she looked so beautiful. His member pulsed with urgent demand. He moved over her, parting her thighs—

Ross woke with a start. He was in his own room, and he was alone. He felt swollen with arousal and instantly grew angry that he'd awakened from his beautiful dream. A breeze of night air swept over him from the open window, cooling his fever. He ran his hands over his face and eyes, dragging himself back to the real world.

God, how he wanted Arianne! His dream had revealed the intensity of his desire. The frustration was agony. He'd never wanted a woman this much.

But his dream didn't reflect reality. She'd never give in to him so easily—perhaps would never give herself to him at all. And why had he dreamed that she was running toward the sea, as if to drown herself? Was this another premonition? Or was it because he'd been investigating Willow's death, and he somehow kept mixing the past with the present? Or maybe the vivid dream had come only because he'd sniffed her provocative perfume?

As the remnants of the dream's driving passion subsided, a heavy sense of foreboding filled Ross again, more strongly than ever before. There was something dangerous happening. He shouldn't need and want Arianne this much. An affair between him and her was doomed to end in heartbreak. Any relationship between a Briarcliff and whatever foolhardy woman got involved with him was bound to be rocky. But for a Briarcliff to become involved with a Monroe was only asking for history to repeat itself.

If Ross could manage to use his head, he'd stay away from Arianne. He didn't want her to be hurt, especially not by him. And he didn't want to learn to care for her and need her in his life, if he was destined to lose her. He might not be as tough as Peter was in enduring a lifelong broken heart.

Ross lay awake the rest of the night, vowing that he must stay away from Arianne for her sake, as well as his own. When dawn came, he'd talked himself into staying away from the hotel for at least two weeks.

CHAPTER SIX

The dream came back three more times, plaguing Ross with fear and frustration. Each time, Arianne was at a greater distance from him as she ran blindly toward the sea, the brooch glistening in her hand. Last night, he hadn't been able to catch up with her in time. He saw her plunge into the waves while he ran to save her, his legs so heavy, moving so slowly, it was as though the beach had turned to quicksand. He woke up in a breathless sweat. He spent the rest of the night worrying whether Arianne needed his protection or needed to be protected *from* him.

Two weeks had gone by so slowly, to Ross they felt more like the passage of two long months. But, despite the recurrent dream he couldn't decipher, he kept his promise to himself and did not go near the Aragon Hotel for fourteen days. During that time, when he was not in court or researching a case, he went to public and university libraries in San Diego and Los Angeles to search out historical information that might pertain to Willow Monroe or Peter Briarcliff. He found little—a few old newspaper articles he hadn't seen before, but which contained no new information, and a published diary written by a member of another prominent San Diego family, who associated with the Briarcliffs at the turn of the century. The diary, written by a man of Peter's age, made mention of how Peter was thought by some to be a murderer because of the mysterious circumstances of his former fiancée's death.

But the man wrote that he knew how "besotted with Willow" Peter was, and that he didn't believe Peter could have murdered her, unless he had temporarily lost his sanity.

Because of his own unsettled mental state, Ross had begun to wonder if temporary insanity was indeed what had happened to Peter that fateful night. The fact that one of Peter's contemporaries had conjectured the same thing made Ross uneasy, for it seemed to confirm his own thoughts. When he drew back and considered how his mind-set had changed from at first being indignant at the idea that his ancestor might have been a murderer, to now looking for ways to explain *why* Peter may have murdered Willow, he realized how he'd been swayed from his original stance. He wondered how his attitude could have changed so. Partly it was due to the fact that he'd found no evidence to clear Peter's name; but then he'd found nothing to confirm his guilt, either.

Arianne had influenced him, he began to realize. She believed so in Willow's love for Peter, and that Willow had been rejected by Peter, that Ross had begun to feel sympathy for her. He also had developed a strong desire for Arianne; and he realized how easily he could hurt her by drawing her into an affair, tarnishing her innocence with his lust, when he had no intention of marrying her.

Ross wondered if that was, more or less, what Peter had done to Willow. And afterward Willow had no doubt felt used and rejected, despite Peter's claim that he was leaving her because of her ill health. So Willow either killed herself or tormented Peter with her heartache until *he* killed her, perhaps not to get the brooch back—which he hadn't—but to try to silence his own feelings of guilt by silencing Willow.

This new theory had been turning in Ross's mind the past several days, and it disturbed him greatly. It made him wonder if, given similar circumstances, he could lose his sense of right and wrong, and do the same thing his great-grandfather may have done. Certainly, he ought to keep his distance from Arianne.

But Ross needed to return to the Aragon Hotel one more time. All his research had turned up nothing for his first newspaper article on the Briarcliffs, and his deadline was next week. He had to come up with something to grab readers' interest, if they were to follow his column over the coming months and be convinced that the Briarcliffs weren't as bad as their reputation.

Ross had thought of a solution to the dilemma. He would stay overnight in Room 302 and report on what did or didn't happen while there. He came upon this idea one day when he'd been reviewing his file on all the news articles and TV clips regarding the Aragon Hotel's ghost. Many of these pieces were done by reporters who had stayed in Room 302, who presumably had invented phenomena for their readers and viewers to devour. Ross decided he might as well follow their example. If he couldn't fight the old scandal with facts, he'd do it with tabloid-style bravado. He could even see his news article's headline—Briarcliff Tempts Ghost's Wrath by Staying in Haunted Room.

When nothing ghostly happened, as he was certain it wouldn't, he could report with humor about his peaceful night in the supposedly haunted hotel room. He could point out that if Willow did inhabit the room, she certainly would have appeared to terrorize the great-grandson of the man who purportedly murdered her. Ross hoped that, in this roundabout way, he could help to dispel the murder theory. If nothing else, such an article would show that the Briarcliffs had a sense of humor about the ghost story—which, Ross's conscience forced him to admit, wasn't true. Briarcliff humor, when it surfaced, tended to be dark and destructive. But for William's sake, Ross wanted the public to think otherwise.

So Ross phoned Alex Howatch and requested a reservation for Room 302 for the following night.

"Arianne?"

Arianne heard her name called and came out of the back room of her shop, where she'd been unpacking a newly shipped box of crystal atomizers. She smiled when she saw Alex near the oak counter, leaning on his walking stick.

"Hi, Alex. How are you?"

"Oh, the humid weather lately makes my arthritis act up," he grumbled. "Listen, I wanted to let you know—Ross Briarcliff is staying in Room 302 tonight. He hasn't been around for a few weeks, and I'd hoped we were well rid of him. Seems we're not. Thought I should warn you that he'll be back on the premises."

Arianne felt alarmed, not for herself, but for Ross. "Why does he want to stay in Willow's room?"

"That's just what I asked him when he phoned for permission yesterday afternoon. Said he's doing it for the newspaper series he's writing. He pointed out that I'd allowed media reporters to stay in the room on past occasions. So I couldn't argue, or he'd charge me with discrimination." Alex seemed vexed. He shrugged his thin. shoulders. "Well, at least this time he'll be confining himself to that room and not snooping around—I hope."

After Alex left, Arianne felt bewildered. She hadn't heard from Ross for two entire weeks. The fact that he actually had stayed away from her after all they'd said the last time they saw each other surprised her. She'd expected him to try to break down her defenses again—she began to realize she wanted him to. She'd spent many nights lying awake, thinking of him, longing to know what making love with him would be like. In the light of morning she would always chide herself for encouraging such reckless thoughts. But soon she even spent her daylight hours dreaming of Ross, of his strong, willful embraces and his burning sweet kisses. There was always combustion when they came together. She yearned for him to walk into her shop, into her life, and make the fireworks begin again.

Was *she* obsessed, as Alex had said Ross was? She had to admit to falling into a jealous disposition whenever she imagined what Ross might be doing. Two full weeks had passed, and the first news she had of him was that he'd be staying in Room 302 *tonight*. No warning. No consideration for her feelings on the matter. Perhaps he'd been too busy with court cases since she'd last seen him to cater to his infatuation with her. Or perhaps, as Arianne had told him might happen, he'd met someone new to be infatuated with. Maybe she, like Willow, was history in Ross's mind. This thought brought a sharp, painful sense of loss in the depth of her abdomen.

Now the fact that he suddenly wanted to stay in the haunted room, when he didn't believe in ghosts, puzzled her. She feared for him, because he didn't understand the possible danger he might be getting himself into. Arianne was afraid of Willow herself, remembering what the psychic had told her. Why hadn't Ross even *tried* to contact her to tell her about his plan, since it was the ghost of *her* relative that he'd be coming there to investigate? After all, Willow was one of their sources of contention.

Maybe that was why he hadn't wanted to tell her.

All at once, it occurred to Arianne that Ross might stop by her shop before she closed this evening, since he'd be coming to the hotel. Maybe he'd planned it that way, to see her in person first and explain to her what he was doing. Her spirits lifted and her newfound hope brought unexpected tears to her eyes. As Arianne listened to her heart, she realized with a profound, silent shock that she wasn't obsessed with Ross. It was worse. She'd fallen in love with him.

She waited the rest of the long afternoon, helping customer after customer, testing her perfumes on dozens of them. When her watch showed five o'clock, she grew nervous, wondering if at any moment Ross might appear at her door.

But he never came. She closed promptly at six, turning the Open sign over to read Closed, telling herself she was glad he hadn't come by. Let him stay in the haunted room and ignore her! But as she tidied up the back room before leaving, the strong sweet scent of violets filled the air, and she found herself falling into a deep sadness. And then she heard weeping again. Nearly every day lately, she'd heard Willow sobbing at some odd moment when she was alone in the shop. And always, the weeping played on her own feelings of loneliness, often making her sink into moments of sheer despair. The downward spiral of sadness she felt coming on now frightened her, and she quickly gathered her things and left the shop.

She walked out onto the beach with some trepidation, thinking she'd run into Ross or else find that Willow had followed her. But neither event happened. She took a long walk by herself along the shore, and Ross did not appear, nor did she sense, hear or smell Willow.

Arianne felt curiously abandoned, though she had feared meeting either of her nemeses. And she couldn't help but continue to worry about Ross, even though he seemed to have forgotten her. His presence in Room 302 would certainly disturb Willow. Arianne remembered how the ghost had knocked over the bottle of perfume when Ross had been in the shop. If Ross stayed overnight in the room Willow had haunted for over ninety years, who knew what might happen to him? Arianne had never heard of any report indicating that Willow had endangered anyone, but the ghost had never had a Briarcliff staying in that room before. And the psychic Arianne had met had warned her that some spirits were evil. Arianne wondered if such a spirit could seriously harm a person. By the end of her walk, she'd decided to try calling the psychic for advice.

Not anxious to go back to her shop because she'd sensed Willow there, she went to a pay phone off the lobby that was enclosed in a glass and wood cubicle. After leafing through her small purse notebook, she found the psychic's number and hoped the woman would be home.

"Claudia?" Arianne said when a woman's voice answered.

"Yes."

"I don't know if you remember me. I'm Arianne Lacey and we met at a party a few months ago."

"Let me think—you work at the Aragon, and you're Willow's great-great-niece, right? We had that long talk."

"Right," Arianne said with relief, "I'm glad you remember. You said I could call you if I needed advice."

"Sure. What's going on?"

"Well, she's been haunting me more and more lately, and—"

"Appearing to you?"

"No, but I smell her violet scent and hear her crying—even tonight, a little while ago, in my shop." Arianne hesitated, not sure how to bring Ross into her story. "One of the Briarcliffs, Ross Briarcliff, has been doing research at the hotel. I think her activity increased when he came on the scene."

"Interesting. How is he related to Peter?"

"He's Peter's great-grandson. You've heard of William Briarcliff, who's running for the Senate? Well, Ross is William's brother."

"Yes, I've seen William on the news. And what research has Ross been doing?"

"He's looking into the Willow scandal, trying to find evidence that she wasn't murdered by Peter. I believe he also wants to debunk the ghost story. Maybe that's why—" Arianne paused to catch her breath, she was talking so fast. "He apparently made arrangements to stay in Room 302 tonight."

"Oh, no."

"Is it dangerous for him to do that?"

"I wouldn't recommend it. Not without someone with him. I have another appointment tonight. If he could put it off till tomorrow, I can go over there and be in the room with him if he wants to make contact."

"No," Arianne said with regret. "I don't think he'd agree to that. He doesn't believe in ghosts. And, from things he's said, I don't think he has a high opinion of psychics, either."

"Then why is he staying in the room?"

"The only reason I can figure out is that he doesn't think anything will happen. He's in the process of writing a newspaper series on Briarcliff family history. The Briarcliffs hate being connected with the Willow ghost story. He may be trying to demonstrate that there *is* no ghost here, which is what he believes."

"So he's sort of challenging Willow to appear by staying in the room?"

"I think so. I haven't talked to him, but I imagine that's how he's looking at it. He probably sees it as something of a joke."

"You'd better warn him, Arianne. Will he listen to you? Oh, that's right," Claudia said, as if a thought had just hit her, "you're a Monroe and he's a Briarcliff. Are you on speaking terms?"

"Yes. Well, sometimes. We have a...an odd relationship."

"In what way odd?"

"We don't get along, but...we're..."

"Attracted to each other?"

"Yes."

"Like Willow and Peter. This is fascinating! I can see why Willow may be agitated, as you say."

Arianne felt frightened, hearing her fears confirmed by Claudia. "What about Ross? He has no idea—"

"Tell him not to stay in the room. If Peter did murder Willow, then Ross may be in great danger. You, too. If you're there, she might even try to possess you. Neither of you should go in that room without a sensitive like me, or someone else, who understands the spirit world. If Ross doesn't believe in spirits, then tell him...oh, tell him you'll die of fright, worrying about him. If he cares for you, he'll—"

"I can't count on him doing anything for me," Arianne said with an unbidden feeling of hurt. "I haven't heard from him for weeks. I didn't even know he was staying in Willow's room tonight. The hotel manager told me."

"I see. Then I don't know what more to say, Arianne. I could give you the name of another psychic I know, since I'm busy tonight. But if Ross won't pay the psychic any heed because he thinks it's all nonsense, then it won't do any good, anyway."

"No," Arianne agreed. "I'll just have to try to stop him myself. I appreciate your advice."

"You're welcome. But be careful. Catch him before he even goes into the room, if you can. Look at it from Willow's point of view. He's a Briarcliff and he'll be invading *her* territory. If she's already agitated by him coming to the hotel, when he enters her room, she'll be all the more affronted. And to repeat myself, you may be in danger, too. She may try to get at him through you."

"You mean, she might make *me* try to harm him?"

"I can't say for sure what she'll do, since I haven't had the chance to make contact with her, but it's not impossible for her to try to take over your mind and body. She seems to identify with you, and if she perceives Ross as her—and possibly your—enemy, then she might do most anything. It's not worth the risk."

Arianne thanked her again and hung up, feeling deeply shaken and almost weak with trepidation. She went to the reception desk and asked if Ross had checked into the room yet. The clerk told her Ross had come in and gone up to the room a few minutes ago. Arianne raced toward the Aragon's old-fashioned brass elevator located in the lobby. She asked the operator to take her to the third floor. When he slid the door open for her, she rushed out and headed toward the south wing.

The hall of the south wing was decorated in the same manner as the rest of the hotel's hallways. Cheerful yellow wallpaper with a small flower pattern covered the wall from the ceiling to the wainscoting. Below that the wall was painted a light green, to pick up the shade of the stems and leaves of the flower pattern. Though the colors in daytime were charming, they took on a less pleasant, sickly hue at night in the pale, artificial light of the crystal ceiling fixtures. The windows along one side of the hall, which faced the ocean—often noted as a curiosity in the architecture, for the rooms ought to have been built to face the sea—were left open. Now that the sun was setting, and the temperature was cooling, Arianne felt a chill as a breeze ruffled the window curtains.

She felt rattled and shivery as she hesitated in front of Room 302. She'd always feared this place. And now the man she both feared and loved was behind the door. Clenching her jaw for bravery, she knocked.

In a moment, Ross opened the door, a look of annoyance on his face at being disturbed. When he saw Arianne, his expression changed to one of confusion.

"Arianne. What are you doing here?" He sounded out of breath from surprise.

"How about you? Alex told me you were staying here tonight. Why?"

"To prove your ghost doesn't exist."

"I thought so. It's for your news article, isn't it?"

Ross nodded. "What's it to you?"

"Ross, I came here to warn you not stay in this room."

He looked as if he was trying to smother a smile. "You've heard my views on ghosts," he told her.

"I phoned that psychic I met, and she said it could be dangerous for either you or me to be in this room."

"Stupid nonsense," he muttered. He opened the door wider, so she could see inside. "Doesn't look any different than any other hotel room to me."

Indeed, the room looked peaceful enough. There was a bed with a yellow flowered bedspread, which matched the drapes. The moss green carpet looked like new and the room appeared very neat. There were even fresh flowers in a vase on the dresser, she noticed.

"Where did the flowers come from?" she asked.

"Compliments of the hotel. I think Alex probably had them sent. He seems worried about what I'll say about the Aragon in my article."

Arianne nodded, knowing it was like Alex to make overtures to those in some position of power. Though the room looked absolutely normal, as Ross had said, Arianne was still fearful. She reached out to touch his jacket sleeve. "Please, Ross, don't stay here. I'm afraid for you."

His expression softened. "Why?"

"Because of what the psychic said."

"Never mind the psychic. Why do you care what happens to me? You've told me more than once to stay out of your life."

Arianne realized that now wasn't the time to pretend she didn't care. "We may not be good for each other, but...it doesn't mean I don't miss you when I don't see you for a while."

A new light entered his eyes, making them transluscent. "You missed me?"

She nodded, saying nothing further for fear she'd say too much. Just letting him know she'd missed him was probably asking for heartache.

Ross's eyes were glowing now with an incandescent light. He smiled and reached around her waist to swiftly pull her to him. She was inside the room before she knew what had happened.

"Ross, no!" she objected as he shut the door behind them.

His eyes darkened. "*No*, what? You just said you missed me. Your eyes said it, too." He held her close and bent his head to kiss her, his black hair falling over his forehead.

"Not here ... Wil—" she whispered before his lips smothered her ancestor's name. And then he swept her up in his warm embrace, his kiss pushing all thoughts from her mind except the knowledge that she was with him again, that this was what she'd been longing for all the past lonely nights.

When he ended the kiss, she clung to him, lighthearted with new happiness. "Ross, why did you stay away so long? Why didn't you come to see me? You knew I wouldn't be able to resist you."

"I wanted to," he said, an earnest quality in his face. "I had so many doubts. I thought of you constantly."

"I couldn't think of anything but you, either," she said, rising on her toes to touch his lips with hers again. She slid her arms up to encircle his neck. He pulled her against him, deepening her tender kiss with his tongue, increasing the feeling of shared intimacy. A small sound of desire escaped her throat when he brought his hand to cover her breast. This was what she'd wanted every moment they'd been apart, she thought as she began to tremble with longing.

His mouth left hers and traveled to her jawline and down her neck in a series of eager kisses so moist and hot, her breathing grew ragged. As his hand cradled her breast, he found her nipple through her knit top. He fondled her, whispering, "I want you." The ache in his voice revealed his deep desire.

Arianne ached for him, too. But she wanted him to know that it wasn't only sexual response on her part. Not any more. "I think I've fallen in love with you," she told him with shy but sincere joy. "I realized it while we were apart. I've never been in love before."

He studied her with an arrested expression, and then his gray eyes turned bleak. "That's a mistake! Don't love me."

"W-why?" she asked, astonished.

"Because I don't know how to love *you*. All Briarcliff love affairs end badly, Arianne."

"But—" She wanted to argue, yet could think of nothing to counter what he'd said. He'd stated her own fears.

He was staring at her, and she could see apprehension making his eyes like slate. "I've had a recurring dream, four times now. I wonder if it's a premonition, though I don't usually believe in such things. But this seemed so real. I saw you running toward the sea—as if you were going to drown yourself."

Arianne felt as if an icy wave swept through her, and she thought of Willow.

"The first time I dreamed it," he continued, "I stopped you before you could go into the waves. But since then, I've dreamed the same thing three more times, and each time I'm farther and farther away when I try to save you. The last time I woke up in a sweat just as I saw you plunging into the water."

"Why am I drowning myself?" she asked.

"I don't know, but you're holding the brooch in your hand. You're in a panic—fear of me, maybe."

"Because you're trying to get the brooch away from me?"

He hesitated. "I'm not sure. If I reach you in time, the brooch seems to be forgotten."

"Forgotten?"

"We fall down together, and we... make love."

"You dreamed about us making love?" Arianne could barely catch her breath. "*Was* I afraid of you?"

He seemed distracted and looked away. "Maybe the dream is just symbolic," he said. She noticed he didn't answer her question. "Maybe it's only a reflection of my own anxieties and desires." He turned his head to face her again. "But I don't want anything to happen to you because of me. It's why I've stayed away and haven't tried to see you." He let go of her and swallowed hard. "I think you should go now, before something does happen between us we'll both regret."

"No, Ross." Arianne feared losing him more than she feared any possible danger. "I . . . I trust you. I love you."

"Then stop loving me!" he told her in a sharp tone. "And don't trust me, either. No female should trust a Briarcliff. I could take you in a minute and leave you the next. You *know* better than to love me. Don't be as foolish as Willow was!"

Tears filled Arianne's eyes and clouded her vision. "Ross, please—"

He grabbed her arm in a tight clasp and began to usher her toward the door. "Leave, before we go too far—before we make love or destroy each other. Or both!"

He pushed her roughly to the door, but when he turned the knob to open it, the door apparently wouldn't open. He drew his hand back in shock.

"What?" Arianne said.

"The doorknob feels like ice."

All at once the two lamps in the room went off, pitching them into darkness. Arianne screamed. Then the lights came back on. She clung to Ross.

"It's Willow!"

"No," Ross said. "Just a temporary power loss."

"But the door—"

Ross tried it again. "It's stuck, that's all." He brought his hand away, rubbing his palm on his thigh as if to warm it.

And then the heavy scent of violets filled the room. Arianne had never smelled the fragrance so strongly.

"Willow's here, Ross. Don't you smell her violet perfume?"

He seemed hesitant, as if not wanting to acknowledge the strange odor.

Arianne began to shiver. "It's freezing in here." She looked around the room fearfully, wondering if she'd see the mist in the shape of a woman that a few guests had reported over the years. But she saw nothing. And then her eyes came upon the bouquet of flowers on the dresser. "Ross!" she screamed.

"What?" he said, still trying the door.

"The flowers. They're all wilted! They were perfect when I came in."

He looked at the bouquet, stunned. "It's . . . probably from the cold. Obviously the heating doesn't work in this room."

"It's the middle of summer," she said, reminding him of the obvious. "The hotel doesn't need heat in summer."

"It's a draft from the windows in the hall, then."

"It's Willow! I *know* her presence. We've got to get out of here!"

"Calm down!" he said with irritation. "There's no such thing as a ghost." He sounded as if he was saying this to convince himself more than her.

The lights went off again. In the darkness, Arianne clung to Ross, both looking for protection and wanting to protect *him*. "She's angry with you, don't you see? Not only are you Peter's great-grandson, but you're denying her existence."

The lights came on again.

Ross's complexion seemed a shade paler as he glanced about the room. Arianne's heart was beginning to thump irregularly, and she placed her fist near her sternum and tapped her chest. She had the feeling of wanting to cough.

"What's wrong?" Ross asked.

"My heart. I'll be okay in a minute." But her heart showed no indication of returning to its normal rhythm.

Ross slipped his arm around her, as if wanting to steady her. "You okay?"

Arianne was feeling faint. "N-no."

When her weight slackened against him, he lifted her off the floor with both arms and carried her to the bed. After he'd set her down on the bedspread, he told her, "I'm going to call for help." She rose up on one elbow, numb with fright as he picked up the phone from the bed stand and placed the receiver near his ear. His forehead creased. He tapped on the phone, then slammed the receiver down. "No dial tone."

This news set Arianne on the verge of hysteria. "She's got us trapped here," she cried, grabbing Ross's arm. "She means you harm!"

He sat on the edge of the bed and gathered her to him. "Shh. There's no ghost. And we're not trapped."

She slid her arms up to his broad shoulders and tried to shake him, though she felt too weak to make much impact. "Ross, she'll be angry if you don't stop ignoring her." Tears streamed down her face as she began to sob. "I don't want her to hurt you."

"Nothing will hurt us," Ross said.

"I love you."

"Shh."

"Don't shush me!" she suddenly objected, feeling a rush of anger out of nowhere. And then her whole being fell into a swoon of deep passion as she clung to his shoulders. "I love you, Peter. I'll always love you. Say you love me!"

He drew back, his eyes wide with alarm. "I'm *Ross*, Arianne."

She felt confused, and then the room began to spin. His arms supported her as she seemed to fall, and then her head met the pillow. As she lay there in a strange lethargy, he hurried to the door. With a fierce movement, he tried the doorknob. Suddenly the door opened, throwing him off balance for a half second. He rushed to the bed, picked Arianne up in his arms and carried her out of the room.

She was coming to her senses by the time they reached the elevator. There were a couple of upholstered hall chairs nearby, and he let her down, then helped her to sit on one of them.

"Are you all right?" he asked, bending down beside her on one knee, taking her hand.

"I think so." She squeezed his fingers to reassure him. "You're not going to stay in that room tonight, are you?"

He shook his head. "I don't want to upset you anymore. I've got to get my overnight case, though," he said. "Stay here and I'll—"

"Don't go back there!" she exclaimed. "Are you crazy?"

"The door's working again. It's okay."

She held tightly to his hand to keep him from going. "You can ask a bellman to get your luggage." Ross thought a moment. "Okay. Let's go down to the lobby. I'll get you some tea to drink. You've had a shock."

Once they were in the lobby, he led her to a couple of leather chairs in a corner near the lobby bar. He ordered tea for Arianne and sat down with her. "Have you eaten dinner today?" he asked.

Arianne had to stop and think. "No," she replied.

Ross looked at his watch. "It's quarter to eight. If we hurry, we can still get into the dining room."

"I'm not hungry," she said.

"You should eat something," he insisted. "That may be why you felt faint and got a little hysterical. Your blood sugar is probably low."

"You know why I got hysterical," she said, rubbing her forehead. "Willow was there."

"Some odd things happened and you assumed it was Willow," he told her.

"Cold spots? The lights going on and off? The flowers? What else should I assume?"

"All those things can be explained somehow."

"Oh, Ross!" she said with exasperation.

"Did you spray perfume on a lot of customers this afternoon?" he asked.

"Yes," she admitted with reluctance, knowing where he was leading.

"So you've been inhaling perfume alcohol all day and you haven't eaten dinner. No wonder you called me Peter."

Arianne bowed her head and shut her eyes to keep fear from getting the better of her again. The fact that she'd spoken to him as if she were Willow speaking to Peter frightened her the most. Had Willow made her say that?

Ross slid his chair closer to hers. She felt his warm, reassuring hand on her shoulder. "It's all right," he soothed. "I'm not angry. You were upset and not thinking straight, that's all."

She opened her eyes and nodded, pretending to agree, knowing he would never believe or understand what had happened. She didn't understand it herself.

The waitress came with the ordered pot of tea. Ross poured her a cup and handed it to her. "Drink this."

She took it and sipped from the bone china cup. The hotel served English-style teas in the afternoon and used fine china. Ross asked the waitress if there were any scones left. She brought some a few minutes later, and he coaxed Arianne to eat them.

Ross was uncharacteristically solicitous, even sweet, and Arianne couldn't help but feel warmed and cared for. If he was like this more often, Arianne knew she would be in danger of falling hopelessly, incurably in love with him. And then what? she asked herself. Could they have any sort of future together?

She finished her second cup of tea. As she set it on the small table in front of her, she told Ross, "I'd better go home now. Thanks for—"

"I'll drive you," he said.

"My car is here. How would I get to work tomorrow?"

"I'll pick you up in the morning. I'm not going to let you drive tonight. Not after nearly fainting a little while ago." He said this with such finality, she didn't argue.

He went to the registration desk, checked out of Room 302—to Arianne's relief—and asked them to hold his luggage for him until he returned to pick it up. Then he took her hand in his and, in a protective manner, accompanied her out of the hotel to his car.

Though she was still shaken by what had happened in the haunted room, thoughts of their earlier, impulsive desire also played in her head. Ross had asked her to make love. She'd almost agreed to do so. He'd even dreamed of them together. The thought of being alone with him again as he drove her home made her heart beat rapidly, both with excitement and fear. If she demonstrated her new-found love for him tonight, might he learn to love her in return?

She wondered if she should invite him in when they arrived at her house.

Ross followed Arianne's directions to her home, located almost a mile from the hotel. He felt edgy. All the goings on in Room 302 had almost unhinged him, though he refused to believe they were due to ghostly interference. Still, there was something unusual about the room, he had to admit, to explain the sudden cold and the lights flicking on and off. And the stuck door. He wondered if Alex had the room rigged somehow, to make these things happen, just to keep the ghost story going and his hotel in the limelight.

He glanced at Arianne, sitting so pensively and quietly in the passenger seat of his Jaguar. Her earlier hysteria made him worry about her, though it was gratifying to learn she cared so much about him. She'd even told him she loved him. She'd said the words so sincerely, too, not like other women he'd known. It was the authentic way she expressed her feelings that disconcerted him the most. He didn't know how to respond. And if she truly loved him, there was that much greater a probability that he'd wind up hurting her.

Ross had never been in love—didn't think he knew how to love anyone. He was bound to break her heart. Sometimes he wondered if his apparent inability to feel emotion could eventually drive him mad. It was said that every human being had emotions, but Ross never sensed he had any, other than anger. There was madness in his family, too. Peter's daughter had gone mad. Even Peter himself might have gone over the edge of sanity that last night with Willow.

Ross had to leave Arianne alone, that was all there was to it. If she loved him, well, she'd have to get over it. She'd be better off without him. He'd just drive her home now and then go home himself. No good-night kiss to make him forget his intentions.

Ross pulled up in front of the house she pointed out. It was an old home, quaint, not large, built in the Spanish style with a tiled roof. The residential street seemed quiet and peaceful.

"I'll walk you to your door and then leave," he told her, so she knew what to expect.

She nodded with hesitance, looking a little wide-eyed and troubled. Ross told himself to ignore the look. He didn't want to wind up comforting her again. He'd found that he liked looking after her—a new and curious trait for him, since he'd never been a care giver in any interpretation of the word—but now wasn't the time to indulge his propensity to nurture her.

He got out, opened the passenger door and assisted her out of the car. They walked in silence up the sidewalk to her front door. He noticed her hands were shaking as she unlocked her door and he waited until she went in and turned on the lights. Now was the time to say goodbye, turn around and *go,* he instructed himself.

"Would you like to come in?" she asked. She looked at him with huge, lambent eyes, their brown picking up the warm lights from inside the house.

All his resolve vanished. "All right." And then he followed her in, his mind gone numb after making his decision; and yet, within himself, he felt alive. He glanced around the cozy, small house, filled with braided rugs, comfortable old-fashioned furniture and an easy ambiance, and he knew at once he'd rather be here than anywhere else in the world. "Is this where you grew up?" he asked, looking at an enlarged framed color photo on the wall, which appeared to be of Arianne at twelve or thirteen. She was beautiful even then.

"Yes. I should take that old picture down. My parents still own the house and I rent it from them. They want a place here, in case they decide to move back. And it worked out nicely for me." She smiled. "They don't charge me much rent. They asked me to keep the furniture, so I have. But that old photo of me should be put in a closet."

"Why? You look so happy. If I had an old photo like that of me, I'd keep it around just to remind myself I could be that way. You must have had a good experience growing up here."

To his surprise, she slipped her arms around his waist and leaned her head against his shoulder. "Ross, I wish I could take away your unhappiness with your family. I can see how it still tears at you. I wish I could make you happy."

In a reflexive movement, he brought his arms around her. "I accept my lot in life, Arianne. You can't change things for me."

Her trembling fingers played with his necktie. And then she looked at him with shy but impassioned eyes that took his breath away.

"Let me try," she whispered, looking so vulnerable as she said the words, he got a weak feeling in the depth of his stomach.

"Arianne—" He knew what she was suggesting, and he knew he should gently tell her no and get the hell out of there.

But he wanted her too much. Already he felt raw stirrings of desire at the very thought of lying down with her. "Are you sure?" he asked, stroking her dark, silky hair.

She nodded. "I've never felt this way before about anyone. I keep thinking about what it would be like. Other men I've met have wanted to . . . to go to bed, but it didn't feel right to me, so I didn't. But with you—oh, Ross, it's all I think about."

Ross smiled a bit. "I've never been asked by a virgin before."

Her eyes clouded. "I know I'm inexperienced, and you're used to women who—"

"Shh. I don't mind that at all." He touched her delicate jawline. "It's your innocence that makes you so ethereal, like a beautiful dream." And then he remembered his own dream, not the lovemaking so much as the premonition it seemed to contain. "But what would this mean for us?"

Confusion filled her eyes. "I don't know. Right now I don't care about consequences. Maybe our relationship will wind up badly." Her eyes brightened. "Or maybe if we fulfill our longings, we can break through the past that hangs over us. You said once that our problems are between you and me, and not due to an unhappy story about our ancestors. Remember?"

He was watching her lovely mouth as she spoke, and he barely heard her question. Her whispery voice and sweet warm eyes had totally mesmerized him. Gathering her close, he bent his head until his lips found hers. Her mouth was soft and eager, and his heart beat faster as he felt her respond. He pressed his hand against her lower back, bringing her pliant body against his swollen member. A whimpering sound escaped her throat.

"Show me what to do," she said, her bright, dark eyes imploring him.

Her white knit top had short sleeves and no neckline because it stretched from shoulder to shoulder, exposing the length of her delicate collarbone. One of the sleeves had begun to slip down while they kissed, reminding him of his dream. Placing his hands on her upper arms, he slowly moved the sleeves downward, exposing the upper portion of her breasts.

"God, you're so beautiful," he whispered.

Arianne began breathing faster, making her breasts plump against the stretched material, but she made no effort to stop him from exposing her body. All at once the garment slipped off her pink nipples and slid downward to her waist.

Enflamed with desire, he bent over her, holding her in his arms and kissed her breast, then suckled her nipple. She made breathless little cries of excitement, her hand stroking the back of his head, pulling him closer as he teased her with his tongue. He kissed the hollow between her breasts, and he could feel her heart beating shallow and fast. It seemed to skip a beat. He glanced at her face. Her lustrous eyes looked dazed with discovered new pleasure, but she appeared to be growing limp.

He stood upright again, realizing he'd been bending her far backward. She wobbled a bit in his arms, smiling as she clung to him. "You make me dizzy," she whispered.

He lifted her, one arm beneath her shoulders, the other under her knees, and then looked around for a bedroom. He saw a bed through a doorway on the other side of the living room and headed toward it. When he laid her down, her arms went over her head on the pillow, and she looked at him with sweet surrender. As in his dream, he tugged off her clothes until she lay naked on the quilted bedspread. He slipped his fingers between her thighs. Her flesh felt slippery and she was clearly aroused. When he touched the quick of her, her body jolted and she gave a high, astonished cry. She was more than aroused, he realized. She was ready.

He tore off his jacket and tie and tossed them aside. Her eyes widened with awe as he unbuttoned his shirt, and she reached up to stroke his chest. When she touched his nipple, he couldn't wait any longer. He unfastened his belt and zipper, then moved over her, parting her thighs.

She started breathing in short, shaky gasps as he began to enter her.

"Are you all right?" he asked.

"Yes." But tears filled her eyes, and then she winced as if with pain. He was feeling an unusual resistance as he tried to penetrate her body, and then he realized it was because of her virginity. She gave a sharp cry and suddenly he was able to slide smoothly into her.

He stopped all motion and searched her face, feeling bad about hurting her. She wiped away a tear with a trembling hand. Her eyes looked startled, as if the pain had been unexpected, perhaps bringing her out of her eager bliss and making her think about what she was doing. Maybe she was reminded of Peter taking Willow's virginity. At least, that was what was now occurring to Ross. He remembered what Peter had written. *Willow sweetly trembled... She was a virgin. Of course, I promised to marry her.*

No, Ross wasn't going to make that last mistake, and Arianne already knew he had no intention of marrying her. But perhaps just now that was on her mind.

"Arianne?"

"Sorry...it hurt for a moment." She reached up to touch his shoulder as he rested his weight on his elbows. "It's better now."

"You want to go through with this?" he asked.

She nodded and wiped away another tear. "It doesn't hurt anymore," she assured him.

"You aren't having second thoughts?"

"No," she said, but he knew she was lying. He could see the uncertainty in her eyes. As if sensing that he was questioning the truth of her reply, she slipped her arms around him to pull him closer. "I want this, Ross. Don't stop."

His throbbing member demanded satiation inside her moist, tight body, and he questioned her no further. Slowly, he slid all the way inside her, delirious with acute pleasure at the way her body fit his so snugly. She closed her eyes and her expression changed to one of awe as he began to move back and forth within her. She made a high little gasp with each forward thrust. Her immediate responses increased his pleasure. When she opened her eyes, Ross smiled as he gazed into her innocent, wanton face.

"Oh, Ross," she breathed. "So this is what it's all about." She returned his smile unabashedly as she stroked his back. "I like this. I like this a lot."

Her words and her look of dazed delight made Ross almost feel as if this was a new experience for him, too. All his former encounters, more physical recreation than meaningful experiences, always accompanied by artificial, pseudoseductive pillow talk—all those memories seemed to mesh and blur. They wound their way out of his mind, like smoke from a spent cigarette. This coming together with Arianne was altogether different, entirely new, and...a little scary. This was so rare, so genuine, he feared no one else would ever satisfy him, would ever make him feel so positive about life, about being with a woman, as he felt right now with her.

He stroked her hair and kissed her, settling the weight of his chest over hers, while her legs came up to wind around his body. After a long kiss, she broke away from his lips, gasping for air, making sighing, urgent little cries. He loved the way she was so uninhibited and vocal, so endearingly naive in her enjoyment of each sensation. She made him feel like a perfect lover, which he'd certainly never thought of himself as being.

Her cries grew more frenzied, tinged with panic now. Her climax was near, he realized, and he felt a surge of anticipation. He eagerly wanted to share the coming moment with her, to fully satisfy her and make her happy as he satiated his own powerful need.

"Ross," she whispered hoarsely, sounding uneasy, even frightened. Her heart was pounding wildly—he could feel its vibrations through her small rib cage. He knew she was on the brink, and the enormity of the sensation must be scaring her.

"Don't be afraid. Let go," he urged. "Let it happen."

"It's too intense," she said between gasps. "I can't... stand it... oh... oh, Ross!"

He drew back and slid into her again, grinding his pelvis against hers when he'd reached his mark. She screamed and gripped him tightly, and then her body trembled with long, erotic convulsions. He looked at her face, and her lovely features were tensed in the sweetest look of bliss he'd ever seen. His own climax came then, as hers was ebbing. He felt his seed pulsing into her. Moisture seeped onto his lashes as he tightly closed his eyes, aware of the beauty and sense of restoration she gave him. He relaxed on top of her for a long moment as she softly breathed his name.

And then he realized—they hadn't used any protection. In his rush and confusion, he hadn't thought of it. This was unlike him, for in all his past relationships, he'd always secretly worried about being delivered with a paternity suit. It was a prime way for a woman to get money from a man of his wealth, and several of his male relatives had been served with such suits. He'd invariably used a condom, never quite believing any woman who assured him she was on the pill.

Concerned now, he kissed Arianne and then rolled onto his back, pulling her into his arms. What if she became pregnant? he worried. He wouldn't want her to have an abortion. He wouldn't want her to be alone, an unwed mother bringing up his child. He'd ... he'd have to marry her. And then he realized why Peter may have so quickly promised to marry Willow—the same thoughts had probably gone through his great-grandfather's head, especially in that day and age.

Ross recalled his theory that Willow may have seduced Peter, to get him to marry her. He couldn't help but wonder now about Arianne's motives. She'd been so anxious. Though she was a virgin, she'd asked *him* to have sex.

Suddenly, Ross felt a clammy chill that started in his limbs and soon reached his heart.

Arianne was still regaining her breath as she lay in Ross's arms. Her heart was doing somersaults, but she took deep breaths and let her body relax. Lovemaking was wonderful! Scary at first, but sheer ecstasy! At least, it was with Ross. After this, she never wanted to be with another man. Ross was so virile and yet surprisingly tender. No, she'd never need to know what other men might be like. No one could be better, could make her feel so utterly fulfilled and happy. She wanted him for always.

And then she remembered that he did not intend to marry. Well, she knew that. She'd be ... his mistress, instead. Her heart began to fill with sadness as reality overshadowed her brief happiness. He was a Briarcliff. One day he'd probably discard her for someone else.

She looked at him as his arms around her slackened and he seemed to grow cold. He did not meet her glance and sat up, his face withdrawn now, almost expressionless. Her heart began to thump with apprehension. Was he going to discard her already? Had he been disappointed with her?

Without a word to her, he got up and began to get dressed. Unsure what to do, Arianne went to her closet and took out her coral silk robe. As she slipped it on and tied the belt, Ross was putting on his suit jacket. He stuffed his tie into his jacket pocket.

"Ross?" she said, coming up to take his elbow. "Would you like some...some coffee or something?" She didn't know what people usually did in these situations, so she improvised.

"No, I'm going home."

"Already?" she said with a shaky voice. "But—"

He turned on her, his eyes like granite. "Look, I warned you not to get involved with a Briarcliff, didn't I? I told you a relationship between us was no good. Don't start whimpering now because you thought it would be different."

His heartless words crushed her. "Ross, I enjoyed making love with you. You seemed to like it well enough, too. Why are you saying this?"

His eyes shifted, as if searching the air for words. "Sex is just sex. I told you that once. We did it. Yeah, it was great. But it's over now. Don't look for anything more from me."

Arianne put her hand over her nose and mouth to try to control her emotion. She felt ready to dissolve into tears.

"And don't tell me you love me, damn it!" His voice sounded odd, strained to the point of breaking. "I don't want you to ever tell me that again!"

He walked out then—out of her bedroom and straight out of the house. Arianne ran to the front window and watched him get into his car, wondering if she should try to call him back, wondering what had suddenly gone so wrong. When he drove away, she ran to the bed, threw herself on the quilt still warm from their bodies and sobbed for the next hour.

Later, when her tears were spent, she lay in the fetal position, hugging her knees to her chest for comfort. Finally she realized what had happened. She'd made the same mistake Willow had made. She'd fallen in love with a Briarcliff who had enjoyed sex with her purely out of physical desire—and then had forsaken her.

CHAPTER SEVEN

The next day, Arianne went to work, smiled at customers, chatted with them and tested perfumes on them, all the while feeling cold and empty inside. She hadn't heard a thing from Ross and did not expect to. She'd walked to work, since her car had been left at the hotel. He'd apparently forgotten or deliberately ignored his promise to pick her up and drive her to work. She hadn't wasted any time at home this morning waiting for him to show up, either. No lovely bouquet of flowers or handwritten note of apology would be sent to her on *this* occasion, she was certain.

When lunch hour came and Doris arrived to take over for her, Arianne decided she needed to get away from people and be alone for a while. She thought of a unique place—the top of the hotel's closed-off south tower.

Once a scenic lookout point for hotel guests, the south tower had been in disrepair and closed to the public for years. Its wooden staircase had rotted. Alex had been in the process of having the tower and other areas of the hotel renovated, but due to difficult economic times, the hotel's budget often fell short of funds. The last she'd heard was that the seven-story staircase had been rebuilt by a team of carpenters, but it hadn't yet been painted. The painting crew usually under contract to the hotel had stopped work due to lack of funds, she'd heard from friends who worked at the hotel.

After picking up her take-out lunch from the hotel's coffee shop, she walked to the end of the south wing to see if the tower was still closed off. The door leading to the staircase had a sign that read Closed for Repair. But when she tried the door, she found it wasn't locked. So, checking to be sure no one was near to see her disobey the sign, she slipped in. The newly built staircase smelled of fresh wood, and there was still sawdust in the corners of the steps. She climbed the seven stories of spiral stairs until she reached the top of the round tower, which had a conical roof and arched openings designed for visitors to enjoy the scenic view. New metal beams crossed each opening about a foot above the waist-level ledges, ensuring that no one could accidentally fall from the opening while looking out at the view.

Arianne went to one ledge and gazed at the seashore far below. The sun shone brightly, and puffy clouds scudded across the sky in the swift breeze off the sea. The waves sparkled in the sunlight as they swept onto the shore. She remembered she was above that point on the beach where Willow and Peter were said to have argued nearly a century ago. It was also the spot where she'd first met Ross. Recalling this only reminded her of the present. Her spirits disheartened, she sat down on the newly made, still unpainted bench and opened up her lunch.

She wasn't very hungry; her throat was too constricted with unshed tears to eat. Soon she put her half-eaten sandwich into the plastic container from the restaurant.

Her chin trembled, and she gave way to the sobs she'd kept inside all morning while she'd pretended to others that everything was fine. She knew her life would never be the same. The man she'd foolishly loved had used and rejected her. She'd given him her virginity and her love, and he'd repaid her by cruelly trampling on her heart. She felt as if she could never entrust her broken heart to anyone again.

As she cried into her crumpled paper napkin, she heard other sounds of weeping, as if coming to her on the wind. She caught the faint scent of violets. The ghostly weeping seemed to sympathize with her own, and she had the feeling that Willow was sobbing along with her, like a comforting, sisterly presence.

Arianne gradually stopped crying and no longer felt quite so alone. She realized with a new sense of calm that Willow meant no harm—not to *her,* at any rate.

That weekend, Arianne made the two-hour freeway drive to Los Angeles to visit her grandmother, Henrietta. Henrietta had recently turned eighty-one. She'd returned home a few months ago after spending some weeks in a convalescent hospital, recovering from a hip fracture. Her doctor had advised her she should no longer live alone. Her only daughter, Nanette, and her two grandchildren, Arianne and her brother, agreed.

So with reluctance mixed with her characteristic plucky humor, Henrietta was in the process of selling and moving out of the house she'd lived in for over fifty years to move to a residence for the elderly. She was leaving the original Monroe house, which she'd inherited from her mother, Katy Monroe Thornton, Willow's sister. Willow and Katy had grown up there, so the house contained a great feeling of family history.

Because of the house's age and vintage architecture, a group devoted to saving old Los Angeles homes from the wrecking ball was making arrangements to buy the house for a fair, though not overly generous, price. They were generous, however, in the amount of time they were allowing Henrietta to go through the place and sort out its contents. Several members of the Monroe family had already put in time helping Henrietta, and today was Arianne's turn.

"I've been looking forward to seeing you," Henrietta said in her high, aged voice. She was the last of Katy's five children. All Henrietta's sisters and brothers had passed away. Her thick, white hair was cut short nowadays for convenience. She wore pink knit pants and a matching top over her plump figure, and orthopedic shoes. "I don't see you often enough." She gave Arianne a kiss and hug. "Come in. I've saved one of the closets for you to help me go through, if you don't mind."

"Sure. Whatever you need help with, Grandma."

Henrietta walked with slow care and led Arianne to a back bedroom of the one-story brick house. "I saved this one for you, because you're my closest relative living nearby. Some of my nieces and nephews have come and been sweet about helping me clear out things. But I'm looking for some important insurance papers, and I think I put them somewhere in this old closet a dozen years ago or more. I'd have your mother help me find them, but she's off in Florida and your brother's in Seattle, so that leaves you. And even you had to drive a long way," she said with regret.

"I'm glad to help," Arianne assured her.

Her grandmother peered at her through brown eyes that had grown dim. "Are you all right? You look tired. Your eyes are red."

Arianne shook her head. "It's just...you know, cramps." Arianne was glad to have a true excuse to explain her wan appearance. And, for once, she was glad to have cramps. It meant her quick calculations driving home that night with Ross had been correct, and she hadn't been in the fertile time of her cycle. She may have been foolhardy enough to lose her virginity with him, but at least she hadn't been careless enough to get pregnant by him. Though, she reminded herself ruefully, using no protection was always a risk, a risk she shouldn't have taken.

"Oh," Henrietta said with sympathy. "I remember what that was like. You want some aspirin?"

"Okay, thanks," Arianne said. "I can get it."

"No, you start unpacking that closet. I'll bring it."

"What am I looking for?" Arianne asked before her grandmother walked out.

"One of those metal boxes with a lock on it," Henrietta said. "I think I know where the key is. But I need to find the box."

Arianne began by taking out the old clothes hanging in the closet and carrying them to the bed. They had a musty smell from disuse. There were old coats and dresses, even a moth-eaten fur scarf. At the bottom of the closet lay a jumble of cardboard boxes, old shoes and some books. Seeing no metal box, Arianne began clearing out everything on the closet floor, sometimes coughing from dust, as she removed the old books and shoes.

She dragged out the largest of the old corrugated cardboard boxes and opened it. There, with a sense of accomplishment, Arianne saw a metal box such as her grandmother had described.

"I think I've found it," she said as Henrietta hobbled back into the room, carrying an aspirin bottle and a shaky glass of water.

"Oh, wonderful. Here you are," she said, handing her the pain reliever. "Take it right away so you feel better."

"Thanks." Arianne swallowed two aspirin tablets and set the empty glass on the floor next to an old shoe. She picked up the metal box. "This it?"

"That looks like it. Now, I have the key..." Henrietta turned to the bed, sat down on an empty spot and picked up an ancient-looking cigar box, whose colorful lid advertised an old brand of Cuban cigars. She opened the lid and poked through its contents with stiff fingers. Her knuckles were enlarged from arthritis. "My mother had this box to keep keys in, and I still use it. Silly, no? I don't know what half of these keys are for. But the one for that lockbox has a ribbon—here it is," she said, picking up one that had a thin red ribbon tied to it. "I put the ribbon on it so I could find it again." She handed the key to Arianne. "Your fingers work better than mine. You open it for me."

"Sure." Arianne took the key, found it worked easily in the lock and opened the box. Inside was a stack of folded legal documents, including a birth certificate. Arianne smiled to herself, wondering why these things hadn't been kept in a bank vault. But she knew older people, who had lived through the Great Depression, didn't always trust banks. She handed the papers to her grandmother.

While Henrietta sorted through them, turning toward the window for better light, Arianne looked in the closet. Almost everything was out now and she could see how deteriorated the old blue rug on the closet's floor had become. She lifted the worn edge a few inches—it came away from its tacking easily—wondering if she should rip it out and throw it away. The house ought to look as clean as possible when it was turned over to its new owners.

When she lifted the rug, she noticed what appeared to be a square cut into the aged floorboards underneath. Pulling up on the rug and flapping the front edge of it to the back, she was astonished to find that there seemed to be a small trapdoor cut into the wood floor.

"What's this, Grandma?" she asked. "This square cut into the floor?"

Henrietta leaned to one side to peer at it. "Well, I don't know. I didn't know it was there." And then she hesitated. "Wait, I do remember. I once saw my mother on her hands and knees, pulling it up. I was only about five. She told me to go away, that she was just cleaning. I remember wondering about it, but then I forgot."

"Should I see if I can pull it up?"

"Sure, go ahead. Probably nothing in there, though."

Arianne dug her fingernails into the crevice formed by the square and was able to raise it up far enough to get her fingers underneath. She lifted the loose floorboards and set them to one side. Beneath she found another metal box, this one looking quite antique. Taking it out carefully with both hands, she showed it to her grandmother.

"My goodness," Henrietta said. "What can that be?" She chuckled with excitement. "Maybe there's money in it!"

Arianne smiled and tried to lift the lid, but the lock was securely fastened. "It looks like it needs a key. Maybe in that cigar box."

She stretched up, reached for the cigar box on the bed and set it on the floor next to her. One by one, she tried each key that looked like it might fit. Finally, she took out an old-looking, small brass key and tried it in the lock. It stuck at first, but then it opened like a charm. She lifted the lid and looked inside.

Arianne gasped and her heart nearly stopped when she saw a fiery, opalescent gleam. She leaned against the closet doorframe, fingertips to her mouth, catching her breath.

"What did you find?" Henrietta asked.

"Grandma, it's the Briarcliff brooch!" With tremulous fingers, she picked up the large milky opal, whose strange inner fires wavered and changed hue in the light from the window, almost as if it was alive. The opal, about the size of a half-dollar, but oval-shaped, was set in gold filigree. A pin and clasp were soldered onto its back. It looked exactly like the brooch in the photo of Willow and the design Arianne had used on her perfumes. The thought that Willow herself had worn it gave her a sense of reverence.

"The Briarcliff brooch? No!" Henrietta seemed confounded. "How could it be? My mother always said it was missing. Unless . . . maybe that's what she tried to tell me the day she died."

"What do you mean?"

Henrietta bit her lip for a moment, then looked at Arianne with a doubtful expression, as if unsure what to say, or perhaps how much to tell. And Arianne began to wonder if there were more family secrets than this hidden brooch.

"When my mother lay on her deathbed, I kept vigil with her all through her last day and night. She was past seventy and very weak. I was her youngest and had remained closest to her, so she confided in me. That day she told me...oh, many things. Her last words, you know. She was almost delirious from the pain of her cancer."

Arianne nodded, her heart beating with expectation.

"Well, one of the things she said was, 'Never tell where it's hidden.' I didn't know what she was talking about. I asked her what was hidden, but she faded back to sleep for a while and never mentioned it again. She must have meant this brooch, and in her delirium, she didn't remember that she'd never told me she had it." Henrietta shook her head. "My goodness. All these years, the Briarcliffs have insisted we had it. And we did. I feel a little ashamed."

"You didn't know, Grandma," Arianne said, reaching to squeeze her hand. "It's not your fault. But why would Katy have wanted to keep it hidden?"

Henrietta shifted a bit on the bed, sighing heavily. "My mother always revered her dead sister, Willow. She used to talk a lot about her in an admiring way. I remember she used to describe Willow as frail and beautiful—like an angel, she'd say. Willow lived in a romantic dream world because she was an invalid and couldn't be as active as others, but she was surprisingly stubborn. Peter was Willow's only love, and my mother bitterly blamed him for her death. When I was young, I used to think she meant that Peter had drowned Willow. Well, the Monroe family always assumed that he'd killed her to get back that brooch, because . . . it was never found."

Henrietta paused, and slowly clenched and unclenched her fist in an unconscious mannerism while her mind seemed to be taking mysterious turns. "But that wasn't so, was it? Because *there* it is. He never got it back from Willow."

Arianne had the feeling that Henrietta wasn't surprised that Peter may not have committed murder to get the opal, though she *had* been surprised to find the brooch here in her home. This confused Arianne. "Go on, Grandma."

Henrietta looked up, apparently startled out of her deep rumination. She wet her lips. "There's nothing more to tell."

"How did Katy get the brooch? Willow was seen wearing it on the beach that night."

Henrietta wet her lips again. "Oh . . . one way or another."

Arianne wondered what her grandmother was keeping to herself. "What else did your mother say on her deathbed?"

"Things that . . . that were meant to remain between me and her. I don't think I should break her trust. It's all so much old history now. Nothing that matters to anyone."

Arianne changed her position on the floor and edged closer to her grandmother. "But it does, Grandma. I've met one of the Briarcliffs—Ross Briarcliff." Now it was Arianne's turn not to tell everything. "He and I have had arguments about the past. In fact, he told me he believed that our family had this brooch, and I denied that we did. Now I discover he was right. The Briarcliffs still claim ownership of the brooch, and I think he's entitled to know it's been found. So I'll have to tell him. But...do you think I should *give* it to him?"

Henrietta looked shocked. "*Give* it to him? I should say not! One thing my mother always said is that Peter had given Willow the brooch as a gift, so it was hers to keep, and that he'd been a cad to ask for it back when he changed his mind about marrying her." She paused, as if thinking. "I suppose *that's* why my mother kept it hidden. She did it for her dead sister. It was probably her sense of justice, because she hated Peter Briarcliff for what he'd done to Willow. So she had to hide the brooch and not tell anyone, because those Briarcliffs never gave us an end to the question of what happened to that opal. My mother secretly kept it out of revenge, so they wouldn't have it."

Arianne swallowed. "And you're asking me to continue keeping this secret, Grandma?"

Henrietta's expression changed and she slowly nodded. "I see what you mean, Arianne. I didn't even know the thing was there, so that made the matter easy for me. But you've found it, and you don't like keeping the secret." She drew in a breath and shrugged her shoulders. "Well, then you take the brooch and do with it as you see fit. You belong to a new generation. Clinging to old ideas and animosities never did anyone much good, I don't think. I'll explain to the rest of the family that I've left it all up to you. I'll have my lawyer write a document stating that I've given it to you alone to handle, so there won't be any squabbles over it in *our* family. It's time we were finished with this Willow business." She chuckled grimly. "If you ask me, I suspect Willow was a little spoiled, her with her bad heart and everyone waiting on her hand and foot, expecting everything to come to her just because she was so beautiful and her health was fragile."

Arianne was only half listening, feeling the weight of responsibility as she studied the gold-encrusted opal in her hand, entranced by its changing colors. What would she tell Ross when she showed it to him, as she felt she must?

She'd been so fascinated with the brooch and the things her grandmother had said that she'd forgotten to check to see what else was in the antique box she'd unearthed. She dropped the brooch in her lap and reached for the box again. With surprise, she found it contained some old letters. She picked them up and examined them, and she realized they were all addressed to Willow Monroe—they were the letters Peter had written her. Arianne's pulse quickened. She'd found them! Now perhaps she would know more about Peter's side of the story.

After putting them in chronological order according to the postmarks, she began reading them, handing each one to her grandmother as she finished them. The first few were polite and full of admiration. *You are the loveliest, most artless young lady I have ever met, and I hope our friendship will grow despite the distance between our homes,* the initial letter said. Another referred to Peter's first visit to Willow's home, the very home in which Arianne now sat. The second to last letter, judging by its

content, apparently was written after their friendship had
evolved into an affair. Peter wrote:

I hope you are not troubled or ashamed by what
transpired between us on my last visit. Though society may condemn what we have done, I can only find
joy in the new depth of our relationship, as I hope you
do. When you told me that you loved me, I was so
moved by your sincerity and so touched at being the
object of your deep affection, that I could not contain myself.

As she read Peter's words of rapture, Arianne could not
help but think of her own experience with Ross and how
he had reacted in exactly the opposite way, with anger, after she'd told him she loved him and had slept with him. If
Ross was reading this now, he would probably say it
proved his theory that Willow had seduced Peter, that she
had put a spell on him by plying him with her words of
love. But Arianne was convinced in her heart that Willow
had been as sincere in her declaration as she herself had
been. She read on.

When you didn't show any sign of displeasure at my
bold advances, I gave in to my boundless desire to be
one with you. Forgive me if I am mistaken, but I felt
that, though you were frightened with inexperience,
you were as filled with emotion as I. My dearest Willow, if I am guilty of taking advantage of you, I ask
your forgiveness; but I confess I do not feel any such
guilt weighing on my conscience. Your tears of joy
afterward, your delightful smiles, your continued
declarations of love for me, make me certain enough
to assume that you are not sorry for what happened,

as I am not. My only fear was and is for your health.
I could feel your frail heart pounding so as I held you.
I must admit it gave me pause.

Arianne wondered if this was what Willow responded to
in her letter when she said, *Don't worry so about my heart.
As long as it beats for you, it will remain strong.*
She continued reading Peter's words:

You have made me love you as I have never loved
anyone before. My beautiful Willow, I adore and
worship you. You gave me the utmost happiness when
you consented to become my wife. We must make
plans quickly, so we will not have long to wait to make
our impulsive union honest in the eyes of God and
society. I have spoken to my parents, and they have
consented to give me the family brooch about which
I've spoken. I shall visit again this coming weekend to
present the brooch, with the proudest joy, to you, as
a token of my love and my intention to make you my
wife.

Arianne couldn't help but notice that Peter's tone here
seemed different than the more terse, possibly smug entry
he had made in his journal, where he seemed to relish the
fact that he'd taken Willow to bed while her parents were
out. She recalled his using the term *guilty pleasure,* and he
even admitted he'd taken advantage of the situation. And
then there was his reference to his *wild obsession* for her,
with not one mention of the word *love*.
Arianne wondered if the fact that he'd saved his stunning testimonial of love for this letter to Willow, and did
not record having any such emotion for her in his journal,
indicated a duplicity on his part. Still, his words sounded

sincere and full of hopeful excitement, and he *did* present her with the brooch. But perhaps his decision to marry her was only because of his obsession for her, not because he'd really fallen in love. Marrying her would make it easy for him to quench his lust whenever he wanted. True love may not have had much to do with it—just as Ross had wanted nothing to do with that emotion.

At least Ross hadn't gone through the sham of offering to marry her, she thought with bitter irony. She supposed that made Ross more honest than Peter. He hadn't spewed forth such lovely words of love as these that Peter had written to Willow. No wonder Willow believed Peter really loved her. No wonder she trusted him.

Arianne could at least be grateful for having Willow's tragic experience to learn from. She felt a keen sisterhood now with her dead relative. Arianne glanced around the small bedroom and at the antique double bed on which her grandmother sat reading, and she wondered if Willow had lost her virginity to Peter in this very room.

Her own experience of pain and tearful ecstasy with Ross came back to her in a rush, making her feel her emotions of that evening all over again. Moisture gathered in her eyes. Blinking, she gave the letter in her hand to her grandmother and picked up the last one to read.

This appeared to be the final note Peter sent. He began the letter by describing his visit to Willow's doctor and detailing what the doctor had told him about her health. And then he wrote:

> My heart breaks as I write this, for I have come to a heartrending decision. I must tell you that our planned marriage cannot be. I wanted to live with you and love you for the remainder of my life. But to do so would likely take away your precious life, my dar-

ling. I could never live with you and not love you as a husband. If you were to die giving birth to my child, I would never survive such a tragedy myself. I must break my engagement to you for both our sakes. We must accept this as our fate and carry on with our lives.

I must also ask you—with a sense of shame and heartfelt sorrow—to give me back the brooch. If it were up to me, I would want you to keep it as a token to remember our love by. But it belongs in my family. I have explained to you our tradition, and my parents would be most upset if the brooch were not returned. I trust you will understand and forgive me.

Lastly, and with a most profound regret, I must inform you that I have asked another lady to be my wife. Who she is, you will no doubt learn soon enough, and her identity is of no importance at the moment. I am marrying another, Willow, so there will be no future temptation for you or I to harbor any hope that our sad situation can somehow be overcome. I will marry her, and that will be an end to our love. I am most dreadfully sorry, my dearest Willow. I loved you as I will never love again. Shed tears for me as you weep for yourself and our lost union.

I wish for you improved health and a long life. Take comfort in the fact that you have a family who adores you and to whom you give great joy—as, for a brief, sweet time, you gave me.

Arianne felt rather stunned as she read Peter's impassioned words. Tears streamed down her cheeks. Perhaps she'd been all wrong about him. He sounded so heartbroken in this last letter. Maybe his feelings for Willow did go far deeper than a zealous sexual obsession. Perhaps he really, truly loved her with all his heart.

Arianne felt confused. She handed the last letter to her grandmother, then wiped tears from her cheeks with the edge of her long cotton skirt. As she smoothed her skirt, another thought came to her. She'd have to show these letters to Ross, as well as the brooch. What would he think of them?

Ross always said that he believed Peter cared for Willow. This last letter would seem to prove him right. But Arianne wondered if the letter would make Ross think about his own treatment of her. Peter had at least rejected Willow with as much tender kindness as he could. Ross had rejected Arianne after their sexual encounter with as much coldness and anger as he could. She hoped reading this letter would have the effect of making Ross feel self-conscious at least, if not guilt-ridden. But she was probably hoping for too much, even at that. Ross wouldn't want to be bothered with her hurt feelings, because they simply didn't matter to him. Now she found that she had to change her opinion of Peter. She had much more respect for him than she did for his great-grandson.

Henrietta folded up the last letter and put it into its envelope. "My goodness," she said softly. "Such pain they went through. Both of them. I think my mother was wrong to despise Peter so. Don't you?"

"I'm not sure what to think right now," Arianne replied. "But I believe you're right, that Peter went through a lot of pain, too. In those days, I suppose there was nothing that could be done medically for a woman with a bad heart. Peter got involved with her before he knew the extent of her ill health. I suppose there was nothing else he could do but break off with her. But I wish he could have stood up to his family and let her keep the brooch."

"Yes, I feel the same," Henrietta said. "But he was from a wealthy family, and those kind of folks always think they should have things their way. Maybe he just couldn't go against all that."

Arianne studied her grandmother's pensive face. "So if Peter didn't murder Willow to get the brooch back," she asked, "and if he did really love her, then how and why did Willow die?"

Henrietta's expression grew solemn for a moment. She bowed her head a bit, handing the small stack of letters to Arianne. She did not reply to the question.

"You know, don't you?" Arianne asked, not wanting to press her grandmother too hard but wanting at least to know for sure that there was something Henrietta wasn't saying.

"Yes, I do know, Arianne. But, you see, I promised my mother on her deathbed that I wouldn't tell."

"But why would Katy tell you about it at all if she didn't want someone to know? She could have just taken her secret to the grave."

"I suppose she felt it was information that should be passed on, so someone in the family would know in case some unforeseen circumstance connected with Willow's death came up. Or maybe she just felt obliged to tell the truth before she died."

"Is there something so awful about Willow's death that it needs to be kept a secret?" Arianne asked.

"My mother thought so. Nowadays...well, it would all be seen differently today."

"Would you consider telling me, Grandma?" Arianne asked in a gentle voice.

Henrietta thought for a long moment, then said with hesitation, "I don't like to break my promise to my mother, even if her reasons seem old-fashioned now. I gave her my word. Why do you need to know about Willow, anyway?''

"Her spirit haunts me at the hotel," Arianne told her.

Henrietta drew back, her eyes widening. "No, really? You mean that ghost story is true?"

"Yes. I hear her weeping. If I could figure out what happened, it might help me understand. And . . . and then there's Ross Briarcliff. He wants to know the truth, too. He's writing an article about it for the newspaper and—''

"The newspaper!" Henrietta shook her head. "Then I can't tell you. My mother certainly wouldn't have wanted the circumstances of Willow's death to be published in a newspaper. And the fact that Willow's spirit is still not at rest only makes me think that maybe my mother was right. I'm sorry, Arianne. I know you're curious. But we must honor the wishes of the dead, mustn't we?"

Arianne fingered the brooch in her lap, wishing she hadn't mentioned Ross's newspaper article. She might have coaxed her grandmother into saying more. Now she might never know what really happened to Willow. She would have liked to have learned every detail of the past when she showed this brooch and the letters to Ross. She would have liked to be able to settle the old issues between their families once and for all. And most of all, she wanted to settle her own brief, sorry past with Ross, forever.

CHAPTER EIGHT

Arianne thought over her options through the weekend. She could simply say nothing to Ross about the brooch and the letters, but she didn't really consider this as a choice. It was her obligation, she felt, to inform him the Briarcliff opal had been found. But how to inform him was another question. Should she write him a letter? Phone him? Make an appointment to see him?

On Monday morning, heart pounding, she telephoned Ross's office. She felt relieved when his secretary answered and said he was not in at the moment. Arianne asked the woman to leave him the message that some artifacts had been found that would be of interest to him, and would he please return her call. The secretary took down the message, sounding a bit mystified as she read it back to Arianne.

Arianne waited all day, helping customers and tidying her shop, but Ross did not show up to see her, as she thought he might, or call. Perhaps he'd decided not to simply because he didn't want to talk to her. Now what? she wondered. She'd have to write him a letter giving him all the specifics, a chore she didn't look forward to. A phone call would have gotten things over with so much more quickly if he'd seen fit to call her back. Now she'd have to write and wait days for his reply. Damn him!

At six o'clock, when she was turning her Open sign to read Closed, she heard the phone ring in the back room. Her heart seemed to stop.

During the days since he'd left Arianne's house, Ross had found himself thinking of her often. In fact, he could think of nothing else. He'd even considered calling her to see how she was. He wondered how she'd gotten to work the next morning, because he'd been too angry to drive her to the hotel as he'd promised. He felt guilty about the way he'd walked out after what had happened between them. And yet he questioned why he should feel any sense of shame. She'd enticed *him*, hadn't she? She'd gotten him so excited with her soft seduction that he'd ignored his resolve not to get involved. He'd even forgotten to take precautions.

It seemed she'd forgotten to protect herself, too. Or had she been hoping to get pregnant so she could expect him to marry her or pay her a lot of money in a paternity suit? It had happened before in his family. Ross had met enough gold-digging females himself that he should have known better and been more careful—even with a virgin. Arianne always appeared so ingenuous, but Willow probably had seemed guileless, too, and she'd ruined Peter's life.

So Ross had reconsidered his idea about calling Arianne and hadn't done it. But now, it seemed, *she'd* called *him*. This bothered him. If there was going to be a phone call, he'd wanted it to be his idea, not a response to her request.

But here he was, sitting at his desk, telephone receiver to his ear, listening to Arianne's phone ring. He felt tense as he clutched the receiver and pondered the message his secretary had given him. He'd been in court all day and she'd handed it to him when he came in. The phrase about some artifacts having been found almost amused him. He'd thought Arianne was different, but she was proving to be just like so many of the women he'd gotten mixed up with. When he ended a relationship, his ex-girlfriend often would find some excuse to call him, some ploy to try to get him back. And Arianne apparently had been clever enough to come up with just the sort of bait he couldn't ignore right now when he was fishing for something— anything—to use for his first newspaper article.

He wondered exactly what artifact she'd come up with, real or invented, to entice him to see her again. Something connected with Willow, he supposed—Willow, Arianne's model and inspiration for twisting a Briarcliff male around her finger.

"Hello?"

The sound of Arianne's high, hesitant voice broke into his thoughts and disconcerted him. She always sounded so damned innocent. It made him go soft inside.

"It's Ross," he said, keeping himself tough by using a tone of annoyance.

"Ross . . . I hoped you'd return my call."

"I'll bet." He put a sarcastic edge in his voice.

There was silence on the other end of the line, as if she was puzzled by his remark. Then she said, "I found some things that I need to show you."

"To *show* me? In other words, you want to make some arrangement to meet with me."

He heard a faint sigh. "Yes, we'll have to meet," she agreed.

"And what is this fabulous artifact you just happened to find?"

Again there was silence. Only now he sensed hostility on the other end of the line. "Why are you taking that sarcastic tone with me?" she asked.

"Why are you finding excuses to see me again?"

"Finding excuses?" she repeated with astonishment. "You think I *want* to see you again? After the way you left things between us? You actually think I'd *invent* a reason to call you?"

"You can deny it all you want, but I know the tactics you women use," he told her. "And it won't work."

She gasped as if incensed. "You are the most insufferable man! Your callous behavior is matched only by your boundless ego!"

She paused, apparently to catch her breath. Ross found himself at a loss. He hadn't expected such outrage—that is, such authentic emotion—undergirding her response. He'd made women angry before, but they usually reacted with more of a method in their indignation, a method designed to make him wind up apologizing. Before he'd dialed Arianne's number, he'd warned himself not to buy into any manipulated guilt trip she might try to put him on. But Arianne was succeeding in making him genuinely feel like two cents.

"I would never talk to you or even look at you again if I could help it," she continued. "But I found the Briarcliff brooch. I thought I ought to tell you."

Ross sat still, replaying her words in his mind. "You...?" He couldn't believe he'd heard correctly. "Did you say you found the brooch?"

"Yes. And Peter's letters to Willow."

"Where? How?"

"At my grandmother's over the weekend. They were buried in a box beneath the floorboards of a closet. I was helping her clean it out when I saw the trapdoor and opened it out of curiosity. My grandmother didn't even know the letters and brooch were there."

"Where are they now?"

"Here at my shop. I brought them with me, figuring you'd want to come by to see them. But I've just closed for the day, so—"

"I'll be there in ten minutes!" He hung up the phone before she could object.

Insufferable was too polite a word to describe Ross, Arianne decided as she slammed her wall phone onto its hook. She'd wanted him to come during her regular work hours, when customers might also be in the shop, so she wouldn't have to be alone with him. Now she had no choice *but* to be alone with him—unless she left now, before he arrived. But that would defeat her purpose. She wanted to get this meeting about the brooch over with. In a huff, she sat down behind the counter and waited, anxiety twisting her stomach into a knot.

Ross rushed up to the glass door of Arianne's shop and tried to pull it open, but it was locked. He looked in and saw her behind the counter. After he knocked hard on the glass, she looked up and came over to let him in. She said nothing as she unlocked and swung open the door for him, her eyes fixed on the marble tiled floor.

She looked beautiful, of course. She wore a long, open-necked dress that reminded him of movies from the 1930s. The dress was made of a thin, crinkled material, printed with pastel flowers, and clung to her curves. Instantly, his mind jumped to the last time he saw her, the night he'd held her in his arms and taken all she offered.

Don't think about that, Ross warned himself. It was foolish of him to go on wanting her when he suspected she may have manipulated him into an affair. He had to keep up his defenses.

"Where is it?" he demanded, taking an authoritative manner.

She closed the door behind him and walked across the small shop to the back room behind the counter. He followed, breathing in the fragrant air laden with the perfumes she'd been spraying on people all day. No, he told himself, he wasn't going to let these scents of paradise weaken his resolve. Nothing could induce him to lower his guard with her a second time.

In the small storage room, its corners stacked with boxes of perfume, she walked up to a small, rectangular worktable, on which she'd left her leather shoulder bag. She opened the shoulder bag and took out a quart-size paper bag. After unfolding this, she drew out a small, padded mailing envelope and a handful of old letters in their original envelopes.

Ross peered over her shoulder at the envelopes and recognized Willow Monroe's name and Los Angeles address penned in Peter's hand. Arianne opened the padded mailer, lined with plastic bubbles for protection, and pulled out a shiny object. Placing it in the palm of her hand, she showed it to him.

He had a sense of disbelief as he saw for the first time the iridescent fires of the splendid opal that Peter's grandfather had brought back from a voyage to Australia. Carefully, he took it out of her hand to have a closer look. It was a stunning piece of jewelry by anyone's standards. The delicate goldsmithing and the large, colorfully hued opal were rare indeed. No wonder the Briarcliffs had been so covetous about keeping it in the family.

Ross looked at Arianne, who was studying him with great, sad eyes. Her gaze threw him. In an instant the brooch moved to second place in his mind. What was she thinking? he wondered. But he was too wary of her to ask.

She might be thinking that she'd told him she loved him and had given herself to him. Ross didn't want to deal with that again. Even if she was sincere about being in love with him, it didn't mean he had to do anything about it. He had no responsibility for her feelings. Although—there was one loose end regarding their impulsive, one-night affair that he felt he needed to get straight with her. He had to find a way to get around to the subject, which was delicate. He ought to be more conciliatory.

He held up the brooch in his hand. "I'm glad you were honest enough to tell me you discovered this. You probably would have preferred not to reveal the fact that your family had it all along, as I suspected. It must be humiliating for you. I appreciate your integrity."

She gave him a tight nod of her head, but he could see from her expression that his words hadn't pleased her. As he realized how bluntly he'd put things, he could understand her displeasure. Tact wasn't a Briarcliff trait; lack of it was. Growing uncomfortable, he set the brooch on the wood table for a moment. She hadn't said one word to him yet, and it was undermining his composure.

He began again. "Look, about . . . about what happened last week—"

"We don't need to talk about that," she said, her eyes fixed on the boxes in the corner rather than on him.

"You're right, it's best to . . . to forget it and go on. I told you it would be a mistake for us to get involved. I wish you hadn't decided to push the issue with me the way you did. Now we're both sorry."

Her eyes suddenly turned on him, huge and glaring. "*I* pushed the issue?"

"You asked me to go to bed with you, Arianne. You can't deny—"

"Only a few hours earlier, in Room 302, you were try-ing to coax *me* into making love. You took me in your arms, pulled me into the room and closed the door. In fact, ever since the very first minute I met you, you've been chasing me and making advances, even after I objected. Just because, when we finally did it, *I* happened to be the one to suggest it, doesn't make it all my fault!" She low-ered her eyes with disdain and shook her head. "The nerve of you, to blame it all on me! I don't know how I ever could have been the least bit attracted to such an insolent man."

Ross believed he knew the answer. "My money, wasn't that it?"

She glared at him again. "Money! I wouldn't want one penny of your tainted Briarcliff money, gotten from a century of your family's ruthless business dealings. I've always been happy enough with my station in life. Maybe other women have pursued you for your wealth, but don't ever, *ever* rationalize your treatment of me by making me out to be one of them. Poor Willow lost her life after she got involved with your treacherous family. I should thank God that you walked out on me when you did. Unlike Willow, at least I can survive!"

Her words stung. Ross felt like giving up trying to talk to her and walking out, but he was determined to con-tinue this gut-wrenching conversation. For his own peace of mind, he had to bring up a point he anticipated would upset her even more.

"All right, what happened was my fault, too," he ac-quiesced. "But Arianne, we didn't use any protection. Has it occurred to you that—"

"That I could be pregnant?" She smiled with angry irony. "Don't worry Ross, I won't come after you, saying I'm carrying your baby."

Somehow he believed her. She'd deal with it on her own, rather than ever tell him; she seemed to hate him so now. He studied her face for a long moment. She looked tired, strained. Perhaps thinner, too. She'd lost weight and wasn't taking care of herself, he feared. He needed to make his position clear to her.

"I wouldn't want you to get an—" he began, then thought of a more tactful way to say it. "I'd want you to have the baby, Arianne. I'd see to it that you were taken care of. We'd . . . I'd work something out with you about that . . . I mean so the child would have a home and . . ." Ross found himself knotted up in his own thoughts, and he knew his words were coming out garbled. In fact, he wasn't really sure what he was saying.

Arianne looked askance, then closed her eyes as if drumming up patience. "Ross, you don't need to think about all that. My period started," she explained, as if he was a bumbling, ignorant male. "That means I'm not pregnant, and you're free and clear. Okay?"

"Oh." He swallowed. "Well, then. That's . . . fine." But somehow it didn't feel so fine to him. He grew aware of an unexpected sense of disappointment. When he recognized what that might mean, he immediately repudiated the thought.

Ross didn't want to be a father or a husband. He'd decided that long ago, and he knew it was a sensible decision. No use producing any more Briarcliff family casualties like himself. This spiteful entanglement with Arianne was new proof of his inability to have a normal, caring relationship with a woman, even a woman who wasn't after his money and said she loved him. He'd wound up hurting Arianne, just as he'd warned her he would when he told her not to love him. Why on earth, he asked himself, would he cherish the notion that she might have had his child? Deal with reality, he told himself. Arianne certainly was.

He glanced at her and realized she'd been studying him while he was distracted in his ruminations. Her brown eyes, sensitive and puzzled, looked into his, as if trying to pull his thoughts out of his mind.

Ross instantly drew down an imaginary curtain on his inner self by looking away from her and stiffening his back. "Did you read Peter's letters?" he asked in a curt, all-business tone, such as he used in court.

"Yes."

"They say anything new?" he asked, picking up the stack and shuffling through them.

"It looks as though you may have been right about Peter, too," she admitted with obvious reluctance. "The last letter, at least, seems to show that he was in...that he cared a lot for Willow. His feelings for her appear to have been genuine. I'll make copies of the letters and mail them to you, so you can take your time reading them and have them for your files."

As he held in his hands the very letters his great-grandfather had written, Ross said, "What do you mean, make copies? I'm taking these with me. Peter wrote them and they belong to my family."

Arianne's dark eyes flashed. "They were written to Willow. They belong to *my* family," she argued. "You wouldn't give me the letters you have, the ones Willow wrote to Peter. You claimed *those* belonged to you, too. In fact, I asked you to make copies of them, and you never have. Just because you're a Briarcliff doesn't mean you can go around confiscating anything that has to do with your family history. There must be some things that legally belong to the Monroes."

Ross knew she had a point, but he wanted to have the letters in his possession. "I'll take them and make copies for you," he told her, stuffing the letters into his jacket pocket. "I'll make the copies of Willow's letters, too. We can sort out later which letters should belong to whom. But I need to take these now. I'm writing that article and they may be useful."

Arianne rolled her eyes. "Of course. Your article. Obviously that's more important than the feelings of the Monroe family. As usual, the Briarcliffs are trampling all over us!"

Ross clenched his jaw. "I'm sorry. I promise I'll make you the copies tomorrow as soon as I get to the office. And then I'll look into the legalities of who owns old letters like this."

"I think I'd like my own lawyer to look into those legalities," she informed him.

Ross nodded. "You're free to do that."

"Thank you! And meanwhile, you feel free to steal these letters out from under my nose."

Something inside Ross snapped. "All right! I'm a ruthless Briarcliff, just as you say. High-handed and superior and anything else you want to call me. It's the way I am, so deal with it!" A heavy new scent seemed to fill the air, but Ross continued in his tirade, paying no attention to the floral fragrance. "I'm taking the brooch with me, too. I know you Monroes think Peter gave it to Willow as a gift, but it belongs to our family."

Arianne began to tremble, rage in her eyes. "I brought the brooch and the letters here only to *show* you. They've been buried on Monroe property for nearly a century, and it's possible they may legally belong to us. I hadn't decided what to do with them yet. I haven't given them to you, and you don't have the right to just take them!"

She reached out and snatched up the brooch from the table. Clasping it to her chest with both hands, her eyes dared him to try to take it from her.

"Arianne, give that to me," he said, stepping toward her. The air seemed supercharged, and the heavy scent began to make him feel slightly ill.

"No!" she exclaimed.

"Don't make me take it from you by force," he warned.

She didn't respond. Her eyes were frantically searching the small storage room. Her breathing grew shallow. "She's here."

Ross paused. He heard a woman weeping now, but it wasn't Arianne. Arianne was standing in front of him, mute and wide-eyed. Ross refused to believe the disturbances were caused by a ghost. The scent could be from some spilled perfume bottle in one of the boxes. The weeping—well, there must be some explanation.

"She's upset," Arianne whispered. Her eyes searched the room again. "With me?" she asked, as if speaking to the ghost.

Ross felt a harrowing shudder go through his body. Was Arianne losing her mind? "You can't see her, can you?" he asked.

Arianne shook her head. "It's just the feeling in the air. She's close to me. She's agitated now, and I don't know why. The last time she came to me, she comforted me."

Ross took hold of her shoulders. "Arianne, you're imagining things," he said, trying to use a soothing tone, but failing. Hearing her talk this way unsettled him to the core.

"No, I'm not!"

"Shh. Don't be upset." With shock, he noticed a thin line of blood running down her finger as she clasped the brooch tightly. Gently, he pried open her grip. The sharp pin from the brooch's clasp at the back had stuck her finger. He set the brooch on the small table. Then he pulled out his handkerchief and pressed it to her bleeding hand. Arianne looked at her finger in surprise, as if she hadn't realized she'd injured herself. "You'll be all right," he told her.

The weeping had stopped now. The room was silent, the atmosphere still thick with the floral scent. There was a sense of suspension, a static electricity waiting to spark. The ceiling lights flicked off and then on again. Arianne gasped in fright.

"I think we should get out of here," he told her.

Taking her hand, he paused to pick up the brooch before he led her out. Arianne tore her hand out of his grasp and reached for the brooch herself.

"You can't take it!" she told him, tears in her eyes. "I have to keep it for Willow."

But Ross stopped her, taking hold of her wrist just as her fingers brushed the opal. With his superior strength, he folded her arm to her waist. "I don't think it's good for you to have it right now," he told her with feeling. "It upsets you. Look, we'll take out a lockbox in both our names and keep it there until we decide who should have it."

"No!" she objected, looking frantic. "It belonged to Willow! It symbolized Peter's love for her. Peter said so in his letter. It was important to her, and I want to keep it for her."

Ross was growing desperately worried about her state of mind. "Arianne, it doesn't make sense to keep something for an imagined ghost. You're not thinking straight right now." He tried to put his arm around her, to steady her quaking body.

"No!" she objected and pushed him away.

All at once, the brooch, lying face up on the table, began to vibrate, its iridescent lights flickering, as if it was coming alive. Arianne screamed and lifted her hand to her chest in fright. Ross didn't know what to make of it.

Suddenly, the brooch levitated off the table and flew in a two-foot-high arc straight for Ross. It hit him smartly in the chest, just to the left of his tie. The brooch fell and landed upright on the floor next to his shoe. The small table began to jiggle, though neither Ross or Arianne was touching it. All at once it turned over in a noisy jolt, dumping Arianne's handbag to the floor.

Arianne screamed once more in horror. "She's angry with you, Ross. She means to harm you!"

Ross began to believe in ghosts. Throwing his arm around Arianne's waist, he pulled her along as he raced out of the room, through the shop and out into the hall. There, feeling relatively safe, they spent a few moments recovering, leaning against the shop's glass window. A male passerby looked at them oddly and continued on his way down the hall.

Shaken, feeling a few shades paler, Ross asked, "Are you all right?"

"Willow must be angry with you for trying to take the brooch and the letters," Arianne said, clutching the lapel of his suit jacket. "She doesn't want you to have her things."

Ross nodded in agreement. "I'm not about to argue with an ill-tempered spook. Keep the brooch." He felt for the letters from Peter, still in his jacket pocket. "But I'll take the letters for now. I'll get them back to you when I've made copies. Do you think *she* will be happy with that?"

Even as he said the words, the sound of weeping surrounded them in the hallway. The air turned frigid. The hall lights flickered. Ross lost whatever composure he had left.

"Damn you, Willow!" he exclaimed. "I'm not afraid of you! When I write about you, everyone will know you for what you were—a pathetic, grasping female!"

"Ross!" Arianne looked horrified at his words.

He took Arianne firmly by the elbow. "Come on, let's get out of here."

She broke out of his grip as the poignant sound of weeping intensified. "*You* get out of here!" she yelled at him. Tears streaming from her face, she looked about the empty hallway, as if trying to determine what direction the weeping came from. It came from everywhere. "Don't worry, Willow," she said in a soothing manner choked with her tears. "I'll protect your brooch and your name."

"Arianne—" Ross said, trying to reach for her though she kept avoiding his grasp on her arm.

"Go away!" she told him. Her voice throbbed with anger and hurt. "Haven't you Briarcliffs tortured us enough? Can't you just leave us alone?"

Ross felt as if he'd gotten a spear in his chest where the brooch had hit him. He wanted to calm Arianne, but he knew now it was *his* presence, even more than Willow's, that kept her near hysteria. The only thing he could do for her now was to leave, as she'd asked.

He turned and walked out, too distraught to say anything more to her. He found himself heading down the hall in the direction of the entrance to the beach. When he reached the sand, cooling in the setting sun, he sat down on a beach chair and looked numbly at the sea. Minutes later he realized his face felt wet in the breeze. He wiped his fingers across his cheek and discovered that he, too, was weeping.

Willow, it seemed, had won.

CHAPTER NINE

After Ross left, Arianne remained in the hallway, crying into her hands. The sounds of weeping gradually faded. A young couple passed by and looked at her, concern on their faces because she was in tears. Arianne decided she'd better go into her shop and compose herself.

She walked to the back room and picked up her handbag and the Briarcliff brooch off the floor and put them on a nearby shelf. Then she uprighted the turned-over table. As she did these things, the smell of violets surrounded her, and she knew that Willow was still present. An idea occurred to her.

Sniffing, wiping her wet cheeks, she walked over to the wall phone and dialed Claudia's number. Perhaps the psychic could advise her. When Claudia answered, Arianne explained all that had just happened.

"I still sense her presence," Arianne said, gazing about her and seeing nothing, yet feeling another personality in the room. "Could you possibly come over? I don't know why she's still here. I kept the brooch for her. I don't know what more she wants from me."

"I have a dinner date, but it's with an old friend," Claudia said, as if thinking aloud. "I can call him and ask to meet a half hour later. I'm sure he won't mind and that will give me time to run over to the hotel. I don't live far away."

"That would be great," Arianne told her with relief.

"Be there in five or ten minutes."

Arianne paced nervously as she waited, and she had the oddest feeling that Willow was following her, pacing, too, with a sense of expectation.

All at once Claudia appeared at the door. Arianne hurried to let her in. Claudia was an attractive blonde of about thirty-five, and she was dressed in a trim suit of apricot linen. She smiled and shook Arianne's hand.

"Oh, your hands are cold," Claudia said with concern. "You're frightened, aren't you?"

"Yes. I made Ross go away. I believe Willow means him harm. I don't think she'd hurt me, but I don't know what she wants. She's beginning to drive me crazy."

"I'll see what I can do. I feel a definite female presence here. And I smell the violet scent you described. You mentioned the brooch that levitated. Do you have it?"

"Sure," Arianne said and went into the back room to get it. She came out and handed it to Claudia. Claudia sat on one of the leather-padded stools in front of the counter. Arianne stood to one side and watched. The psychic held the brooch in her hands, her forearms resting on the wood counter, and closed her eyes. She seemed to meditate.

"Yes, I'm clearly getting her name, Willow." Claudia sat quietly, eyes still closed, speaking softly. "She's quite agitated. I can sense her distress. She feels something is all wrong. It's...about this brooch. She's...oh, I believe she's upset because you've misread her."

"I've—"

"Shh." Claudia was silent for a while, concentrating. Arianne's heart began to palpitate as she waited, and she forced herself to breathe more slowly. Then Claudia spoke again. "I'm getting the name Briarcliff." Claudia opened her eyes. "That's it. She wanted you to give Ross the brooch."

This didn't sound right to Arianne. "But she made it hit him in the chest. It was as if she threw it at him."

Claudia nodded. "Because she wanted him to have it."

"I hadn't thought of it *that* way," Arianne said in confusion. "But why does she want to give the brooch back to the Briarcliffs?"

Claudia meditated for a long moment, her eyebrows tensed in concentration. "I'm getting the name Peter. She wanted Peter to have it." Claudia looked at Arianne. "Peter was the man she loved, who gave her this brooch?"

"Yes."

"Then that must be why she's been so troubled. She'd always wanted Peter to have the brooch. It's why she's not at rest. And now she wants you to give it to Ross."

This didn't make sense to Arianne, because she knew that Willow and Peter were seen arguing on the beach the night she died. They were arguing because she wouldn't give him the brooch.

"Wait," Claudia said, gripping the brooch tightly. She was silent for a long moment. "I'm getting the words *letter* and *file*. A . . . a letter is in a file." Claudia looked up. "Does that mean anything to you?"

Arianne shook her head. "No, I don't think so. We've found the letters Peter wrote to her. And the Briarcliffs have always had the letters she wrote to Peter. I don't know of any other—"

"Maybe it's still hidden. She seems to want it to be found."

"Hidden in a file?" Arianne asked. "What file?"

Claudia concentrated again. "Here at the Aragon. It's the reason she won't leave the hotel. She guards the letter." Claudia nodded, as if satisfied she understood her reading of Willow.

"The Willow File?" Arianne whispered, remembering the old file drawer Alex had once shown her. She remembered it contained very little, and she couldn't recall any letter among its contents.

"I don't know," Claudia said, puzzled. "But I sense she's calmer now. You see," she said, turning to Arianne, "spirits get upset when they can't communicate what they want us to know. I'm clairvoyant, which makes things easier."

"Can you see her?"

Claudia smiled. "I caught a glimpse of her there, near you. She's young, dark-haired, quite beautiful. Old-fashioned white dress with a high collar. A very feminine spirit. She's not dangerous, as I told you some are. She's just an unhappy ghost and not an evil entity. I don't think she means to harm anyone." Claudia looked at her watch. "Well, I ought to be going. My dinner date is waiting. Are you all right with this? Any questions?"

Arianne didn't want to keep her, since she'd been so kind to come on a moment's notice. But she couldn't help but ask, "Do you know why she died? What happened that night?"

Claudia grasped the brooch again. "I'll give it a try." She closed her eyes. After a long moment, she said, "I see darkness. The ocean. Great sorrow and hopelessness. The waves overtake her. And...that's all." Claudia opened her eyes and shook her head.

Arianne felt disappointed, but she was glad to have learned as much as she did. "Thanks for coming, Claudia," Arianne said with sincerity, taking the woman's hand. "I was so confused by what was happening."

"Your confusion is normal," Claudia said, rising to her feet. "That's why I was given this gift, I believe. To help those living who have to deal with ghosts, and to help the spirits find peace. If you want, I can come back sometime and see if I can help Willow go toward the light and move on to the next realm. She's stayed here because some matters important to her have been unresolved since her death. But if we can assure her that those things have been taken care of and tell her that she's free to go, then she may at last find her peace."

"That would be wonderful," Arianne said. "I'll look into that old file again and see if I can find a letter. If I need to, I'll call you again. Do I owe you anything for coming?" Arianne remembered Ross's comment that psychics were paid for their services.

"Oh, not this time. It's been an honor to be called in for such a famous ghost," Claudia said with a smile. "Well, I have to go now. Keep me posted."

"I will," Arianne said and walked with her to the door, where they said goodbye.

Feeling calmer, but still perplexed, Arianne went to the counter and picked up the brooch. She studied the lights within the opal, the varying shades of orange and green radiating from its milky depths. So much trouble had arisen over the magnificent stone, at the beginning of the century and now again toward the century's end. She wondered why Willow wanted the Briarcliffs to have it. This went against everything the Monroe family had believed about her wishes throughout the century. Arianne couldn't help but question if the psychic might have been mistaken. The brooch had definitely levitated toward Ross. Did it fly through the air to go to him, or to strike at him?

Arianne pondered the matter, still reluctant to give the opal to Ross after she'd fought to keep it on Willow's behalf. Despite what the psychic had said, Arianne began to feel unsure of what she should do. And she wanted to be sure, because she was certain that once it was in Ross's hands, she'd never see it again.

As she turned the brooch, watching the inner lights of the gemstone glimmer and flash, all at once she felt it vibrate. Frightened, she wanted to let go of it, but somehow she couldn't. Her fingers clutched the brooch, despite her wish to drop it. The scent of violets surrounded her, and she could feel Willow's presence in a more compelling way than she'd ever felt it before. She had a vision of the ocean and felt a great, sudden sorrow. Tears started in her eyes because of the deep remorse she felt, and she found herself walking out of the shop, clutching the brooch.

Next she was hurrying down the hall toward the entrance to the beach. She burst through the doors into the darkness outside. The sky was full of stars. The air was cool. Ahead lay the sandy beach and the serene waves of the ocean. And then she felt two invisible hands on her shoulders, pushing her forward. She knew it was Willow. The ghost was hurrying her onward, making her run as fast as she could toward the sand and the sea.

Ross was still sitting on the beach, thinking through all that had happened. The sun had set and he remained in the darkness, worrying about the ghost, which had turned out to be real, and its insidious influence over Arianne. He wondered if Arianne was still in the hotel, if he should try to find her and see that she was all right.

But Arianne clearly hated him. So did Willow, who seemed to protect her. He wondered if he could ever make things right between him and Arianne. Why was he always so brusque around her? Why did he doubt her? Why did he always lose his composure and do and say the wrong thing? Perhaps Willow had some devilish influence on him, as well. Not that a Briarcliff needed an angry spirit to make him act like a boor and say hurtful things. Briar-cliffs just had a knack for being nasty. And Ross realized he was becoming one of the prizewinners in his family for having this ability.

Ross leaned forward in his chair, feeling restless for some reason. He'd been sitting here depressed and dejected for half an hour or more. But suddenly he felt uneasy. Something was wrong. Arianne—

He looked to his left and was stunned to see her running across the sand headlong toward the ocean—just as she did in his recurrent dream. She was crying and there was a wild aspect to her eyes. A rush of adrenaline shot through him. Ross leaped to his feet and took off after her, fearing, as sometimes happened in his dreams, that he wouldn't overtake her in time. He ran as fast as he could, kicking up sand behind him.

He reached her just as she stepped into the farthest stretch of the waves on the sand. Catching her to him, his arms around her waist, he pulled her backward onto dry sand. She twisted and fought him for a moment, her dress slipping off her shoulder, and then she went limp. He was a bit off balance, and all he could do was help her fall slowly to the sand, so she wouldn't hurt herself. Kneeling, he cradled her head and shoulders in his arms.

"Arianne!"

She seemed in a daze as her eyes fluttered open. When she saw him, however, she appeared to recognize him immediately. She sat up, but Ross continued to hold on to her, fearing she'd try to get up and run for the sea again.

"Are you all right?"

"Yes," she said, brushing her hair out of her face. It was then that Ross noticed she was carrying the Briarcliff brooch in her hand. She looked at it and then at him. "That's why she made me run to the beach," Arianne said, as if just now realizing. "Because you're here." She held out the brooch. "She wants you to have this."

He looked at the opal, perplexed and not anxious to take it. "Willow? She made you run here?"

"I had a vision of the ocean," Arianne said, wide-eyed, her body seeming to vibrate with inner intensity, "and then I felt her hands on my shoulders, pushing me in this direction. I felt her sorrow."

"Because she died near here?"

"Because she wanted me to give you the brooch, and she was distressed because I hadn't." She looked at Ross. "Earlier, in the shop, she wasn't angry with you. When she levitated the brooch at you, it was because she wanted you to have it. Claudia, the psychic, told me. After you left, I called her, and she came over. But then after Claudia left, I began to have doubts about what she'd said. That's when Willow compelled me to come here, to give you this. Take it, Ross. Willow wants you to have it."

"You're sure?"

"Yes, now I'm sure. Willow's made it clear. Please take it."

"Will she leave us alone then?"

Arianne shook her head, her eyes beleagered. "I don't know. All I know is that she wants me to give it to you."

With reluctance, Ross took the brooch, not really wanting it anymore. "You scared the wits out of me, rushing toward the waves like that. It was like that recurring nightmare I had, where I saw you running to the sea, as if you..."

"No, I don't think I was going to drown myself. Willow wouldn't have wanted that. In her way, she's just trying to make everything right. We don't always understand her ways, though. The psychic tried to explain that to me."

Ross slipped the brooch into his jacket pocket. He hesitated, then reached to tenderly stroke her hair. "I'm sorry about the things I said. I hate it when you're angry with me." He took her hand and brought it to his lips.

Arianne gently pulled her hand away as his mouth brushed her knuckles. "Ross—"

"Let me make up with you," he urged in a low, soft voice. "Maybe there's hope for us after all. I had that premonition and now it's come true—both parts of my dream." With his arms around her, he pulled her closer. "Only in reverse order. In the dream, I stopped you from running to the sea, and then we...made love...." He ran his fingers over her delicate collarbone beneath her long hair. He felt a warm frisson tremble through her in response to his touch.

But she pushed herself out of his embrace. "No, Ross," she whispered, bowing her head as she pulled her dress into place. "Don't talk about that."

"There's still a strong pull between us, Arianne. I can feel it. We can't deny it. Let's...try to be friends, at least."

"Friends?" She attempted to laugh, but it came out more like a painful sob. "I don't think you and I could ever be friends."

He exhaled slowly and a twinge of pain began to curl in his abdomen. "You're right," he had to agree, though he wished it weren't so. "Whenever we're together, desire always rears its formidable head. And then we get angry, because we don't know what to do, because old family animosities get in our way. History has spoiled what we might have had together."

She twisted her fingers into her long hair as she seemed to fight back tears. Suddenly she sat up straight. "I have to go."

Ross hated to part with her again. She was like some rare butterfly he couldn't hold on to, or might even crush in his rush to capture her—or in his fear of being captured by her. God, he was a mixed-up piece of work, wasn't he?

"I wish you'd stay," he said as she got to her feet. Reluctantly, he stood up, too.

Her expression looked cool and resigned. "I've given you the brooch. Everything's finished now between us. Goodbye, Ross."

There was a finality in her tone that set him on edge. Who was she to decide when they were through with one another? He couldn't help it—with a surge of possessive energy, he reached out and pulled her into his arms. When he tried to kiss her, she turned her head to one side to avoid his mouth. He pressed his forehead into her hair. "How dare you say goodbye?" he told her in an intense whisper. "We're *not* finished. Not as long as I'm breathing!"

She wrenched herself away from him, her eyes wide with fright, as if he'd threatened her. He hadn't meant to. He'd just wanted her to understand his passion. She stared at him for a stormy moment, then hurried away, her long dress blowing in the wind as she ran toward the hotel.

"Arianne!"

She didn't turn around. He knew better than to try to run after her. Soon she'd disappeared inside the hotel.

Ross realized he'd probably blown his last chance with her. Maybe she was right to run from him. He acted like a maniac half the time nowadays. In the past, he'd often been overbearing and brusque, but he'd always been civilized. She brought out something in him he hadn't known he'd had until he met her—passion, the word that had come to him just a second ago. From where inside him did such a passion erupt? This feeling he had was more profound than physical attraction, more elevated than earthy lust. He'd never felt this way before, and he didn't know what to do with himself, how to handle it. Somehow he was obsessed with the notion that he was meant to be with her.

Ross had never believed in fate before. Why believe now that he and she were destined for each other? He'd already made love with her, and he'd destroyed the beautiful moments they'd created together with his suspicions and his inbred temper. How could he ever hope to win her back after that? Or even after the way he'd frightened her just now? He didn't deserve to. He didn't deserve *her*.

He looked bleakly toward the sea. And then, for a moment, he heard the echoing sound of weeping from somewhere... and a swift scent of violets.

CHAPTER TEN

Arianne was assisting a customer while waiting for Doris to replace her for lunch when Ross walked in. His unexpected appearance surprised her and she immediately became edgy, but she tried not to let it show. She rang up the sale and said goodbye to the cheerful woman, who walked out with a half-dozen bottles of perfumes she'd bought as gifts for friends. When the lady was out the door, Arianne turned to Ross. He carried a large brown envelope in his hands and wore a tentative expression on his face.

"I brought the copies of the letters that I promised you—Willow's letters to Peter and hers to him." He held out the envelope over the counter for her to take. "I'll look into who should own the originals."

"Thank you," Arianne said, lifting the envelope out of his hands. She avoided his eyes. It was hard to look at him. He appeared so handsome and urbane in his expensive, three-piece suit, and yet his relentless, intrepid nature frightened her. He kept on wanting her, and somehow, when she was with him, she felt the same wild desire for him. They both knew their relationship was hopeless. Still, he wouldn't leave her alone. Not as long as he was breathing, he'd said. Those words had sent a chill down her spine last night, and they did now, too, as she was reminded of them.

"I want to apologize for last night," he said. "You ran off looking frightened. I didn't mean to—"

"Never mind," she said quickly, afraid to even discuss it with him. "It's okay."

"No, it's not okay."

He had an unusual humility today. She wondered why. "Let's not talk about it," she said.

"How can we get past these things if we don't talk?" he asked. When she had no reply, he bowed his head, then tried a new tack. "I never properly thanked you for the brooch. On behalf of my family, I *do* thank you."

Arianne made an effort to smile. "You're welcome."

His somber face brightened at her reaction. "Why don't we have lunch together?"

She was glad she had a ready excuse to decline. "I can't, Ross. Later, I'll grab a sandwich and eat here in the shop. I need to go upstairs and look at the Willow File."

"Why?" Ross appeared surprised now. "What are you looking for?"

"A missing letter. I forgot to mention it, but last night when the psychic was here, she got the words *letter* and *file* from Willow, as if a letter was hidden in some file. Maybe she meant the Willow File. I thought I'd look at it again."

Ross nodded, his forehead puckered in thought. "I saw that file. It contained an old perfume bottle, newspaper clippings and her photo. Alex said everything else was on display. I never saw any letter."

"Neither did I, though it was some time ago when Alex showed me the file. Maybe the letter is there somewhere and we both missed it. Weren't there some old menus, too? It could be mixed in with those. Or stuck underneath that cardboard box."

"It's possible. Are you going right now? I'll go with you."

Arianne paused, wishing she hadn't told him all this. "But Ross, this information came from Willow by way of a psychic. Why would you want to bother? You don't believe in ghosts or psychics."

"After last night, I'm a believer. And you won't get rid of me that easily," he said. "If there's any new information about Willow, I want to see it."

"For your article," she surmised in a dry manner. "I know that has first priority for you right now."

"Don't make assumptions about my priorities," he told her in a testy voice. In a softer tone, his eyes unsettlingly serious, he added, "Anything that has to do with Willow and Peter seems to have an effect on you and me. If there's a new development, then I want to be there with you when you search for it."

Arianne did not argue, sensing the truth of his statement. Anything having to do with their ancestors did affect them in some peculiar, time-transcending way.

When Doris arrived to take over for the lunch hour a few minutes later, Arianne and Ross left to go to the file room upstairs. Ross began heading down the hall that led to the lobby, but Arianne directed him to a nearby fire escape stairwell.

"This is faster," she said, "and more direct."

As they climbed up one flight on the metal steps of the empty stairwell, Arianne grew aware of how alone they were. She wished she'd taken the longer but more public route Ross had been about to take. The hotel's main hallways were usually bustling with people at midday. She felt isolated here, and she also could feel Ross breathing down her back, almost literally, as he climbed the stairs close behind her.

When she arrived at the door on the next landing, he reached around her to open it, and they both grabbed for the doorknob at once. When their hands met, he hesitated only a moment, then slipped his arms around her and drew her against him, her back to his chest.

"Ross—"

"Shh. Let me hold you. I wanted to last night, but you ran off. Don't run now."

She felt his lips on the side of her neck through her long hair. He pushed away her hair and kissed her ear, her jaw and her neck. Arianne's breathing quickened. His hand crept up to her breast. His fingers pressed into her soft flesh through her blouse, fondling her with sweet gentleness. She closed her eyes at the pleasure that gave her such pain. She tried to tug away his hand, but she went weak when he unbuttoned her blouse, then slipped his fingers beneath the material.

"No, Ross," she breathed.

"It's our destiny to be lovers," he murmured insistently. "Accept it. Don't fight it."

"No!" She extricated herself from his arms and stood with her back to the door, facing him. "I've learned a good lesson," she told him, regaining her composure. "I'll never lay down with a man again unless he can tell me, with all his heart, that he loves me. I said those words to you, Ross. And you told me then that I shouldn't love you because you couldn't love me in return."

"I didn't say I *couldn't*," he told her with emphasis. "I said I didn't *know how*."

She bowed her head with sadness. "What's the difference?"

"There's a lot of difference—"

Arianne looked up again, not wanting to hear any more of his convoluted explanations. "It doesn't matter a hill of beans, Ross, because I'm not in love with you anymore." She told him this forthrightly and insisted to herself that she meant every word. "So there's no use stroking my hair, kissing me or fondling me, because I have no intention of ever sleeping with you again.'' She buttoned her blouse with swift, trembling fingers. ''If that's all you want, I'm sure a man of your wealth can easily find some other female to accommodate you.''

''It's not all I want!''

''No? Then what do you want?''

He hesitated and his angry gray eyes seemed to cloud over with confusion. ''Why is it you can't just talk to me? Why do we always have to wind up shouting at each other?''

''When do you ever just talk? Whenever we're alone, your hands are on me in two seconds and talking seems to be the farthest thing from your mind.''

''All right, all right,'' he said, putting up his hands. ''I just...I can't help wanting you. I never mean you any disrespect. If all I wanted was a female body, then you're right, there are plenty of women....'' He paused and seemed to regroup his thoughts. ''Look, I know you were a virgin. Giving yourself to me was special and unique. That's the way I'll always remember our night together.''

''Lovely words,'' she jeered. ''But then you walked out.''

''I got suspicious.'' He lifted his shoulders. ''It's my nature. Wealthy people have to be, or else we'd be taken advantage of every day of the week. But, as I've told you, if you'd gotten pregnant, I...I probably would have married you.''

Married her, she thought. No, he hadn't said that before. He'd only said he'd see that she was taken care of. ''But you don't want to get married,'' she reminded him.

''I know!'' he said, gesturing for emphasis. ''That's what I'm saying. You're special to me.''

Arianne couldn't help but be touched, in a roundabout sort of way. "Well, it's a good thing you didn't have to marry me, then," she said. "Can you imagine how long a marriage between us would have lasted? Maybe two days. And then you'd be walking out."

He seemed irritated. "Why say that?"

"For reasons you've stated yourself. You're not the marrying kind. You don't know how to love a woman. And you come from a family that has a long history of miserable marriages." She studied him, thinking she was discovering a new insight. "Are you imagining that because I'm special to you, you and I might somehow have a *real* relationship?"

She paused and he stared at her, his gray eyes wide.

"No way!" she told him.

Instantly, he lowered his eyes. She could sense his whole demeanor change. His back straightened and his eyes were like gray steel when he looked up. "You're right," he said, his tone aloof and terse. "None of us Briarcliffs knows how to have a real relationship. We tend to mistake sex for passion and passion for devotion." His manner was all business now. That rare hint of vulnerability had disappeared. And so had any remaining glimmer of desire. "Thanks for reminding me of my warped value system. I'm sorry for any embarrassment I've caused you. I'll make it a point never to physically touch you again. You can feel safe around me." He straightened his tie. "Shall we go on to the file room?"

Arianne suddenly felt as if she'd overstated her case. "Look, I'm sorry if I've hurt your feelings," she said with hesitance.

"Feelings?" He laughed, but there was no mirth in his eyes. "Briarcliffs don't have feelings. We just...are. Like plants. Like Venus's-flytraps. We get someone in our grasp and destroy them, usually. You're lucky. You've escaped. That's...why you're so special. You're smarter than the rest.''

''Ross, I didn't mean to—''

''No need to discuss this anymore. I think we've finally come to the end of the road.'' His tone was ironic and philosophical now. ''Our interlude, our little tale of woe, is finally finished. Our paths crossed—roughly. But that was inevitable. The Briarcliff path is always rough. And now we'll go our separate ways. We've probably learned something from each other, though. So, let's shake hands and have an end to it.'' He started to extend his hand, but then withdrew it. ''No, let's not. A handshake is a sign of friendship, and we've already established that we can't be friends. So we'll be...acquaintances. How's that?''

With reluctance, Arianne nodded. She felt bewildered, not knowing what else to say at this point. Yet every sense and instinct told her this conversation with him was ending in the wrong way.

A whiff of violets met her nostrils and she looked up. Ross paused and seemed alert, as if he'd smelled it, too.

Willow. They both said the name at the same time in the same hushed tone of voice.

''Why is she here?'' Arianne asked.

''Maybe she's waiting for us to check out her file,'' Ross said, looking around the empty hall. The air was turning frigid. ''Let's go.''

They opened the door and walked down the hallway to Alex Howatch's office. Alex had the key to the file room. When they walked in they found Alex talking to his elderly secretary in his outer office. He greeted them with his usual cordiality.

''Arianne,'' he said, taking her hand. ''And Ross,'' he added with some surprise as he shook Ross's hand. ''How nice to see you.'' He gave Arianne a secret glance, as if to say, *Are you all right? Why are you with him?*

Arianne smiled and tried to look calm, though she wasn't. She was still upset, both by her conversation with Ross and then by Willow's presence. ''Alex, we'd like the key to the file room. We want to look at the Willow File, if you don't mind.''

''Of course not,'' Alex said easily. He turned to his secretary. ''Would you find them the key?'' While she opened a desk drawer, Alex turned to Ross. ''I haven't seen you for several days. I thought you were finished with your investigation.''

''Arianne came up with a new clue,'' Ross said, his tone cool and a little sardonic. Arianne could tell Ross didn't like Alex much.

''What's that?'' Alex asked as his secretary handed him the key.

''There were disturbances in my shop yesterday,'' Arianne told him.

''Willow?''

''Yes,'' she said, abbreviating the story. ''So I called in a psychic—remember my mentioning once that I met a clairvoyant at a party?''

''Yes, yes,'' Alex said with interest, leaning on his walking stick.

''Well, she came in and held the brooch, and—''

''Brooch?''

She'd forgotten he didn't know about that yet. ''I found the Briarcliff brooch hidden in a closet at my grandmother's house last weekend.''

Alex's mouth dropped open. ''You don't say!'' He turned to Ross. ''You must be pleased. Has Arianne shown it to you?''

''She gave it to me.''

"Gave it—" Alex covered his abrupt reaction with a smile. "You must be thrilled to have it back."

"Anyway," Arianne continued, sensing the undercurrents between the two men, "before I'd given the brooch to Ross, I had the psychic hold it. We both felt Willow's presence in my shop. Willow conveyed the words *letter* and *file* to her, and the psychic felt there was some letter hidden somewhere that Willow wants us to find."

Alex squared his thin shoulders and his characteristic refined manner grew even more careful. "I see. And you trust this person, this psychic?"

"Yes, I have reason to."

Alex turned to Ross. "What do you think of all this?"

"I want to see the Willow File," Ross said in a clipped manner, ignoring the question.

"Very well," Alex said, handing the key to Ross. "Go ahead. I'll follow you, if you don't mind."

"What if I do?" Ross said.

"I'm afraid I must accompany anyone who goes into the hotel's private file room," Alex replied, lightly stomping his stick on the carpeted floor in a proprietory manner.

"Of course he should come with us, Ross." Arianne was distressed at his attitude toward the white-haired manager she'd known all her life and enjoyed as a friend. Ross, it seemed, was quickly falling back into his arrogant demeanor. She was glad she'd said those things to him a little while ago. Every once in a while he seemed to show a softer, kinder side, but she knew better now. Ross was as hard and as tough as a coconut shell, which could fall from a tall palm tree to the hard ground intact—and knock someone off their feet on the way.

Ross turned and walked out of the office with the key Alex had given him, leaving them to follow. When they all had entered the file room, they gathered around the old wood cabinet with the drawer marked The Willow File.

"I'm afraid one of you will have to open it," Alex said, resuming his usual politeness. "It's the bottom drawer, and I can't bend down that far. Hurts my knees."

Arianne began to step forward, but Ross shooed her away. "I'll do it," he said in a peremptory manner. He went down on one knee and pulled the file drawer open. Arianne peered into it over his shoulder. It looked the same as she remembered. Ross picked up the stack of historic dining room menus and handed them up to her. "Look through these," he told her.

She took them and laid them on the top of a cabinet behind her, then began turning them over, one by one. As she did this, she kept an eye on Ross, who was taking out the old box that contained Willow's artifacts. He turned it over in his hands, and Arianne could see for herself that nothing was stuck to the bottom of the box. Ross opened the box then and checked its meager contents—the perfume bottle and the old photo of Willow.

"Nothing," Ross said.

"There's nothing mixed in with these menus, either," Arianne told him, finishing going through them. "What about the news clippings?"

Ross handed them to her, muttering that he'd looked through them all before. Then he went down on both knees and peered closely into the drawer, at every corner and at the back and front and sides of it, feeling the wood, as if testing for some secret compartment.

"There's not a damn thing in here that we missed," Ross said.

"I could have told you that," Alex retorted a bit smugly as he leaned on his stick. "But I knew you must see for yourselves. I'm afraid that psychic was full of rubbish."

Arianne looked up from the newspaper clippings she was checking. She smelled violets again. All at once Alex's stick jumped out from under his hands, as if it had been kicked away. Alex lost his balance and stumbled forward. Arianne moved to steady him, taking his arm.

"Alex, are you okay? What happened?" she asked, astonished.

Alex caught his breath for a moment and steadied himself against the file cabinet. "I don't know! It was the oddest thing. The stick just popped out from under me."

Arianne picked up the stick, which had fallen to the floor. As she did, she glanced at Ross. From Ross's expression, she could tell that he was thinking the same thing as she. Willow had done it. She did not say this to Alex, afraid to alarm him any more than he was already.

"That letter must be somewhere, Ross," she said to him softly, knowing it was a sign from Willow.

"I know." He looked over the file cabinet with searching eyes. "Where? The file drawer above it?"

"No, no, it's got a set of old glass vases stored in it," Alex said, regaining his composure. "Well, look if you must," he said when Ross opened the drawer anyway. "I'm telling you, there is no hidden letter. If there was, wouldn't I know about it? I've been the hotel's manager and historian for over forty years."

Indeed, the drawer above, which Ross had opened, did contain nothing but a large, matching set of slim flower vases that must have been used on the dining room tables in years gone by. After peering into it thoroughly, Ross closed the drawer.

"Well, we can't go through the whole file room," Ross said, sounding frustrated.

"No, you certainly cannot!" Alex said. "I think it's time you leave."

"But we need to find it," Arianne argued, feeling increasingly nervous.

All at once, an angry energy seemed to surround them, and Willow's scent grew stronger.

"I smell violets," Alex said with surprise.

A sudden, jangling noise startled them. The bottom drawer, which was still pulled out, had begun to vibrate on its own. The box inside jiggled in response to the movement of the drawer. Ross stepped away and stood beside Arianne, slipping his arm around her as if to protect her. Arianne was barely aware of this as she stared at the dramatically vibrating file drawer. Now the whole cabinet shook slightly.

"It must be an earthquake," Alex exclaimed.

"Nothing else but the cabinet is shaking," Ross said.

"Maybe she's trying to show us." Arianne felt her heartbeat growing erratic with apprehension. She wished Claudia was here. The psychic would know what to do.

Suddenly, as if with one grand effort, the drawer slid forward and came completely off its runners inside the cabinet to rest on the floor in front of it. All motion stopped then. And there, lying inside the cabinet where the drawer had been, on the bottom of the wood casing, was a yellowed white envelope.

Ross quickly rushed to pick it up. He brought it to Arianne.

"There's something written on the envelope," he said, showing it to her.

"The note inside," she read, "was found behind the radiator in Room 302, during hotel remodeling in October, 1929."

Alex looked very shaken. His hands were trembling as they fumbled with his stick. "That's nothing. Just an old stray piece of paper that missed the trash, that's all."

Neither Ross nor Arianne paid him any attention. Arianne unsealed the envelope and took out the sheet of old hotel stationery folded up inside. She gasped. "It's Willow's handwriting." She began to breathe unsteadily as her heart skipped beats. "It's dated the night she died." The letter fluttered in her unsteady hand so much that she couldn't read the writing.

"Are you all right?" Ross asked her, touching her shoulder.

She handed the letter to him. "You read it to us. I'm too rattled."

He gave her shoulder a steadying squeeze, then took the letter from her. He read aloud.

To My Beloved Parents and My Dear Sister, Katy,
It is very late and you are all still at cards. I met with Peter, and we quarreled. Nothing has gone as I had hoped, all because of my precarious health. At last, I see that I cannot hope to ever have a normal life with a husband and children. The sadness is that I did not accept this truth sooner, before I ever met Peter and made him and myself so unhappy.

I realize that I have been selfish and inconsiderate, even to you, who have looked after my every wish with so much love. To always be an invalid and a burden to anyone who must live with me is my apparent fate. This is a fate I intend to avoid. I cannot go on without Peter, and I won't be his torment any longer.

His brooch, which I will set beside this letter for you, I leave in your care. I wish you to give the brooch back to him at your first opportunity. The opal rightfully belongs to his family, and I wish now that I had been sensible enough to give it to him myself this evening. I had lost my perspective, trying so hard to keep him and to convince him that I possessed the good health necessary to become his wife and bear his children. When you return this brooch, tell him that I loved him more than life itself.

Now, my dearest ones, I will free us all from the burden of my poor heart. I have always loved the sea, and it shall be my grave. Don't mourn for me long, or be sad on my account. You gave me much happiness, and I am only doing what is best for us all. I would have died soon anyway and given you great cause for shame. Katy knows.

Goodbye,
Willow

"So," Ross said pensively, "she did kill herself." He seemed sad and disturbed by the words he'd just read. But then he folded the letter and seemed to pull himself together. "Peter's name is finally cleared." He handed the letter to Arianne.

She opened it and skimmed it while Ross put the drawer back in its place. The last few sentences perplexed her. Why did Willow say she would die soon anyway and give her family cause for shame? And then the words, *Katy knows*. Did Arianne's grandmother know what Katy knew? Was that the secret told at Katy's deathbed?

Arianne sniffed the air and tested the atmosphere, wondering if Willow was still present. But she smelled no violets and the electric energy that had affected her moments ago had disappeared. Willow, perhaps, was satisfied now that her final letter had been found, proving that Peter hadn't murdered her and that she'd intended the brooch to go back to him. Arianne finally knew what Willow had wanted, what had kept the ghost haunting the

Aragon. All these years, Willow had been trying to clear the name of the man she'd loved.

Arianne bit her lip as moisture glazed her eyes. She felt so sad for Willow, and for herself, too. Nothing was working out between her and Ross, either. She told herself she knew better than to want a relationship with him. But reading Willow's last request to tell Peter she loved him, Arianne felt her own emotions for Ross stirring in response. Arianne blinked back her tears and tried to get a grip on herself. It seemed ironic that Willow had admitted that she'd lost her perspective when she was with Peter. Arianne had the same tendency, to lose her common sense when Ross came near her. Maybe she still loved Ross, but that didn't mean she should want him in her life. Not if she had any sense left.

Lost in her thoughts and still recovering from reading Willow's last words, Arianne realized something was brewing between Ross and Alex. The two men had begun exchanging sharp words.

"I have no idea," Alex was saying in a defensive manner.

"*No* idea how this letter got hidden underneath the drawer?" Ross grilled him. "You once bragged to me that this hotel's popularity is due to its colorful history. Solving the old mystery of what really happened to Willow wouldn't be good for the Aragon's business, would it?"

"I'm sure it doesn't matter one way or—"

"Is that why you kept this piece of evidence secret all these years?"

"I did no such—"

"Don't give me that. You *knew* it was here!"

"Ross," Arianne said, "don't yell at him."

Ross turned to her. "He's duped us both, Arianne. Keeping Willow's final letter secret prevented Peter's name from being cleared of murder and hurt my family's reputation. And you and your family could only go on believing Willow had been murdered, because you didn't have anything to prove otherwise."

"But maybe Alex didn't know," Arianne said. "Maybe it was there under the drawer before he came to the hotel."

Ross turned his accusing eyes to Alex. "But he was too eager to deny the letter was here, too anxious to get us out of the file room. Why else but because he was afraid the hidden letter would be discovered?"

Alex bowed his head, his hands still shaking. His aged shoulders slumped. "Yes, it's true." He looked at Arianne and smiled sadly. "Thank you for trying to defend me, my dear. I hope one day you will forgive me."

"You knew?" Arianne said with shock.

"Yes, I knew," Alex said, standing straighter and becoming calmer now that he apparently had decided to give up his ruse. "When I became manager here over forty years ago, the previous manager, an elderly gent, took me to this room and pulled that drawer out. He showed me the letter. It had been discovered during the major remodeling here in the late twenties. A workman had found it behind the radiator in Room 302 and brought it to him. The previous manager, like me, had a reverence for history. He saw the value of the letter at once and, as you see, took care to note its time and place of discovery. He also knew that the letter would be newsworthy, since Willow was already thought to be haunting the hotel and drawing the interest of visitors. In fact, he told me that she caused problems when they were redecorating Room 302. Wet paint brushes would fly through the air and the new wallpaper wouldn't stay up."

Alex had begun to lose his self-consciousness and was clearly enjoying telling them a story he'd had to keep to himself for so many decades.

"He decided to hold on to the letter for a while," Alex continued, "so he could choose when to reveal it to the best advantage for the hotel. You see, the stock market crash and the bank failures were drawing all the headlines. No one would take much interest in an old letter written by the Aragon's ghost, maybe not even the Briarcliffs, when everyone was worried about their life savings being lost. So he hid the letter away, there under the Willow File so he would easily remember where it was. He told no one.

"Time passed. He held on to it through the Great Depression and the Second World War. Things began to settle down in the 1950s, and he told me he considered revealing the letter then. But by that time, he'd grown to cherish his secret. He said that he enjoyed the power he felt in possessing the key to a mystery, which only he was in a position to reveal or not reveal.

"He told me all this when I took over. He was quite up in years by then and glad to have someone like me, who also loved historic things, to pass on his secret to. His advice was that I choose the best time to reveal the letter so as to draw attention to the hotel and bring in business."

"And that time never came?" Ross asked. "Why didn't you ever reveal it?"

Alex smiled and rocked his stick back and forth as if enjoying an idea in his mind. "You see, I came to view the situation as he had. I also came to relish the notion of being the sole keeper of this artifact, of being the only man who could solve the mystery of why Willow supposedly haunts the hotel. And, as you said yourself, I decided

Willow has more drawing power as a mysterious spirit than as a deceased woman about whom we knew everything.''

''And,'' Ross said, ''admitting you had the letter would draw questions about why it was hidden so long—questions you wouldn't want to answer, because they would incriminate you for withholding evidence. The Briarcliffs need this evidence now more than ever.''

Alex nodded. ''Yes, you have a point. Though I actually might have let you see the letter—if I could have. I know the Briarcliffs are a powerful family, and I had no wish to antagonize you. And Arianne thought she was being haunted by Willow lately. Perhaps the letter would have set her mind more at ease, too. Not that I ever really believed there was a ghost here, though I tried to keep an open mind.''

''You told me you believed the ghost reports,'' Arianne said with surprise.

''Because you believed them, my dear. And the hotel guests did, too. I didn't want to argue, especially not with you. I'm fond of you, so I pretended to go along with your ideas. And who was I to dispute you, when you said you'd heard her weeping? Perhaps you had. But your father and I, well, we had a more rational point of view on it all.''

''Let's get back to what you said before,'' Ross interjected. ''What do you mean, you would have let me see the letter if you could have?''

''My arthritis,'' Alex explained. ''I couldn't kneel down to reach the letter—haven't been able to these past five years.''

''You could have told me where it was,'' Ross argued.

''But then you would have known, because of the notation on the envelope, that it had been purposely kept hidden all these years. I needed to protect myself, knowing that someone like you might be likely to sue me. If I had decided to reveal the letter to you, I would have taken it out of the envelope and perhaps mixed it in with those dining room menus, so that you would seem to come upon it yourself. I would have made it look as if it had been in the drawer with Willow's other things all along, but had been overlooked. But I couldn't because of the stiffness in my knees. So I had to keep the secret to hide my own stealth. I suppose now you *will* sue me—or the hotel, or both." Alex lowered his eyes, as if finally fully realizing his mistake. He looked at Ross then, keeping his balance with the aid of his stick. "I'm sorry, Mr. Briarcliff. If you choose to sue, I hope it will be me and not the hotel. We're in bad economic times. The hotel doesn't need any bad publicity."

Arianne grew concerned. She couldn't admire what Alex had done, but she felt he'd meant no one any real harm. He'd only followed in the misguided footsteps of his predecessor. Perhaps she was too forgiving, but Alex had always been kind to her, in fact to everyone at the hotel. All the hotel employees liked him. She hoped Ross could overlook Alex's dishonesty.

But Ross seemed quite angry. "So, it was to keep up profitable ghost publicity that you let this letter go undiscovered. And in the process, you continued to allow my family's reputation to be injured. I ought to sue you *and* the hotel! Why should I care if the hotel gets bad publicity? You never gave a damn about clearing Peter's bad reputation! You never cared how we Briarcliffs looked in the public eye. You *wanted* everyone to think Peter murdered Willow, and hid the evidence that proved he didn't!"

"Ross, please," Arianne quietly objected, a little afraid to interrupt his tirade, but feeling she must.

"Please what?" he said, turning on her. "Please let this go unchallenged? Justice is certainly on my family's side in this situation. I intend to see to it that justice is served!"

"But, Ross, what about all the people who work here at the hotel? Including me. If you sue the hotel or Alex, the bad publicity would hurt our business, even put people out of work."

Ross exhaled and remained silent for a long moment, his hard eyes fixed on the closed Willow File drawer as he seemed to consider his options.

"All right, I won't sue," he said at last, with a hint of reluctance. "A lawsuit wouldn't make the Briarcliffs look good, either."

"I hope you won't even reveal Alex's deceit," Arianne said. "If the public learned the Aragon's manager hid the truth at the expense of the Briarcliffs only to ensure the hotel's popularity, the hotel might fall out of favor. Many of the employees have worked here for years. They might lose their jobs and lose their benefits. The truth may be on your side, but is it right to put people out of work just to polish your family name?"

"My brother is running for the Senate," Ross told her heatedly. "He can do a lot of people a lot of good if he gets elected. And he needs our family's name to be cleared of accusations that aren't true. I don't want to put hotel employees out of work, but I do need to make this letter public. I intend to publish it in my article, so that Peter's name will be cleared once and for all."

"But people may ask where and how the letter was found," Arianne said.

"Can't we make up a story?" Alex asked.

"I don't think we should lie to cover up a deceit," Arianne told him. "We could be found out and things would only be worse."

"Right," Ross agreed. "I'm publishing the letter. I won't say in my article how it came to light. But if people ask, I'm going to tell them. I'm not going to be part of a cover-up, especially not for you," he said to Alex.

"Oh, Ross," Arianne said with distress, "isn't there some other way?"

Ross shook his head. "I'm sorry, but I have to do what I have to do."

Arianne supposed Ross had every right to be concerned about the Briarcliff name and to get good publicity for his brother. Why should he worry about the hotel or its employees? And then she paused, as the word *publicity* played in her mind. Perhaps there was a way to make everyone happy.

"Why don't you hold a press conference?" she asked Ross, her tone bright with a new idea.

"A press conference?"

"I found the brooch and Peter's letters at my grandmother's house," she pointed out. "Why not have a press conference and show all the items at once that have recently been discovered, including Willow's last letter? Everyone would assume that the final note from Willow was found along with Peter's letters and the opal at my grandmother's. If a reporter should ask about Willow's last letter in particular, then, of course, we would have to say it was found in the hotel's file room and Alex's deceit may come to light. But if no one asks—and why would they?—then the issue won't come up and the hotel's reputation will be preserved."

"Wonderful idea!" Alex proclaimed.

"A press conference would be a good adjunct to the article I'm writing," Ross murmured, as if thinking aloud.

"In fact," Arianne said, another notion popping into her head, "why don't you and I hold a joint press conference? I'll tell everyone how I found the historic artifacts in my grandmother's closet, and that I concede that the Monroe family has unfairly blamed the Briarcliffs for Willow's murder all these years. I'll officially give the brooch back to you, and we can shake hands in front of the cameras—you a descendant of Peter, and me, a relative of Willow's."

"Sounds good," Ross agreed, a little smile on his lips. "Except you'll have to present the brooch to my brother. He's the eldest, and the one the brooch should go to."

"Oh, of course," Arianne said, feeling disappointed for some reason.

"It'll be great publicity for William," Ross went on. "With an event like that, we'll get TV coverage. In one swoop, Peter's name will be publicly cleared, William will be presented with the brooch, a symbol of tradition in our family that puts a nice, authentic spin on things, and everyone will be reminded that he's running for the Senate. Perfect."

"Yes," Arianne agreed. "Alex's deceit won't come to light, and the hotel's reputation will stay intact. Everyone will have what they want."

Ross studied her. "What about what you want?"

The question surprised her. "I don't want anything from anyone," she told him coolly. "I'm just happy to have all this settled."

Ross's demeanor, excited for a moment, seemed to slip back into a grim, glacial calm. "Good," he said. "I'll speak to my brother and see when he can be free for the press conference, and I'll let you know. If we can make it on the same day as my article appears, that will be ideal."

Though the press conference had been her idea, Ross was taking over and behaving as if he was in charge. Well, she knew nothing about arranging press conferences, anyway. Let him take charge, Arianne decided. "You'll have to give me back the brooch, so I can present it to your brother," she reminded him.

"Right," Ross said. "But first, I'll get it cleaned and mounted in a velvet jewel case."

"Can we have the press conference here at the Aragon?" Alex asked, his eyes alight. "It would be good publicity for the hotel, too."

Ross's face took on a sardonic expression and he shook his head, obviously miffed at Alex's nerve. Arianne was afraid he'd say no. But instead, Ross sniffed with irony and said, "Sure, where else?"

"We'll have it on the south lawn," Alex said with enthusiasm. "The Aragon has held press conferences there before for other celebrities. I'm sure you'll be pleased."

Arianne couldn't help but smile at the fact that Alex was so undaunted at being found out. And Ross seemed satisfied with the solution. Arianne was relieved. She hoped that once the press conference was over, she could go on with her life and have no further visitations from her ghostly ancestor, Willow, or from Ross Briarcliff.

At home that evening, Arianne phoned her grandmother. After asking how Henrietta was getting along with her plans to move, she told her about the discovery of Willow's last letter and read it to her.

"How sad. Perhaps I misjudged Willow," Henrietta said after she'd heard the letter. "She seemed to appreciate her family. And one can admire how hard she tried to overcome her physical frailty. It's too bad. But I'm glad that letter has come to light. My mother told me about her suicide note, but I didn't know it still existed."

"What did Katy tell you about it?" Arianne asked.

"She and my father had been playing cards with her parents, and she left them for a minute to go to her parents' room. Her mother wanted a headache remedy, and Katy had offered to get it for her. When she went to the room, she was stunned to find the brooch and the note from Willow on the dresser. She read the note and realized Willow intended to drown herself. Then she hurried out into the hallway to look out the hall window, which faced the beach. It was dark, but in the moonlight, she could see no one on the beach. She feared Willow had already killed herself, as she probably had."

Henrietta sighed and took a moment to catch her breath, or perhaps recall the details of the old story. Arianne waited, keeping her patience. She hoped Henrietta would leave nothing out. Soon her grandmother continued.

"My mother said she stood in that hallway in great distress, the note in her hand and tears streaming down her face. All at once she heard her parents' voices down the hall. Apparently her mother had decided she'd had enough of cards because of her headache and the late hour. Katy didn't want her parents to see Willow's note and know that Willow had killed herself. You see, in those days, to commit suicide was a shameful, terrible thing. For example, Willow might not have been allowed to be buried in the church cemetery. It was said the soul of a suicide had no peace after death." Henrietta chuckled softly. "Perhaps it's true, since Willow's spirit isn't at rest."

"What happened?" Arianne asked.

"My mother crumpled Willow's note and ran back into the room. She didn't want to throw it in the wastebasket, because it might be found. So she tossed it behind the radiator, so no one would see it. She told me she would have liked to have picked it up again when no one was looking and burned it, but it was stuck so far down between the wall and the radiator that she couldn't reach it."

"So Willow's parents never knew she killed herself, and they assumed Peter had murdered her," Arianne said, piecing things together.

"Yes. My mother confessed to me, on her deathbed, that she had let them believe Peter murdered Willow because my mother felt, in her heart, that he had killed her will to live when he rejected her. She said her mother would become hysterical if anyone so much as wondered out loud if Willow might have killed herself. So no one spoke of it. My mother would hush them if they did; she was so protective of her mother and her dead sister."

"And what about the brooch?"

"My mother never told me about the brooch specifically—except when she was delirious, and she admonished me to never tell that something was hidden. I didn't know then what she was talking about. Since she threw away Willow's note and didn't want her parents to know about it, she also couldn't tell them that Willow had requested that the brooch be returned to Peter. And my mother harbored such a hatred for Peter, I believe she wanted her parents to keep the brooch as a form of revenge on him.

"Her mother died several years later, here in this house. My mother, father, my brothers and sisters and I—I'd been born and was a toddler by that time—moved here to live with her father, my grandfather, whose health was failing. I suppose my mother found the brooch in her mother's things and hid it in the closet, maybe even on that day I walked in on her."

"Is there any more to the story?" Arianne asked. "Anything else about Willow that Katy told you before she died?"

"Oh . . ." Henrietta finished the word with a sigh. She seemed reluctant to say any more.

Arianne decided to prod her a bit. "At the end of the suicide note, Willow wrote, 'I would have died soon anyway and given you great cause for shame. Katy knows.' Do you know what she meant by that?"

Henrietta gave another long sigh. "I suppose now that you know everything else, I might as well tell you. Though my mother may turn in her grave. Can't you guess, Arianne?"

Arianne had an idea she'd been toying with. "Was Willow pregnant?"

"Yes," Henrietta said with relief. "There, I didn't have to tell you, after all. Willow had confided to my mother that she believed she was going to have Peter's baby. She hadn't told her parents. I remember my mother said that Willow had refused to see a doctor, partly because of the shame of it, Willow being unmarried and all, and partly because she was afraid of what her doctor would tell her. She probably knew she wasn't strong enough to carry a baby to term. But still, she hoped Peter would marry her, as he'd promised, and that somehow her baby would be born safely. I guess she wasn't always realistic about her physical condition."

"Did Peter know?"

"I don't think so. My mother said that she was the only one Willow had told. Willow had been given the brooch and was already engaged to marry Peter when she began to suspect she was pregnant, so at first she may have thought she'd tell everyone else after she was married, when it would look better. Then Peter changed his mind about marrying her, apparently because he'd talked to her doctor about her health. Katy said she advised Willow to tell Peter about the baby, and then he'd *have* to marry her.

But Willow said she wanted Peter to marry her for love, not because he had to. Well, he didn't marry her. And she killed herself. When she wrote that she would have died soon anyway, I imagine she meant that she knew she would die in childbirth, or even before, from the stress on her heart. And being unwed, she would have brought shame to the family. Moral codes were altogether different back then."

"Yes, I know," Arianne said. "Poor Willow."

"Yes," Henrietta agreed. "Being beautiful and charming doesn't guarantee you happiness, does it? Not if you don't have your health." Her grandmother hesitated. Then she asked with concern, "You have heart palpitations, don't you? I remember your mother telling me. But your doctor said—"

"Yes, Grandma," Arianne reassured her, "my doctor said I'm fine. He told me that many people have the type of occasional arrhythmia I have, and it's not serious. It's just that I feel my heart jump, especially if I'm tired or upset, and it makes me aware of my heartbeat. I even asked him once if I can have children, and he said there wouldn't be any problem. I'm perfectly healthy."

"I'm so glad," Henrietta said. "I wouldn't have wanted you to have somehow inherited Willow's heart condition."

"She must have had some congenital defect," Arianne speculated.

"So when *are* you getting married and having children?" Henrietta asked, taking a lighter tone of voice as she shifted the conversation to tease her granddaughter.

Arianne chuckled a little sadly. "I don't know. I have to find the right man first." Thinking of Ross, she added, "Not every man you meet would make a devoted, caring husband."

"No, indeed," Henrietta agreed. "It's better to wait and find yourself a good one."

"Yeah," Arianne said, drawing out the word with a long sigh. "But I want to be in love with him, too. I may have to wait quite a while."

After Arianne said goodbye and hung up, she slumped in her chair and felt depressed. She wished Ross could have been the right man for her. No other man would ever have the same impact on her, would make her want to melt with one touch. But she reminded herself of what Ross had said. Sex was just sex. She knew love had to be there, too. And Ross couldn't give her that.

The next morning, at the perfume shop, Arianne got a brief phone call from Ross. In a thoroughly all-business tone, he informed her that he'd spoken to his brother and to Alex. "The press conference will be held at one o'clock tomorrow. Does that fit into your schedule?" he asked.

"Yes, that's fine. Am I supposed to make a speech when I present your brother with the brooch? I'm not used to public speaking."

"Just a few words will be fine," he told her. His tone warmed a bit. "Knowing my brother, he'll take it from there." There was a hesitant pause. "How are you? Any more visits from Willow?"

"No, nothing since we found the letter. Maybe she's put to rest at last. By the way, I spoke to my grandmother. She said Katy had told her, and asked her to keep it secret, about the suicide note. Katy found the note and threw it behind the radiator so her parents wouldn't know that Willow killed herself. Apparently she thought it would be too great a shock for them. So Willow's parents found only the brooch and Katy never told them Willow had meant for it to be returned to Peter. Katy was the one who hid it in the closet."

"I see. Well, that answers all the questions, then."

"There's something more," Arianne said. "Willow was pregnant with Peter's baby."

There was a long pause. "She was?"

"She didn't tell Peter," Arianne explained. "She wanted him to marry her because he loved her, not because he'd...he'd gotten her pregnant." Arianne couldn't help but think of her own exchange with Ross about the possibility that she'd gotten pregnant. "When he didn't marry her, she decided to end her life. Apparently she'd finally faced the fact that she would die having the baby, and she didn't want to bring the shame of being an unwed mother on her family. That's what those last lines of her letter meant."

"I see." Ross's voice sounded surprisingly grim. "And Peter never knew. She ought to have told him."

"I can see why she wouldn't tell him," Arianne said. "Just like when you told me that you'd have married me if I had been pregnant. I wouldn't have wanted you to marry me for that reason."

There was a stony silence. "You wouldn't want to marry me for any reason."

This statement made Arianne grow tense and puzzled. She wasn't sure if he meant that she would never choose him to marry, or if he meant that no woman who was wise *should* choose him for a husband. In any event, she was surprised that he'd made the comment at all. She tried to find something to say. "Ross, if you—"

"See you at the press conference," he said abruptly and hung up before she could finish, as if not wanting to hear her argue with him on the subject.

Arianne hung up her phone in a daze, both because of Ross's cross attitude and because of her bafflement. Why had he needled her about the topic of marrying him? she wondered. He didn't want to get married, and he didn't love her, so why say that to her? And then she wondered ruefully at the words she'd been about to say to him. *Ross, if you loved me, I'd marry you.*

She was glad that he'd interrupted her. It wasn't something she ought to have said. As she'd told him, she *didn't* want to marry him for very good reasons—and she didn't want him to go around thinking that she did.

"The press conference is all set," Ross told his brother later that day. Ross had stopped by William's house after work before going to his condo. William was waiting in the living room for his wife, who was getting dressed. The couple had a local political function to attend that evening.

"Arianne will present the brooch?"

Ross nodded. "She was a little nervous about speaking in public. But she'll be fine. She's...tougher than she looks."

"So how are things going with her?"

Ross drew his brows together, irritated at the question. "Things aren't going anywhere with her. They never were."

"I thought—"

"You were mistaken."

"Okay," William said lightly. "I'll be glad to finally meet someone from the Monroe family. This will be a historic event for the Briarcliffs, eh?"

"Yeah," Ross said. "Historic."

William edged closer, eyeing his brother. "What's eating you?"

Ross exhaled. "Arianne just learned more about Willow from her grandmother. Willow was pregnant with Peter's child when she died."

William's puzzled blue eyes shifted to the floor and then to Ross's face. "That's a shame. And it's a new twist to the old story. But it happened nearly a hundred years ago. Why should it put you in such a funk?"

"Because everything could have been so different. It makes me angry and then depressed."

William scratched his cheek. "I'm not following you, Ross."

Ross realized he hadn't been very clear. He was so enmeshed in his thoughts, he assumed William was on his wavelength. "If Willow had been strong enough to have her child, she and Peter would have married. He...he loved her. Arianne found his letters to her, and they show that he genuinely cared for her. It was more than just an obsession."

"Or a spell she'd put on him?" William teased.

"Okay, okay," Ross said, not amused. "But what if Peter had married her and she'd been able to carry the baby to term, and survive the delivery herself? They might have been a nice, happy little family. Peter would never have wed Isabelle and become so ruthless as a result of his horrible marriage. Our family's heritage might have been altogether different. Peter and Willow's child would have been much more likely to marry happily, and their grandchildren would have, too, because they had a positive example to follow. You and I might have had decent parents. Think how different our lives might have been."

William seemed to reflect on this for a moment. "I suppose the family would have evolved differently. You're right. But it didn't happen that way. No use wishing otherwise."

Ross stuffed his hands in his pockets and took a turn about the room. He didn't like his brother's *so what* reply. It seemed inconsiderate, when Ross had spent the afternoon stewing about what Arianne had told him. "I've gone my entire life wishing I'd been born into a different family," he told his brother. "The fact that our family could have been nurturing instead of destructive upsets me. I should think it would upset you, too."

"I've let all that go, Ross. I have my own family now. Why wish for what might have been? You can't go back and change anything. You have to live with what is, get past it and move on."

Ross nodded, agreeing with reluctance. "I know. I never learned how to do that."

"Find someone who makes you want to focus on the present and the future, so you don't dwell so much on the past. Get married. Make a new life. Look upon today as the first day of the rest of your life—well, today's a bad day for you. How about tomorrow?"

"I should get married tomorrow?" Ross said dryly.

"Well, start looking for the right life partner tomorrow."

"Maybe the right woman wouldn't think I was right for her," Ross said, walking toward the window.

"Why wouldn't you be right?"

"I don't know how to form a lasting relationship with a woman." Ross turned and looked across the room at his elder brother. "How is it done?"

William spread his hands. "It's not like there's a step-by-step guidebook you can follow. You find a woman and you take the plunge. Then you work it out together, day by day, year after year. And there is help available, if you don't have smooth sailing. Marriage counselors can be very enlightening. I haven't mentioned it before, but Marlene and I have been to one.''

''You have?''

''Sure, several years ago. I assumed I'd probably need advice along the way, being the product of such a cold marriage, so I didn't hesitate to get some when the need arose. Therapy can help anyone get past a dysfunctional family. But having a loving, understanding wife is the key thing for most men.''

Ross tilted his head and studied the plush carpet beneath his feet. ''What if I can't be loving and understanding in return?''

''Why do you think you can't be? Just because our parents weren't? We aren't our father and mother, Ross.''

Ross wanted very much to believe his older brother, but he knew himself too well. To him, the situation seemed entirely hopeless.

CHAPTER ELEVEN

"Are you Arianne?"

Arianne turned to find herself looking at a man whose features were similar to Ross's, but whose eyes and hair were lighter in color. "Yes."

"I'm William Briarcliff, Ross's brother."

"I thought so," she said with a smile. "I've seen your picture in the paper." She extended her hand. "It's nice to meet you."

They were in a meeting room of the Aragon Hotel, near the hotel's picturesque south lawn. Arianne had been waiting with Alex and some hotel staff people for the time to go out and speak to the reporters who were gathering on the lawn outside. Ross hadn't arrived yet.

"My brother has mentioned you," William said. "I thought you must be Arianne since you look a little like Willow Monroe in that old photo. Ross said there was a resemblance."

"Too much of one for him, I think," Arianne said with a dry chuckle.

"Don't pay attention to his dour attitudes. Underneath, he's a teddy bear."

Arianne laughed. She'd have never compared Ross to a teddy bear in a million years. But his brother certainly had a sunny disposition. It was amazing how different brothers could be. She wished Ross... Oh, there was no use wishing. Ross would never change. He probably didn't even want to, not really.

She wasn't sure if *she* would want him to. There was still something compelling about his dark, intense nature that drew her, even as it frightened and saddened her. Ross was a man she ought not be attracted to. But she was. She'd have to get over him, once this press conference was done and she never saw him again.

"So you're going to present me with the infamous Briarcliff brooch," William said.

"I'm happy to have it go back to your family," Arianne told him with sincerity. "I didn't even know we had it. Did Ross tell you it was hidden underneath the floorboards of a closet?"

"He did. Just between you and me, it would have been fine with me if it had stayed hidden. I've made it a point to ignore my family's history. And my wife said she doesn't particularly want the obligation of wearing it. She's never liked opals. But I am glad that this old feud between our families is ending."

"So am I," Arianne agreed. "Maybe you'll both like the brooch once you see it. It's a striking piece of jewelry. Is your wife here today?"

"No, she had a women's charity luncheon to attend. She's my best campaign asset, so I didn't want her to cancel her plans for this. If I know Ross, he'll get me all the publicity I need for this press conference. He comes up with better ideas than my campaign manager."

"Does he?" Arianne asked with interest. She hadn't known anything about Ross's political talents or his relationship with his brother.

"What do you think of Ross?" William asked.

The question took her unexpectedly. "I...well, he's..."

William lifted his eyebrows humorously. "A lot of people have that reaction to my brother."

Arianne laughed even as she sensed his joke was meant to help her recover from her confusion. And all at once she wondered—did William suspect she and Ross had feelings for each other?

Ross walked into the hotel meeting room carrying the letters, which had been encased in plastic covers, and the brooch, which was in a black velvet jewel box. He immediately spotted Arianne. She wore an old-fashioned dress and had her hair pinned up, looking very much like Willow today. William stood next to her, smiling. She was laughing, apparently at something he'd said.

A pang of jealousy shot through Ross. She never laughed so freely and easily with him. Things—people—always seemed to come to William so easily. Did he have to charm Arianne, too, and make Ross's image suffer by comparison in her eyes?

Then again, Ross thought with angry resignation, what difference did it make? He had no relationship with her. Never would. She'd told him that herself. *Let* her laugh at his brother's wit. Ross had other things to think about—this damn press conference, for one. He'd be glad when it was over.

Ross walked up to them, and William greeted him. Arianne silently nodded her hello when Ross turned to her, the smile gone from her face.

"We've been making friends," William told him.

"So I see," Ross said, trying to hide his black mood and keep his tone cool.

"I saw your article in the paper this morning. Great job," William said, clapping him on the shoulder. "You used some effective quotes from the letters to put Peter in a better light."

"Yes," Arianne agreed. "You were evenhanded in the way you wrote it, too."

"No Monroe bashing, you mean," Ross quipped darkly.

"I was thinking," William said, "we ought to invite members of the Monroe family to the Briarcliff mansion sometime—have a festive reconciliation party." He gave Ross a conspiratorial grin. "We'll send Dad out of town."

"I'll go out of town with him," Ross muttered sarcastically, in no frame of mind to think about planning a party in which he and Arianne would have to pretend to be friendly.

Arianne looked stricken by the comment. Her shoulders fell and she lowered her gaze. Ross wished he hadn't made the remark when he saw her reaction. But the damage was done.

"What kind of thing is that to say?" William asked him in a stern manner rarely used by him. "This whole press conference is meant to show that the old feud between our families is settled."

"It's okay," Arianne murmured, apparently recovering from the comment. Her beautiful face wore a stoic expression.

"She knows what I'm like." Ross spoke to his brother with anger directed more at himself than anyone else. "I'm a Briarcliff of the old school, not spiffed up and polished like you. Our father isn't fit to host a reconciliation party and neither am I."

"Ross—"

"Save the speech," Ross shot back before William could finish. "I'm not redeemable." He turned his eyes harshly to Arianne. "She learned that the hard way."

Ross was taken aback to see tears well in her eyes as she looked at him with an earnest expression. He felt that odd, sinking sensation in the pit of his stomach again. He stopped breathing for a moment, it was so profound. A thought pounded in his brain. She might be the one person who *could* redeem him.

But she wouldn't have him. He'd hurt her too much already; that was probably why she was blinking back tears now. He'd walked in only two minutes ago, and already he'd made her cry. He'd better walk away, or she wouldn't be composed enough to speak at the press conference, he told himself.

He handed her the velvet box. "Here," he said in a quieter, more reserved manner, "present this to William. You two are good at peacemaking. I'm sure you'll make it a nice ceremony." He turned to his brother. "I'll give these letters to the hotel staff to put on display for the reporters."

He found William studying him, looking curiously empathetic, with a certain gravity in his features, as though his mind was working. Ross didn't know what to make of it, and at that point didn't care. Someone was signaling them that it was time to go outdoors and begin the press conference. He glanced at Arianne as he turned to go. She was drying her eyes, her gaze to the floor, as if not wanting to interact with Ross any further. He couldn't blame her. He left to walk over to Alex and his staff, who were hovering nervously by the door, motioning everyone to hurry.

A few minutes later, Ross looked out at the fifty or more reporters and TV people arrayed in front of them in the bright sunshine. A podium and microphone had been set up on the smooth green lawn, which was enclosed with colorful beds of flowers. Alex had already introduced the participants and given a brief history of Willow Monroe and Peter Briarcliff. He pointed out the newly discovered letters on display. Then he quipped that this was an important occasion for the Aragon Hotel, especially its resident ghost. This got a good chuckle from the audience. The old man didn't miss a trick, Ross thought. Alex invited Arianne to the microphone then, mentioning that she ran the Aragon Perfumery and was descended from Willow's sister, Katy.

Ross felt that clutch in his stomach again as he watched her walk up to the podium, looking slender, shy and lovely. She leaned into the microphone and spoke, her voice soft and high. It was an ultrafeminine voice, one he could listen to forever. If only things were different, he thought. If only *he* was different....

"I found the Briarcliff brooch and some old letters in a closet at my grandmother's house," Arianne was saying. "They'd been hidden there for over three-quarters of a century. I'm happy they've been recovered, both for the historical value of the artifacts, but also because it settles a question that has been argued between the Briarcliffs and the Monroes through the century. Willow's last letter proves that she drowned herself in the sea, and that she wished the Briarcliff brooch to be returned to Peter."

Arianne paused to pick up the velvet box, which she had set on the podium. She turned and asked William to step up next to her. Then she opened the box and held it up for all to see. The gold of the newly cleaned brooch shone in the sunlight, and the large opal flickered iridescently with its mysterious inner flames in hues of green, red and orange. There was an appreciative murmuring in the audience, and cameras clicked.

"So, to fulfill Willow's last wish, I'm presenting this to you," she said to William. "I'm told that you are the eldest son, and so it should go to you."

William smiled and took the box from Arianne, kissing her on the cheek as he did so. As the audience applauded, Arianne stepped to one side of the podium, where she'd been standing before.

"Thank you, Arianne," William said. "I, too, am very happy that these old questions have been settled. You were historically correct in giving this brooch to me," he said, glancing again at the brooch as he held the box. "Our family tradition was that it be handed down to the eldest son of each generation, on the occasion of that son becoming engaged to the woman he'd chosen to be his wife. The young man would then present the opal to his bride-to-be as a token of their impending marriage."

William paused, as if considering his words. He looked at the audience and smiled. "However, I'm going to break that tradition. I was never all that interested in family history, to tell you the truth. And I'm already married and have two wonderful children to prove it, so receiving this brooch would seem a little anticlimatic to my wife."

The reporters grew silent, apparently sensing something unexpected and interesting was coming.

"My brother, Ross, on the other hand, has always appreciated family history, and he knows a lot more about it than I do."

Ross's head went up as he heard his name mentioned. What the hell was William doing?

"He also isn't married yet. So it stands to reason, in my mind anyway, that this brooch ought to go to him. Therefore—" he turned to Ross "—I'm going to pass it on to my best and only brother. Ross?"

Ross stood on the grass dumbfounded. He glanced at Arianne, who was looking at him, wide-eyed with surprise. She began to clap her hands as the rest of the audience applauded. Obviously, there was nothing else to do but go up to the podium as William wanted him to.

When he reached the podium, he said to his brother, avoiding the microphone, "Are you nuts?"

"No, but you are," William said as he handed the velvet case to him. William stepped to one side, leaving Ross alone at the microphone.

Ross was used to public speaking, but at this moment, he hadn't a clue what to say. His mind raced in all directions. "This was unexpected," Ross said with irony to those gathered. "That's why William will make a great senator—he's always coming up with new ideas."

As the reporters chuckled, Ross glanced again at Arianne. She was smiling, looking as though she was genuinely happy for him, as if she'd wanted the brooch to go to him all along. Ross wondered why she should be pleased—he'd been so boorish a few minutes ago. He knew that she wanted to be patient and forgiving, and that he usually hadn't let her.

As he looked at her, something inside him clicked. Suddenly the chaos in his mind stopped swirling, and things seemed to fall into place. It was time to wake up, he realized. Here he had an opportunity to make a grand gesture, to try to amend all the hurt he'd caused Arianne. Here was also the opportunity for him to take a new path in his life and make a grasp at happiness. Ross wasn't a gambler, but he decided to go for broke.

"As my brother mentioned, I'm not married. In fact, I'd had my mind set to remain a bachelor. But I've met someone who seems to have changed my mind." Ross stared straight ahead, not daring to look elsewhere. "Since this brooch is to be worn by the bride-to-be of the Briarcliff who possesses it, I want to present it now to the young woman I'd like to be my bride—if . . . if she'll accept it.''

His fingers numb with nerves, he fumbled to remove the brooch from the case's velvet lining. The audience watched in fascinated silence as he walked the few steps to where Arianne was standing. He kept his eyes lowered, but when he reached her, he looked at her, holding out the brooch in his hand.

''Will you take this?'' he asked.

Arianne's brown eyes grew lustrous with shock. Her mouth dropped open, and her lower lip quivered in confusion. ''Ross . . .'' she murmured, apparently not knowing what to say.

''I want you to have it, to wear it for me.''

''W-why?''

He smiled. ''I love you. I didn't think I'd ever say those words to anyone. But I can finally say them now, to you.''

Tears flooded her eyes as she smiled at him with happiness.

''Will you take the brooch?'' he gently prodded, still holding the opal in his hand. ''Everyone's waiting for your answer.''

Apparently unable to speak, she nodded. Grinning with joy and relief, he pinned the brooch to her dress, below the top button. It was a bit difficult, since he wasn't used to working with jewelry clasps, and Arianne stood unsteadily as she breathed in tearful gasps. When he'd gotten it fastened, he took her by the shoulders and kissed her tenderly on the forehead.

The audience applauded warmly. Shutters snapped as photographers came close and gathered around the couple. One said, ''Can we have a photo of her alone, wearing the brooch?''

Ross gladly stepped aside, leaving Arianne to quickly wipe her eyes as reporters vied for a good spot to photograph her. She smiled, tears still in her eyes, looking happy and fulfilled.

A sudden sense of déjà vu came over Ross. She looked exactly like the vision he'd had of her, his brief premonition, that day in her shop. A feeling of awe crept over him. *So this was meant to be,* he thought. He smiled, knowing in his heart that he'd finally done the right thing, that this would work out, that he at last would be happy. And so would Arianne.

The photographers asked him to get into the picture then, so he stood next to her, slipping his arm around her waist. He could smell her perfume, and he drew her even closer. She leaned against him, as if she felt a little limp with surprise and joy.

He bent his head and whispered in her ear, "I was afraid you'd say no."

She glanced up at him. "Last night on the phone, I started to tell you that I'd marry you if you said you loved me."

"Really? And I hung up on you," he said in a self-chastising way. "I seem to sabotage my own happiness. I'll change, Arianne. But you'll have your work cut out for you, putting up with me sometimes."

Arianne grinned as she reached up to touch his chin. "I'll manage," she whispered. "I'll put a spell on you."

She kissed him on the mouth, and everything, even the clicking cameras around them, faded in the warmth of her lips.

"I know where we can be alone for a while," Arianne said, taking Ross by the hand. They'd been surrounded by people congratulating them ever since the press conference had ended. William expressed his pleasure at Ross's decision and Arianne's acceptance of the brooch. Even Alex wished them well. Hotel employees who knew Arianne and had watched the press conference came up to offer good wishes. And reporters wanted to get the whole story about how a Briarcliff elected to marry a Monroe. Finally, Ross had whispered in Arianne's ear that he wanted some time alone to talk to her. Everything had happened so fast.

"Where are we going?" he asked as she led him down a corridor of the hotel.

"To the south tower. Nobody goes up there."

"I can see why," Ross said, as they came to a door on which there was a sign that said, Closed for Repair.

"Never mind that," Arianne said, opening the door. "It's all fixed, just unpainted."

They were out of breath by the time they reached the top of the spiral staircase that led them to the circular observation area beneath the tower's conical roof.

Ross walked over to the ledge overlooking the beach far below and the vast expanse of the ocean. "What a magnificent view!" he said.

Arianne came up and wrapped her arm around his. "Isn't it," she agreed. She looked at him. "It's nice to be alone."

He turned to her and touched the brooch at her collar. "Are you sure you should have accepted this? It means you've officially agreed to marry me. It'll be all over the papers tomorrow and on TV tonight."

"I know."

"We haven't known each other long," he pointed out. "Maybe we should have an extended engagement."

She smiled. "Not too extended."

He studied her, his expression concerned, his gray eyes shining with intensity. "Are you really sure you want to take me on? I'll try to be considerate and not fall back into my high-handed manner, but there are bound to be times when I forget. It's a trait I learned from my father that I don't like about myself. I intend to change, if I can. I don't want to hurt you ever again."

"I'm not perfect, either," Arianne said. "I can be stubborn. You'll have to put up with that from me."

"That'll be a piece of cake compared to all that you may have to deal with, between me and my family. It's a good thing you're the one with the patience in this relationship."

Arianne tilted her chin in a sad way. "Not patient enough, I'm afraid. I'd given up on you. What made you change so suddenly at the press conference?"

"I was mixed up about my emotions and felt hopeless about trying to change anything. But with the opportunity my brother handed me—I think he was playing matchmaker—I saw the chance to try to turn things around between us and make everything right. My mind suddenly focused, and I saw the simple truth. I'm in love with you. That's what I was afraid to admit to myself, what I didn't think I was even capable of experiencing and didn't know how to deal with. I was always afraid history would repeat itself. Peter lost Willow. I decided that didn't mean that I had to lose you."

Arianne felt touched by his earnest words. "You won't lose me. I . . ." She hesitated. "You told me once never to tell you again that I . . ."

"Forget what I told you." He encouraged her with a tender smile. "Say it."

"I love you, Ross," she told him with feeling.

"I don't know why you should, but I'm glad you do."
He leaned down to kiss her. As she tilted her chin, he
slipped his arms around her. Her body melted against his
chest as he pulled her close. His mouth on hers felt warm
and deliciously insistent. That instant fire that always ignited between them flared again. She drew her arms
around his neck as his hands roved over the contours of
her back, her shoulders and her waist. They slid up then
and he pressed the heels of his hands against her breasts.
He pushed his pelvis forward and she smiled when she
could feel his arousal through the full skirt of her light
cotton dress.

"Oh, Ross, I want to make love," she whispered. "I
thought it would never happen between us again. I've
longed for you."

"We could rent a room in the hotel," Ross said as he slid
his lips hotly down her neck, "and raise a few eyebrows."

She chuckled with delight. "What about here? Now? No
one will find us up here."

He brought his head up and eyed her with humor.
"You're daring for a recent ex-virgin!"

She ran her hands over his shirt and began to loosen his
tie. "I just want to make our new happiness complete. I
want to erase all the heartache between us and start anew.
Let's make love, Ross."

"There you go, asking *me* again," he teased as she began to unbutton his shirt.

"That way you don't have to look like you're seducing
me. I'm helping you to shatter your old image," she told
him as she undid his last button.

"Sounds good to me," he said. He kissed her again as
he unbuttoned her dress down the front to the waist. The
heavy brooch pulled down one side of her collar onto her
chest. He pulled apart the dress, revealing her lacy bra.

"You're so exquisite," he said, running his fingertips over the rounded contours of her flesh above the lace.

The bra unfastened in the front. Eager for more, Arianne let go of him to undo it. She closed her eyes as he took over and pushed the bra away, sliding his big gentle hands over her breasts. The slight roughness of his palms on her sensitive nipples sent electricity through her body. She felt as if she would swoon under his touch. Sensual stirrings flared deep inside her, demanding even more.

"Arianne," he whispered. "I want you." He kissed her throat hotly while he continued to fondle her breasts.

Arianne was as eager as he, but she wasn't sure how to go about it. "On the bench?" she asked.

He turned to look over his shoulder at the narrow wood bench. "Doesn't look very comfortable. You'd better sit on my lap," he said with an inventive gleam in his eye. Taking her by the hand, he walked with her to the bench.

He sat down in the middle of it and looked at her, his hands at her waist, his eyes devouring her. "You look damn sexy half undressed."

Arianne didn't want to waste any more time. She bent to take off her panties. "Shall I take off the dress, too?"

He chuckled at her eagerness. "No," he said as he unbuckled his belt. "I don't feel as secure up here as you do. You'd better stay partly dressed just in case someone comes up. Lift your skirts and sit astride me."

Her heart beating wildly with anticipation, she did as he instructed. He slid his warm hands over her thighs beneath her skirt, then found the quick of her with his fingertips. She was already slick, and a shot of radiating pleasure sped through her body. She gasped with delight. Reaching around to her derriere beneath her full skirt, he urged her downward. She felt him slide deep within her and closed her eyes at the fulfillment of being one with him again.

They began to move together in the age-old rhythm of lovemaking. She leaned in to kiss him, her hair falling forward over her bared breasts. As her body moved in gentle thrusts with his, she felt the heavy brooch lightly tap the top of her breast. His mouth left hers and traveled down her throat as she tilted her chin upward in ecstasy. He pushed her hair and the brooch aside to caress and then suckle her breast.

"Oh, yes," she encouraged him and made little noises of pleasure as he teased her higher and higher into arousal. Soon her breathing grew ragged and her heart began to pound.

He thrust into her harder and reached underneath her skirt again to touch her. Shock waves went through her. "Ross...oh, Ross..." she exclaimed in the same rhythm as their bodies moved. Her heart began to palpitate, but she ignored it, knowing it would set itself straight again. All she could think about was the profound tension that was building in the lower part of her stomach.

She stretched up and leaned forward to be closer to him, and he buried his cheek into her breasts for a moment, then kissed the hollow between them. "You are the sexiest woman!" he breathed. "I'll never get enough of you. I want to love you forever."

She smiled at his words even as she began to breathe in sobbing gasps as the tautness in her body built to an intolerable level. All at once she felt as if she was in suspension for a moment, and then she cried out as her body burst with a frenzy of sensual convulsions. Ross held her tightly as he reached his own climax. She continued to feel rapturous sensations in descending waves, and she sighed and then laughed with joy.

Suddenly the sound of laughter surrounded them. Arianne knew it wasn't her own. The gentle scent of violets swept over them in a breeze.

"Willow," Arianne whispered to Ross. "She's happy for us."

At the end of the day, Arianne walked with Ross along the seashore after dark. The beach was empty and the waves lapped on the sand quietly, glistening in the moonlight. They made plans as they strolled, deciding to set their wedding date for six months ahead. Arianne touched the brooch at her throat and said, "William seemed to like me, but what about the rest of your family?"

"My father will give you a hard time, no doubt," Ross said, holding her hand as they dodged the edge of a wave sliding toward them. "But don't let him scare you. He'll come around. Briarcliff men have a weakness for beautiful women." He kissed her hair. "Will your family accept me?"

"My parents will like you, I'm sure. And so will my grandmother. Some of my cousins may raise their eyebrows, but I don't see them much, anyway."

"I imagine there will be some furrowed brows among my cousins and aunts and uncles, too. They'll all get used to a Briarcliff marrying a Monroe, in time. Although they may accuse you of plotting to get the brooch back by marrying me."

Arianne laughed. All at once, just ahead of them, a mist formed in the darkness. They hesitated in their steps. Arianne glanced at Ross. "What's that? Water vapor from the sea?"

"I don't know," Ross said. "The ocean is too calm for it to be spray from the waves."

As they watched, the drifting mist began to lose its vagueness and form a shape—the shape of a woman. The scent of violets filled Arianne's nostrils.

"It's Willow," Arianne whispered, struck with awe, for she'd never seen Willow appear before.

The apparition hovered in the atmosphere for a long moment, and Willow's face, as she appeared in her photo, became clearer. She seemed to be looking at Arianne. And then the face and figure faded into a mist again, which began to move away toward the sea. When it was over the waves, it gradually disappeared. The scent of violets disappeared, as well.

"She's gone," Arianne said, holding tightly to Ross's hand. "Forever—I can sense it. She appeared to us to say goodbye. She's at peace now."

Ross slipped his arm around her as she continued to look at the spot where Willow had disappeared. "So are we," Ross said. "She saw to it that we would be, didn't she?"

"You're right," Arianne said with wonder. "She wanted us to be together, to have what she and Peter couldn't have—a lifetime of happiness."

* * * * *

Welcome To The
Dark Side Of Love...

AVAILABLE THIS MONTH

#27 HANGAR 13—Lindsay McKenna
Mac Stanford didn't believe in the supernatural, yet what else could
explain the eerie events in Hangar 13? To compound matters, he
had to enlist the help of shamaness Ellie O'Gentry. She challenged
his view of reality, while his powerful attraction rocked her safe world.
And all the while, the menacing spirit in Hangar 13 grew ever more
deadly....

#28 THE WILLOW FILE—Lori Herter
When Arianne Lacey encountered the darkly handsome stranger on the
beach, she couldn't know the fateful history they shared, nor the fated
attraction. Ross Briarcliff's great-grandfather had allegedly killed
Arianne's great-great-aunt, Willow, pitting the families against one
another for all time. Ross was determined to solve the legend surrounding
her ancestor's death—a legend that seemed very much alive in
Arianne....

COMING NEXT MONTH

#29 LOVER IN THE SHADOWS—Lindsay Longford
Molly Harris teetered between the brink of madness and imminent
murder charges. Three episodes of amnesia had coincided with three
killings, making her doubt her innocence, as did enigmatic detective
John Harlan. Harlan's logic told him she was the one, but the shadowy
cover of night offered him different answers—and a dangerous attraction.
To save Molly's life, Harlan faced the ultimate test—exposing his dark
side....

#30 TWILIGHT MEMORIES—Maggie Shayne
Wings in the Night
Rhiannon and Roland de Courtemanche had roamed the earth several
lifetimes over, but until the present they had only their private pains to
heal and only their immortal souls to protect.... Hunted like animals by a
relentless pursuer, they strove to save the life of a child, and to ensure
their endless love for all eternity.

**Relive the romance...
Harlequin and Silhouette
are proud to present**

A program of collections of three complete novels by the most requested authors with the most requested themes. Be sure to look for one volume each month with three complete novels by top name authors.

In January: **WESTERN LOVING**   Susan Fox
   JoAnn Ross
   Barbara Kaye

Loving a cowboy is easy—taming him isn't!

In February: **LOVER, COME BACK!**   Diana Palmer
   Lisa Jackson
   Patricia Gardner Evans

It was over so long ago—yet now they're calling, "Lover, Come Back!"

In March: **TEMPERATURE RISING**   JoAnn Ross
   Tess Gerritsen
   Jacqueline Diamond

Falling in love—just what the doctor ordered!

Available at your favorite retail outlet.

REQ-G3

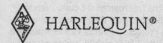

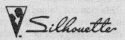

WELCOME TO THE
DARK SIDE OF LOVE....

HANGAR
13

LINDSAY McKENNA

Eerie, *disturbing* things were happening in Hanger 13—
but Major Mac Stanford refused to believe in supernatural
occurrences. He was doubtful about enlisting the aid of
shamaness Ellie O'Gentry, but he couldn't ignore their
undeniable attraction—or his desire to help her challenge
a menacing spirit....

Don't miss bestselling author Lindsay McKenna's first tale
from the dark side of love, HANGAR 13, available in
March from...

♥ SILHOUETTE®

Shadows™

SHLM

It's our 1000th
Silhouette Romance
and we're celebrating!

Join us for a special collection of love stories by the authors you've loved for years, and new favorites you've just discovered.

**It's a celebration just for you,
with wonderful books by
Diana Palmer, Suzanne Carey,
Tracy Sinclair, Marie Ferrarella,
Debbie Macomber, Laurie Paige,
Annette Broadrick, Elizabeth August
and MORE!**

Silhouette Romance...vibrant, fun and emotionally rich! Take another look at us!

As part of the celebration, readers can receive a FREE gift AND enter our exciting sweepstakes to win a grand prize of $1000! Look for more details in all March Silhouette series titles.

**You'll fall in love all over again
with Silhouette Romance!**

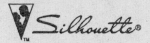

MEN OF COURAGE
by
Lindsay McKenna

It's a special breed of men who defy death and fight for right!
Salute their bravery while sharing their lives and loves!

Be sure to catch this exciting new series, where you'll meet
three incredible heroes:

Captain Craig Taggart in SHADOWS AND LIGHT (SE #878),
available in April.

Captain Dan Ramsey in DANGEROUS ALLIANCE (SE #884), May.

Sergeant Joe Donnally in COUNTDOWN (SE #890), June.

These are courageous men you'll love and tender stories you'll
cherish...only from Silhouette Special Edition!

MENC1